the Pink

JANE HOLLAND

Copyright © 1999 Jane Holland

First published in 1999 by Hodder and Stoughton
A division of Hodder Headline PLC
A Sceptre Paperback

The right of Jane Holland to be identified as the Author of
the Work has been asserted by her in accordance with the
Copyright, Designs and Patents Act 1988.

10 9 8 7 6 5 4 3 2 1

All rights reserved. No part of this publication may be
reproduced, stored in a retrieval system or transmitted
in any form or by any means, without the prior written
permission of the publisher, nor be otherwise circulated
in any form of binding or cover other than that in which
it is published and without a similar condition being
imposed on the subsequent purchaser.

All characters in this publication are fictitious and any
resemblance to real persons, living or dead, is purely coincidental.

A CIP catalogue record for this book is
available from the British Library.

ISBN 0 340 73856 1

Printed and bound in Great Britain by
Clays Ltd, St Ives PLC

Hodder and Stoughton
A division of Hodder Headline PLC
338 Euston Road
London NW1 3BH

For the players

Acknowledgments

For their encouragement and vision, my thanks go to Jane Bradish-Ellames at Curtis Brown and Neil Taylor at Sceptre. I would also like to thank the World Ladies Billiards and Snooker Association for being such an inspired and inspiring group of women. The happiest and yet most challenging period of my life was the six years I spent on the world circuit. I hope this book encourages even more women into the sport.

'What does not kill me, makes me stronger'

Friedrich Nietzsche, from *Twilight of the Idols*

I'm Zoë. I'm standing in a snooker club car park at nine o'clock in the morning. I'm wearing a ruffled evening shirt and a clip-on bow-tie, with pink silk knickers under my trousers. Having silk against my skin helps me concentrate. I have an aluminium cue case under one arm and tatty Mr Bear, one ear missing, under the other. It's a freezing winter morning and I'm about to play the Ladies Scottish Classic.

I know what you're thinking. *Women don't play snooker.* Well, I'll let you in on a secret. They do. In fact, I've just devised a game strategy for today's epic confrontation. It's going to be a kind of 'live and let die' morning.

I grind my cigarette out underfoot, noting with some consternation that my breath is still smoking on the icy air. Already, my mind is racing ahead to tomorrow morning when I will probably be forced to spend several hours defrosting the car locking system before I can set off home. The landlady at my B&B seemed unimpressed by today's request for an ice-scraper and some hot water for the windscreen, imagining no doubt that anyone who comes to Scotland at this time of year unprepared for the rawer elements is 'a bit of a wee prat'.

Tricksy turns up at last, backing her car lopsidedly into one of the last available spaces. Tricksy's not her real name. It's a nickname whose origins are lost in the mists of time, though I believe it has something to do with her strange tendency to disappear whenever it's her round. She has insisted I walk in with her, mainly because she is under the impression that anyone who has to turn up alone at a ladies' tournament is a fairly sad person, but also because she likes me to look after her cue while she dives into the toilets to fix her make-up.

As she walks swiftly across the club car park, swinging her snooker cue like a Mafioso about to do a hit, I hunch deeper into my thin jacket, suddenly realising that the moment of entering the club cannot be put off any longer. 'Ready for the kill?'

Tricksy nods sharply, then frowns. 'Where are your kids?'

'Kevin's already taken them inside. It was too cold out here.'

'What is he, your coach or your babysitter?' When she sees my expression, Tricksy grins. 'Don't look so worried. It was only a joke. Once I'm out of the Plate, I'll do my shift too. As agreed.'

'Thanks, Tricks. I won't forget this.'

'You're playing Sylvie, aren't you?' When I nod tensely, Tricksy looks at me pityingly. 'You had to face her one day, I suppose.'

As usual, Tricksy is wearing her 'lucky' blouse, the one that cost her only a tenner when she picked it up in Portugal a few years ago. Of course, when Tricksy says it's 'lucky', that doesn't mean she plays like a

World Champion whilst wearing it, simply that she's successfully managed never to spill curry on it and that she occasionally loses by less than her usual fifty-point margin when it's on her back. The difference between winning and losing, as you may have already guessed, is only a matter of perspective to some players.

'Well, then,' I mutter unconvincingly, looking up at the darkening sky. Another snowstorm is imminent. There's a tightening in my stomach now. The aluminium cue case is suddenly icy in my hand. 'No point hanging around. Let's get in there and rip 'em apart.'

The camaraderie is false. In snooker, it's every woman for herself.

1

The first thing you notice is the silence. Not to mention the space. It always seemed such a small living room when Adrian was here. Now the sofa feels about ten foot long and the bed goes on for ever. But at least I have absolute power over the remote control. So I stretch the full length of the sofa and drown the silence with the opening bars of *Coronation Street* at top volume. I don't know what it's like with husbands, since Adrian always refused to get married ('it's just a piece of paper, sweetheart'), but boyfriends do tend to dominate the channel selection process.

Now I can watch whatever I want on television. I am the Master Zapper. I can change channels whenever I want. Back, forth. Back, forth. *Home and Away*? No problem. Ten seconds of the news? Go for it. No one here to complain even if I go completely mad and switch from the news, to a late film, to adverts, then back to the news within a one-minute time span.

It's not all sweetness and light, though. The kids are unsettled by Adrian's sudden absence. Jemima asks awkward questions, seven years old now and perfectly able to understand what's going on. Tom, still only four, cries at the smallest incident and clings to me at bedtime. He misses his daddy. They both do.

But I don't relent, not even when Adrian phones that first weekend. 'Zoë? It's me. You doing anything?' Pause. 'I'm not doing anything.' Longer pause. His *most* charming tone. 'We could do nothing together.'

Oh yes, like I've never heard that old chestnut before. In fact, I think it was his first chat-up line, finding me leaning on a wall outside a mutual friend's party, ostensibly getting a breath of fresh air but actually trying to escape some bearded drama student in dungarees and Jesus sandals who'd captured me in the kitchen. I remember that line well and, taking Jemmy and Tom as prima facie evidence, it worked on that occasion. Nostalgia makes me smile, but sorry Adrian, I'm not falling for it this time.

I put on my briskest voice. 'Actually, I'm rushed off my feet here. So many things to arrange.'

'Really?' Surprised pause now. Adrian clearly hasn't anticipated failure as a possibility. After a ten-second delay, pride kicks in. 'Well, I'd better . . . Oh. Hold on. Someone's at the door, Zoë. I'll have to ring off.'

I hold the *burrrr* of the telephone to my ear for a moment after he's hung up. This sort of situation would normally have me in tears, but for some reason I'm not crying. Maybe I'm over him already. Maybe we were never really in love. It happens. Couples mistake lust for love, and later, when lust turns into habit, they mistake habit for love as well. Problem is, there's nothing you can mistake kids for except kids. And I'm the one left holding the babies. But I can't sit around all day, reading *Cosmo*, watching Australian soap repeats, and trying to pretend I can be happy as an unemployed single mother. What I need is a serious lifestyle rethink.

Back in the late eighties, when I was still naive enough to believe that love would last and that beefburgers were safe to eat, I knew a guy called Kevin.

He wasn't particularly significant in my life except for the fact that he loved snooker. Kevin loved snooker with a passion that most men reserve for football, so it came as no surprise when he asked me and Adrian and another guy to make up a four-hander one Saturday afternoon.

In those days, there was a club right in the middle of town, just one big room above a furniture store with reinforced floors for the eight full-size tables it could hold. It closed down a few years later, but at that time it was the only real snooker club in town, so most weekends and evenings it was fully booked. Kevin had managed to get this one table booked for the afternoon for himself and some work mates, but they hadn't shown up, so he went round the pubs looking for anyone he knew who might fancy taking advantage of this pre-booked table. The short straw fell to us, and off we went, with me protesting all the way about not knowing the first thing about snooker and having some shopping to do instead.

Kevin was only a little guy, about five foot five, but he knew his way around a snooker table. He showed me how to use the rest, which was a very useful piece of information considering I was shorter than he was and needed it for practically every shot at first. He wasn't even remotely condescending about the situation, merely grateful that someone had given him a game, although to be honest, I wouldn't have noticed if he had been condescending. I hadn't had enough experience of snooker players in those days to know the difference between someone being helpful and someone taking the piss.

I still remember walking into that club for the first time. You had to squeeze your way round a narrow, winding staircase on to the top floor of this building, and when you emerged at the head of the stairs, you were right next to table three. The windows were all blocked off with black boards, so the only light in the room came from the gold fringe-trimmed shades over the snooker tables. After the darkness of the stairs, these hanging lights were dazzling. I remember shielding my eyes and gazing away down the full length of table three. After playing on pub pool tables, this snooker table looked like a football field. 'I can't even see the other end.'

'You'll get used to it,' Kevin said. 'Come on, I'll sort you out a cue.'

Armed with a rack cue and a lopsided square of old

green chalk, I followed Adrian, Kevin and his mate uncertainly down the hall to table seven. 'Best table in the house,' Kevin's mate said cheerfully. Somebody put fifty-pence in the meter, and after a few agonising seconds where the lights flickered on and off like a scene from a third-rate horror movie, the bulbs finally brightened and we could see the table underneath. The cloth was torn in several places and the middle pockets were cut against the bias so that you had to be spot-on with your potting, but the cushions still had some life in them and the pack of red balls was less scarred and battered than those on other tables.

To my surprise (and Adrian's), I acquitted myself rather well on that occasion, making a twenty-five break straight off.

Kevin took this as a sign from the gods. 'You should play more often,' he told me, looking over my stance with an appraising stare. 'You're a natural.'

'I don't have the time . . .'

'You should make the time,' Kevin said sternly. Then he turned to Adrian. 'You ought to give her some lessons, or at least bring her down for a game some evenings. She might surprise you.'

At this point, Kevin had that man-to-man look in his eyes which says, 'I'm being straight with you here, mate, so listen up,' and Adrian responded by squaring his shoulders with an answering man-to-man look that said, 'I agree that you're an expert, so I'm willing to give you the benefit of the doubt, just don't waste my time and stop looking at my girlfriend's bottom.'

It was settled.

Friday nights we went over to the club for a few frames and more than a few beers, and some weekends I used to trot over to the club on my own for a bit of coaching from Kevin. He wasn't an official coach, he just knew one end of a cue from another, which was more than could be said for Adrian whose concept of potting a ball invariably involved making the white bounce off the cushion and on to the floor without ever making contact with the red.

So Kevin took me under his wing, and for a few months it was a cheerful enough arrangement. He was one of those guys whose age you can never quite place, ranging from thirty-five on a good day to about fifty on a rainy afternoon, largely depending on whether he chose to wear his stained Columbo raincoat or his Starsky and Hutch brown leather bomber-jacket.

On his thirty-something days, he was a useful ally, teaching me how to hold the cue properly and keep my head still on the shot. But the rain seemed to depress him. On wet afternoons, we simply played against each other like everyone else in the club, with Kevin grunting occasionally when I played the wrong shot or failed to get out of an easy snooker.

'What did you do that for?' he would ask irritably.

Why does anyone do anything? Why is the black worth seven points and the yellow only two? Why did the chicken cross the road? 'It seemed like the right thing to do at the time.'

'But it wasn't, was it? Look where you've left me!

Right on top of the red, and with an easy pink to follow. If you can't listen to what I'm telling you, it's just a waste of time your coming down here at all. We might as well pack up now and forget the whole thing.'

So I'd pacify him by apologising, and playing cagey for a few shots. Then the squabbling would start again. Eventually, Adrian got tried of my complaints and put his foot down. 'I don't like it. We barely know the guy. Just tell him you don't want to play any more, and that'll be an end to the situation.'

My role model in those days was not Little Red Riding Hood, but Cinderella in her pre-pumpkin days. It never occurred to me to question my boyfriend's decision, I merely complied. I said goodbye to Kevin, and to my brief but fascinating acquaintance with snooker, and stayed at home. But soon after I had stopped going to the club, I got a parcel from Kevin through the post. It was long and slim and heavy, and it contained a two-piece cue in an aluminium case. There was a brief note with it: *Don't let the bastards grind you down.*

I hid the cue away on a top shelf in the garage and never used it. Adrian would not have understood. At that point, I wasn't sure I understood. I didn't even know why Kevin reacted to the weather like a human barometer, his spirits plummeting alongside some internal needle, but despite his strange ways, I will always be grateful for his incredible belief in me, not to mention that parting advice, so unfathomable at the time. Looking back, though, I reckon Kevin must have been psychic.

I ring my mother. 'I'm going to start playing snooker again.'

'Oh no, darling. That's the worst thing you can do.' She hesitates, and I can hear her thinking frantically. When I was playing before, she spent half the time shuddering in case the neighbours found out, and the other half trying to persuade me to take up knitting or flower-arranging. 'Why don't you get a nice job? Just something during the day, while the kids are at school?'

'I've made my mind up, Mum. I always wanted to play snooker seriously, but Adrian never approved.'

'Nor do I, Zoë. You know I hate to think of you in those smoky working-men's clubs. It's not natural for a woman.'

'Mum, stop living in the past. Snooker clubs aren't like that any more.' Okay, this is a little white lie, but there's no point telling my mother the truth. Truth only confuses the issue. 'I'll be fine. I've got talent, I know that. I just need to find out how far I can go with it.'

'And the children? After a relationship break-up, children need a mother to be there for them, not to go out . . . *hustling* . . . or whatever it is you plan to do at that club. I saw something about that on Oprah Winfrey the other day.'

'I'm not Paul Newman, Mum. I just need to do

something I'm reasonably good at, something competitive. I'm bored sitting at home.'

'Then get a job.'

I sigh. 'Do you realise how expensive childminders are? Or were you planning on looking after the kids for me during the holidays?'

My mother hastily backtracks. 'Oh well, please yourself. You know I don't mind helping you out occasionally, but I've got my own life to lead. You can't expect me to look after children full-time at my age.' She makes a tutting noise. 'I don't know where I went wrong with you, Zoë, I really don't. You're an unfit parent. And now you're going to desert my grandchildren when they need you most, and probably turn *them* into unfit parents as well.'

I wince. My mother's just scored first blood on the emotional blackmail front. She always knows exactly where to strike for best effect. But I set my jaw grimly. I'm capable of putting on the psychological pressure as well. 'Jemmy and Tom will be fine. I'll only play snooker when they're at school . . . unless their loving granny could take them for the odd evening?'

She sighs exaggeratedly. Why is it that mothers always know how to sigh in a particular way that lets you know just how much you've hurt them, without opening themselves up to accusations of overdramatisation? It must be an instinctive mothering skill which I make a mental note of never inflicting on my own kids. But my ruse has worked.

'All right, Zoë, suit yourself. But if it all goes horribly

wrong, don't come running to me. What with the way your father's been behaving . . . well, I won't burden you with my problems.' This is my cue to dutifully ask her what's wrong. 'Oh, don't mind me. Least said soonest mended. What the eye doesn't see . . . well, he's been doing it for years. Why should I take offence now?'

'What's her name this time?'

She sighs. I know my mother. She always makes a fuss about Dad's 'other women', but she never actually takes action. The worst she's ever done is lock him out of the bedroom, and even then, she relented half-way through the night and dragged him off the sofa and back upstairs. Later, she claimed she was worried about his back problem flaring up again. 'Sharon. She works in the laundrette. The first I knew of it was when he stopped putting his underpants in the washing-basket. *She* does them for him now.' My mother makes a clacking noise under her breath. 'Sharon. Such a classy name. Thirty-three, the sort who still wears blue eyeshadow, and if those breasts are real . . . well, I'm Doris Day.'

'Do you want me to come round? Have a word with Dad?'

'What good would that do? He's a man. Men do these things at his age. Unfortunately, your father's been doing them since we got married.' She tries to sound suitably martyred. 'No, you carry on with your . . . snookering. But I must have failed in my duty as a mother. It's not normal behaviour, Zoë.'

I know what my mother's thinking. *Snooker's a man's*

game. Who do you think you are, taking on the entire male establishment? It's not that my mother's old fashioned, you understand, she just finds it hard to accept that a grown woman would want to set foot inside one of those grimy back-street clubs. To her, those places were created by long-suffering women, to keep men out of their living rooms but firmly off the streets.

'Not like that!' Bob says, bending me forwards over the table like a rag doll, my forehead grazing the green cloth and my right arm stuck out behind me like a chicken leg. He knocks one of my feet sideways, kicking me with his hobnailed boot. 'Spread your legs. There . . . that's better.'

Bob's the local coach. It took some persuasion to get him to coach me, but here we are now, with him pushing and pulling at me in a way that reminds me strangely of Adrian. But I keep these thoughts to myself. Bob does not seem like a man who would appreciate that remark. Instead, I stick to the obvious. 'I feel ridiculous.'

'You look ridiculous,' he says sharply, letting go.

I rise abruptly, bringing the cue up at the same time and nearly smashing a bulb in the overhead shade. The whole contraption sways violently, shooting its huge shadows across the club. He puts a hand up to steady it, watching me. I rub my wrist awkwardly, frowning. 'That hurt.'

'I told you it wouldn't be easy.'

I know his type. Good at his job, competent at

handling the half-dozen or so lads who come to his Saturday morning coaching sessions, but totally at sea when it comes to teaching a woman how to play. I put my cue away, watching him as he leans back on the bar and orders a pint. In another few years, his hair will be completely gone, but at the moment he's still raking it over his prominent crown, shining now with the faint sweat of the middle-aged. He has two afternoons off a week and, as far as I know, he spends them both in the snooker club, regardless of the weather or the time of year. He has his own reserved seat just under the telly, and Bet, the owner, pulls him his usual as soon as she sees the blue glint of his Volvo pulling up in the car park.

Still nodding over his own omniscience, Bob knocks back half his pint in one fluid movement, his adam's apple bobbing dramatically up and down. He puts one hand to what used to be his lower abdomen but is now simply part beer-belly, part chest, and gives an only slightly muffled belch. He watches me in vain for a reaction. A typical local coach: once skilful, but now approaching retirement with all the inevitability of autumn, his hair falling out, his teeth not far behind and his cue arm rather suspect under pressure.

Whoever once said of older men 'there may be snow on the roof, but there's a fire in the hearth', was not referring to Bob. When he isn't coaching young lads, he's out in his three-door company Volvo, selling double-glazing to housewives and retired couples. 'It's a living,' he always says, but the gleam in his eye is neither irony nor long years of alcohol abuse taking its toll, but pure satisfaction. Bob enjoys that daily grind. Boredom has become a part of his mental make-up, to the extent that he no longer dreams of avoiding it or heading off into the sunset with a rucksack and an Ordnance Survey map, but actually welcomes it with open arms: the safe, the familiar, the excruciatingly predictable. For him, I come into none of those categories.

'Women, you see,' he says flatly, as if this demands no further explanation.

'Women?'

'Not built for it. Not like men. It's a man's game . . . stands to reason.' Bob catches my eye, falters. 'Although, of course, I suppose . . .' He tails off into his pint, suddenly finding the pale-gold dregs fascinating as they stream back down along the glass.

'Same time next week then?'

'Tuesdays are difficult. Can't you come on Saturdays like all the rest?'

'My kids,' I remind him. 'It's hard to find a babysitter first thing on a Saturday morning. They're at school on weekdays.'

'Of course,' Bob says smoothly.

Too smoothly. He already knew what I was going to say. Irritation flashes up inside me like a tiny electric shock. I can feel my mouth tighten. Almost proud of my restraint, I keep my hands behind my back. 'What are you saying, Bob? That I should knock it on the head?'

'Well . . . it is a bit difficult, love. You understand.'

Oh yes, I understand. Only too perfectly. I glance around the club. From the smiles of the other men within earshot, it's obvious they also understand.

I'm suddenly acutely aware of myself: overlong hair tied back hastily, the unironed shirt that I just had time to grab from the washing-pile before organising Jemima's and Tom's school clothes; my old trainers with their flapping soles and the long grey trail of mismatched laces.

I nearly overslept this morning. The tentative scratch at the bedroom door woke me just before eight, leaving me exactly twenty minutes to wash, dress and get the kids organised before bundling them off to school. The last thing on my mind was my appearance. Actually, it could be worse. Once or twice, I've caught myself trying to leave the house wearing slippers instead of shoes, and on one memorable occasion, I spent a full five minutes struggling with my blue woollen gloves before I realised they were Jemima's. Since then, I've purchased accessories on a strictly colour-coordinated basis.

I look at Bob's neat pinstriped shirt. He has one of those razor-edge creases along each arm, and matching creases along his trouser legs. His shoes are past their best, but immaculately polished. 'I can see your wife doesn't play snooker.'

'Certainly not. She's a woman.'

I smile grimly. I knew this wasn't going to be easy, but I hadn't actually thought of redefining the word 'difficult' until today. I go back to the table and collect my cue case. I'm aware of their conspiratorial whispering at the bar, suddenly reminded of a school trip to the South of France, when a tiny insect crawled inside my ear at the beach and only came out when some kind soul held my head forcibly under the water. Long after I had been debugged, I could still hear that irritating buzzing in my ears. Like water torture, it gets inside you and grinds you down, slowly but surely.

I set my jaw, facing Bob with what I hope passes for sang-froid, but is actually a combination of bravado and sudden nausea. 'I'll try and make it on Saturday.'

In retrospect, I'm sure I only imagined the look on Bob's face, the astonished expression of a card-sharp whose winning hand has just been trumped by a greenhorn.

I've always been a worrier. My close friends call it paranoia, but I know what they're up to. They're just trying to catch me off guard, so I won't be prepared for disaster when it strikes.

Accordingly, a few months later, when I spot an advertisement tucked away in one of the snooker magazines, *'Leicestershire Ladies' Open Tournament'* (with a few smudgy black-and-whites of the top women players just to give me a visual idea of what I'm up against), I start to worry.

Should I enter this tournament? If I do, will I suffer the ultimate humiliation of losing in a first-round match? If I don't enter, will I ever be able to face myself in the mirror again? If I dare to enter this, my first serious snooker competition, will the heavens fall, just as Chicken Licken so terrifyingly predicted they would do when I was only six?

I decide to do the traditional thing. I go round and ask my mother. My mother is practical as ever. She puts down her copy of *Good Housekeeping* and looks me straight in the eye. 'Don't waste your money, Zoë. You'll only lose.'

I send off the cut-out entry form straight away. By return of post, I get a polite but photocopied letter and a list of nearby accommodation, plus details of parking and facilities for the disabled. It's official. In a few weeks' time, I will be a gibbering wreck in some Leicestershire snooker club, dropping my cue every time I chalk it while my opponent calmly mops up the colours.

The whole situation is beginning to resemble one of those Japanese game-shows, where contestants undergo Inquisition-style tortures in order to get on television, yet still jump up grinning and waving over the closing credits. I must be mad. These women in the photographs, poorly reproduced or not, have the look of underfed piranhas. I am about to dip not only my cue but my entire body into the whirlpool of international ladies' snooker, and I fully expect to lose both of them.

Turning up for my first world-ranking tournament turns out to be less terrifying than I imagined. The small Leicestershire club only has twenty tables, and the bar area is roughly the size of a pre-Second World War outside lavatory. After signing in, I develop a sudden overwhelming urge to visit the toilets, probably brought on by being in a similarly sized space. But on opening the door to the ladies, I nearly fall over a woman.

'Don't move an inch!' she exclaims, on all fours. 'Contact lenses. I've dropped one.'

I lean back on the door jamb, watching her. There's a queasiness in the pit of my stomach which seems to have no connection with the bacon butty I consumed so rapidly on my way here. Suddenly, I realise what it is. I've left my cue propped up against the bar. Alone. Friendless. Unprotected.

I start to back out, mumbling something.

'Wait!' she shrieks as I shuffle backwards. Leaning forward, she picks something up off the floor. With her fringe hanging over her face, and the strangely dishevelled figure she cuts on the green and white lino, this woman reminds me briefly of the manic Mrs Rochester in *Jane Eyre*. Any minute now, she'll leap to her feet and sink her teeth into my arm, then rush off to find the nearest stairs to the roof. But as I try to make good my escape, she tugs at my trousers with her one free hand. 'Thanks. You had your foot on it.'

I hesitate, wondering whether to beat a hasty retreat and protect my cue or give in to my now burning desire to go to the toilet. 'Is it broken?'

She examines it minutely. 'No,' she decides eventually, then to my horror she licks the shiny little thing and sticks it straight back in her eye. 'Just a bit flatter, that's all.'

I make my way round her towards a cubicle. The cue will have to wait a little longer. I'm not going to make a spectacle of myself by dragging it in here with me, and if I don't hurry I'm going to miss the draw. *The draw*. The two most horrific words in the language right at this moment. I might draw the World Champion, or even the County Champion, or even this woman, getting up off her knees now and brushing down her dress-trousers and psychedelic orange blouse.

'I'm Tricksy,' she says, holding out a hand. She has strange objects that resemble television aerials dangling from her ears. It's like being introduced to one of the Clangers. 'Have they done the draw yet?'

'I don't think so. I'm Zoë.'

She lets go of my hand and looks me up and down in a critical fashion. Her eyes narrow on my heels. 'First time?' I nod. 'No heels allowed. Still, you might be lucky and the referee won't notice. Good luck . . . and if you draw me, don't worry. I'm not a seed.'

When she leaves, I stand there for a moment, my hand on the toilet door. Not a seed? How wonderfully cryptic. I'm somewhere deep in B-movie territory. It's *Attack of the Pod People* without the popcorn. What sort of world have I got myself mixed up in? No heels allowed. Obviously, I'm doomed to shortness in this brave new world of comfortable shoes.

But somehow, those first jumping nerves seem to have deserted me for a strange, almost evangelical euphoria. There are about fifty women in this club, all of them self-proclaimed snooker players, and I'm one of them. Bar the heels, that is.

Steve Davis once said that all good players have 'authority' in the way they hit the ball. By my reckoning, 'authority' is somewhere between a clean stroke and a punch. Strong. Smooth. Accurate. Carried through and beyond the object ball by its own inner momentum. And the first time you do it, the very first time you get that spot-on connection between white and object ball, the feeling you get is like your first orgasm combined with your first taste of Häagen-Dazs ice cream. As close to heaven and hedonism as it's possible to get. Did you hear that incredible contact? Congratulations. You've just hit the ball properly.

It happens like this. Here I am in my first ladies' tournament, chalking my cue whilst considering a tricky black, when suddenly across the room I see a shot. Not just any shot, but an unforgettable, mesmerising, just-watch-this-pink-you-suckers shot. It's so unexpected to see a shot of this calibre hanging round a Leicestershire snooker club on a rainy Sunday afternoon that I straighten instinctively, stop chalking my cue and stare. 'Who the hell is that?'

My opponent, who introduced herself as a nursery-nurse from the Outer Hebrides, glances over. Her face drops, which is a revelation for me as I was just beginning to wonder whether plastic surgery was responsible for her persistent lack of expression. She is clearly impressed by the tall redhead opposite. 'That's Sylvie . . .' and she adds some unpronounceable foreign surname that goes straight over my head.

'Not British then.'

The face lapses back into its customary blankness. 'Finnish.'

'The game?' I can't resist the bait.

One plastic eyebrow raises itself slowly. 'From Finland. Your shot.'

I chalk my cue again, fix my eyes on the black. It lies six inches from the pocket, an acute one-quarter angle, almost a cut, pulsating on the green cloth like some malignant cinder from *Quatermass*. I see in my mind's eye that smooth backward pull, the slight hesitation, then the forward thrust across the table straight through the ball and on towards some hitherto unimagined universe. Only afterwards rising from the shot, totally cool, almost indestructibly so.

I re-enact what I saw, and it happens. It actually happens. I hear it as ball strikes ball, a controlled explosion of sound instead of the rather laboured clunk-click that I'm accustomed to expect. It's like watching someone else play. The black shoots smoothly into the pocket, and the white zings off the cushion and back into position as if pre-programmed. I punch the air, making a strangled whooping noise that draws eyes from around the room. At this point, my dour Scottish opponent begins to resemble a Cabbage Patch doll even more than before.

The referee appointed for our table 'harumphs'

under his breath at my behaviour, replacing the black, one beady eye fixed on my face as I hurry round triumphantly to my next red.

'Eight,' he murmurs disapprovingly. He straightens up, adjusting the lapels of his penguin suit. Then his eyes fall to my heels. Something flickers in those eyes. His voice sinks even lower, almost to a whisper. 'Flat shoes next time, please.'

I ignore him, too excited by the strange phenomenon. It's happening, I'm playing well, I'm reaching my form. My arm swings in perfect synchronisation with my wrist. My head barely moves. I have Stephen Hendry's absurdly concave back, arching like a wooden bridge under an unbearable load. I have Steve Davis's totally professional nonchalance as I prepare to lunge. I have Jimmy White's nervous genius in the slight turn of my cue just before the hit. Then something happens with my feet, a momentary shift on the shot or possibly the onset of Parkinson's disease. Clearly I have overdone things by including Jimmy White's nervous genius. The red rattles, but does not drop.

'Eight,' the referee repeats with undisguised satisfaction.

My opponent has clearly not been wasting her weekends off in the Outer Hebrides. No picking wild flowers or counting sheep for this one. Ball after ball falls into the pockets, almost by accident from where I'm sitting. Was this bloody woman born in a snooker club? I don't bother arguing with the dodgy free-ball situation. She looks like she flosses with other people's 'm not going to risk a strong right-hook ...meone who can mix knock-off Doc Martens with yellow slacks (the ones with elasticated waists) and get away with it. As the last black surrenders and the goat-girl bares her teeth in a humourless smile, I shake her hand, numb under the chill of defeat.

There's nothing worse than losing. Except possibly losing a first-round match to an extra from *The Sound of Music*.

Two seconds after I've packed away my cue, the Finnish redhead of unusual height swans past with the look of someone who's just wiped the floor with her opponent, an all-leather customised cue case in her hand. Even away from the table, she has the eyes of a striking snake, uncannily accurate and deadly. I would kill for that look. It must scare the pants off the men she plays. And she still looks cool. Untouched by that brief scuffle back on table ten, the ruthless dispatch of yet another stumbling unseeded player.

Some people are just built better. Bomb-proof. Made to last. Others, including myself, have a tendency to shatter at the first tentative knock. This one is indisputably a runner, a stayer of courses, a winner, the real McCoy. She's also unbelievably tall.

'Excuse me?' I hiss nervously in her direction.

The giraffe haughtily turns her head. Even at this distance, I can see the disdain in her face. Bloody hell. What are you going to do now? Congratulate her? Offer to stand her a cup of tea at the bar? You can barely afford to buy one yourself. Ask her what her secret is, when you know as well as the next woman that it's all in the wrist? Maybe I just wanted to know whether she was a natural redhead.

'Yes?'

There's the faintest wisp of a foreign accent, just enough to confirm her identity. She waits impatiently as I squeeze along the wall, my cue catching the legs of an adjacent referee. I stumble, apologising profusely.

Those deadly eyes narrow on my face. 'What is it?'

My mouth opens like a goldfish. I see her looking down at my free hand, waving emptily at my side. No winning sheet. Attila the Hun from the Outer Hebrides has got it. I came away from that match with nothing but my wounded pride. Embarrassment floods over me and I suddenly remember the time I fell backwards off my chair in fifth-form geography and everyone saw my knickers.

'If you remember what it was you wanted,' Sylvie says, and I'm horrified to hear a sarcastic note in her voice. I shrink to the size of a pinhead, backing away. Not only am I a nobody, but a lack of substance is clearly written all over my face. 'Do let me know.'

I could have said anything here. It's that situation where you walk away afterwards and immediately think of all those smart replies you could have pinned to the air like butterflies, too bright and fast for her to follow. That peculiarly effective brand of smart-arse remark that allows you to stroll away laughing, secure in the knowledge that nobody in the room realises you're haemorrhaging internally. But for some reason my mouth has seized. The room swallows me up. I'm getting smaller by the second.

Sylvie laughs. Before I can react, she turns on her heel and walks away, swinging that case as though it were a freshly severed human head.

At that moment, my future is mapped out for me. Such arrogance, such blind hubris! What gives one human being the right to say 'I'm better than you', even if their subtlety in not *saying* so but simply demonstrating it is more embarrassment for your sake than courtesy? I have never seen myself through someone else's eyes like this, and it hurts. All those childhood instincts, especially those that made me want to curl up in the bottom of the wardrobe after some painful remark, come flooding back. The best way to punish that sort of arrogance is with a cue. Wipe the smile off her face. I'm out of this tournament now, but there's always next time. I can practise. Hard.

2

There's a magnetic pull to it. Every time I walk into a snooker room, I feel it. It's best when the club has only just opened for the day: tables draped with long white dust-sheets like occupied slabs at the morgue, the dark Masonic shape of a triangle propped up against the green hanging shade, the steadiness and strength of those carved wooden legs.

I drag back the dust-sheet, reveal the field of the cloth, still deeply furrowed from yesterday's hands. With the light off, it's like looking down at night on some silent waiting place which will be a battleground by dawn. I pull the balls out of their pockets, trickle them across the cloth, watch them glisten like fat slugs as the light blinks on above them. I have a vague awareness of being ridiculous, but I can't shake off the table's mesmerising pulse, the way this baize comes off on your fingers like dust from a butterfly's wings or that powdery pollen inside a tulip petal, green pelt left under your nails for days. Even the acrid smell of the chalk, inescapable.

I suppose this light, the glare of unshaded bulbs once you're underneath the hooded gold fringe, must attract me like a moth. I know each time I raise my cue that I'm going to fail at some point, but I can't resist. Mary Pickford, the American actress, once said 'this thing we call failure . . . is not the falling down, but the staying down'. That's how I'm going to approach every shot from now on, every game, every practice session, even world-ranking tournaments. The baize is like a green river, studded with bright stones. There are crocodiles waiting there for the unwary. The pockets gape like their open jaws. I'm dazzled by the reflections. I stare into the river, gripping my cue. It's a weapon, a yardstick, a balance. Without it, I may fall into the river like a wasp into a jar of honey; drowning, seduced by the sheer luminosity of this game.

Okay, ha ha. You may laugh at this, but if you can't be passionate about something, even if it's only *a ball game*, what's life worth living for? Everyone has a passion for something. For some women, it's a man. For rather more ambitious women, it may be a career. For a sad minority, it's crocheting or gardening or flower-arranging. I have a passion for snooker. It's not easy to explain why, but there's an air of romance about the game that I find irresistible. It's nothing glaringly obvious, just a subtle combination of things that keeps me enchanted: the weight of the cue balanced in my hand, the hum of the overhead light as it warms up, someone calling the score on a distant table, the tense smoky atmosphere of a league match, even the quiet click of balls that comes back to me night after night in my sleep. But most importantly, it's a feeling of intimacy. The awareness that there's something happening between you and the table, something no one else can interfere with or destroy. Something an outsider could never understand. Every player experiences it differently, and that's what makes it special. It's a feeling of belonging in the midst of exile. Besides, the daily practice, the desire to play world-ranking tournaments, these represent my chance to get even with all those people who've tried to keep me out of snooker, and I refuse to go about it in a half-hearted fashion.

Competitiveness is not attractive in a woman. From a man's point of view, that is, not to mention my mother's. Men may feel admiration, even respect, for someone they consider to be a ball breaker with all the charm and vulnerability of a JCB, but they rarely *like* you, and even more rarely wish to sleep with you. Once you start exhibiting a tendency to beat men at their own game, they close ranks. Political correctness may drag a chilly smile out of them occasionally, but beyond that, you're on your own. Being a woman player is not a wise career option for the squeamish or easily offended. Let's face it, the vast majority of men who play snooker are those same men who hang half their bottoms over work-site scaffolding and wolf-whistle mindlessly at anything in a skirt, even Billy Connolly.

Have you ever noticed that it's just when things are

going well that disaster strikes? Only a few days after deciding to put my back into some serious practice, Jemima falls sick. Being the eldest, she likes to set a good example to her younger brother by doing things properly. Not only does she throw up over the neat pile of ironed clothes on the kitchen table, but she manages to pass on a particularly virulent strain of gastric flu to Tom. Soon, both of them are tucked up in bed, feverish and unable to sleep, while I struggle to concentrate on the new snooker manual Bob has lent me. Every fifteen minutes, someone bangs on the floor and calls out weakly for more water or blankets, or fewer blankets, or to be sick. It becomes almost a game, a grim unspoken challenge to prevent me from reading.

I crack first, ringing Adrian one evening to see if he will sit with them while I get out for a quick practice.

'You ought to stay with them,' he says accusingly. 'You're their mother.'

'It's only gastric flu, Adrian. And they're over the worst of it. Jemima's already sitting up reading. It's hardly a life-threatening condition.'

'What the hell do you want to play snooker for, anyway?'

I allow him to rant on for a moment, then break in, unable to stop myself. 'I've got another world-ranking tournament soon. It's really important that I practise.'

'Who do you think you are, Zoë? Steve Davis? Get real,' he says angrily, then finishes in a cutting tone. 'You were the one who wanted children. You've made your bed . . . now you've got to lie in it. Don't expect any help from me in living out your sad little fantasies.'

I put the phone down, and listen at the foot of the stairs for a moment. There is silence from the kids' bedroom. Maybe they've both fallen asleep at last. I let myself out of the back door and stand for a moment on the porch, breathing in the quiet evening air. It is still quite warm. A dog is barking somewhere along the straggling line of houses. The evenings are getting lighter. I can smell fresh-cut grass. Someone is still mowing their lawn in the half-light. I can just see Mr Patterson moving to and fro in his rolled shirt-sleeves, three houses down.

Suddenly, there seems to be something comforting about the steady rhythmical buzz of the mower as one of my neighbours reduces his lawn to an even briefer square of green. The children are asleep. The house is quiet. A bus trundles cheerfully past me and down the hill, steamed-up windows shuddering. I glance at my watch. The news will be on soon. I can make myself a sandwich and settle down in front of the television.

I nip upstairs briefly, just to check on the children. Jemima has fallen asleep over her book and I retrieve it, putting it quietly back on their toy box. Her mouth is slightly open, but she is breathing normally at last. I put a hand to her forehead, relieved to feel cool skin under my palm.

Mr Bear, her favourite teddy, has fallen out of bed. I stoop down and prop it up beside her pillow. As I step back, his one remaining eyeball glints at me in a sinister fashion. I've tried hundreds of times to throw him out, but Jemmy won't let me. At seven, she's too old to admit to being scared of the dark, but I know she secretly is. One of Mr Bear's prime functions is to keep watch for her once the light's been put out. If she wakes up and Mr Bear's not there, tough as old boots and guarding her against bogey-men and nightmares, I will probably have to come back up again to calm her hysteria.

Tom is lying on his back, one leg sticking out from under his duvet, his small face flushed. He's surrounded by soft toys, a knitted caterpillar lying across his stomach, grasped possessively in his sleep. I tuck him back in automatically, checking to see if his temperature has risen at all in the last hour. But it seems to have fallen slightly, so I turn the light off in their bedroom and make my way downstairs.

On the third stair from the bottom, I pause. What am I telling myself? That this is all life holds for me and that I should be grateful to have a home and children like these? For a moment there, I was slipping into some age-old excuse, where women persuade themselves that they actually enjoy being tied to the home. Where the pitter-patter of tiny feet is all we live for. Where a sandwich or a late film is the height of female luxury. If I was going out to earn money, no one would call my ambition a fantasy. People would nod and sigh, and say how awful but ultimately necessary it is for a single mother to leave her children. But to entertain ambitions beyond being able to pay the rent is somehow unwarranted, outrageous, even unnatural for a woman in my position.

I make the sandwich, watch the news and end up nodding off in front of the umpteenth showing of *Casablanca*. It is somewhere between Rick and Ilsa saying goodbye on the tarmac, and the bottle of Vichy being cast into the waste-paper basket, that I realise what a pragmatic woman Ilsa is. It's not noble to throw away true love for the sake of a cause, but it shows great understanding of the nature of love. Rick was only Rick because Ilsa left him. If Ilsa had stayed with him, they would have settled down. He would have taken her love for granted, opened a new café, and spent most of his time in it. She would have borne him several children, ruined her figure, and lost all sense of romance. But with Victor Laslo as a partner, the adventure is always just beginning.

Three weeks later, I'm in the club one afternoon as usual. MTV is on in the bar, and through the partition I can hear R.E.M.'s 'Shiny Happy People'. It's particularly apt because someone has left the back-door open and the sunlight is streaming into the club, making it difficult to play shots into the top left-hand pocket but catching every spinning particle of dust in an incredible light-show. There's a woman laughing in the bar, and the cleaner is sitting outside on the step, shoes and socks off, pulling up dandelions almost absentmindedly. I've been here two and a half hours already, bent on solo practice. I've missed a straight stun blue into the middle pocket three times, and under my jeans, my pasty white legs are screaming to get out into the sunlight.

To focus my mind, I concentrate on my breathing. Buddhists do that too. I'm not sure I'm entirely enamoured of the bit where they press each nostril alternately before lapsing into meditation and drifting away on to a higher plane, but childbirth taught me two important things: one, breathing exercises are absolutely pointless faced with pain of that intensity and two, if you inhale slowly and deeply for any length of time, eventually you fall asleep. The vital thing to remember is to stop before you get drowsy. But it's not only a calming technique, it's helps you focus too.

I blot everything out: the sunlight on the table, MTV's unintelligible Swedish presenter, the rhythmic click-crunch of beheaded dandelions, even Bet still shrieking with laughter through the glass partition. In: one, two, three. Out: one, two, three. Soon, all I can see is the blue. I pull back, breathe, lunge elegantly. The ball disappears. I chalk my cue methodically, get down to the unlikely cut on the red into the top right-hand pocket.

The telephone rings.

It rings seven times. It's like being in a doctor's waiting room. Answer it someone, for God's sake. After about another thirty seconds, by which time most sensible people would have hung up and tried again later, Bet strolls through to the phone. She picks it up, still laughing at something on the telly, then holds it up reluctantly at me. 'For you, Zoë.'

Who the hell can this be? The kids are at school and my mum's at the hairdresser's. Images flash through my mind: my mother, burnt to a crisp under a defective dryer, my eldest impaling herself on the working end of a hockey stick, my youngest abducted during a routine visit to the local swimming baths. Some apologetic voice at the other end, asking whether I was alone or if I wanted to sit down. I close my eyes. 'Hello?'

'It's me! Tricksy! I tried you at home, then rang directory enquiries for the club number. I knew you were keen, but playing in the afternoon's a bit much, isn't it? No job? Oh, you've got kids, haven't you? Well, I suppose kids are enough work for anyone.' Tricksy hesitates as if waiting for a reply, then launches herself cheerfully back into the conversation. 'I'm going to be in your neck of the woods this week. Sales convention. Did I tell you I'm a rep? Never mind . . . we'll cover that later. How about drinks? No, a game. How about a game Friday night?'

'That sounds great.'

'Seven-thirty all right? Where's the club?'

There's only one snooker club in this one-horse dorp and a blind man with a stick could find it in five minutes flat. 'When you reach the only set of traffic lights on the High Street, turn right. You can't miss it.'

'Fine. We'll show the men there a thing or two.' Tricksy giggles.

It's a long time since I heard anyone giggle and for a

moment I'm back in the first year at school, swopping *Star Wars* stickers behind the bicycle shed, long before sophistication hit me in the form of disintegrating Silk Cuts (stolen in ones and twos from my mother's coat pocket while she was watching telly), or later still, the juicy taste of gossip still fresh from some sixth-former's pyjama party. Like the sunlight on the table, her irreverent laughter is something that lifts my spirits. Why can't I be more like that? Amused by the whole situation, casting care to the winds and just playing for the sheer joy and hell of it.

Suddenly, the last half-hour before I have to pick the kids up from school doesn't seem so long. I can fit another line-up routine into that time, easily. It's strange how always being the public enemy can drain your energy. Having Tricksy at the club will be wonderful for morale: *see, I'm not the only woman who plays snooker.*

'Remember. Mine's a large vodka and coke,' Tricksy adds hurriedly as I go to put the phone down.

So much for girlish innocence.

On my way to pick up the kids from school, I'm suddenly reminded of that incisive line in *Tootsie*: 'I've always hated women who treat other women as stand-ins for men.' Is that why I'm so pleased that Tricksy's coming to town? Is it some desperate desire for company, anyone's company, in the absence of male attention?

It's been over a month since Adrian moved out. All

that rebound shit I'd steeled myself to face has not yet materialised. Funnily enough, the double bed's much more comfortable with only one occupant, and there have been no tossing-and-turning incidents so far, or bleary-eyed 'wee small hours of the morning' bouts of insomnia. True, I did go through a short phase of turning the radio or television on after the kids had gone to bed, disliking the eerie silence without *him*. But you can get used to silence, don't you? In the end, it's almost comforting.

And there's been none of those frantic Monday-morning weigh-ins, standing in the bathroom in just bra and knickers, shifting from one foot to the other on the scales to see if that'll make any difference to a three-pound weekend gain. No Saturday-night take-aways. No Sunday-morning fried breakfasts in bed. In fact, it's the first time I've lost so much weight without the ulterior motive of capturing some man's eye across a crowded supermarket aisle. I just can't be bothered to cook for myself. The kids seem happy with my half-hearted efforts at nutrition meals: beans on toast, chicken salad, scrambled egg. But most nights it gets to about midnight before I realise I haven't eaten all day, then I manage a few slices of toast and wonder why my jeans are so loose the next morning. Far from trying to catch men's eyes, I've barely noticed they exist.

Maybe I'm living in denial. But sod it, what if I am? It's about time someone else did all the running. Even if I do 'get off' with someone (is that still the correct terminology?), there are too many things I've forgotten about when it comes to dating. After all, it's been a long time. I started living with Adrian before the AIDS epidemic was forced out into the open. What do people do now on a first date? Go for a blood test?

Last time I dated, I was only nineteen. At that age, the back seat of a car is comfy enough for any position, even one memorised from a hastily cribbed *Kama Sutra*, and a satisfactory chat-up line is somewhere between a grunt and an elbow in the ribs.

Where do women in their late twenties *go* to meet men? The local laser disco seems an unlikely place for anyone pushing twenty-five, and the last time I ventured into a bar, it was all cocktail umbrellas and under-age drinking. The only males in sight were almost as desperate as me, still wearing INXS T-shirts under their suit jackets and raving about Irvine Welsh's latest book. Most of them didn't even look as though they were old enough to shave. Besides, even if I meet a reasonable man about my own age, it's odds-on he'll already be married, with a wife who 'doesn't understand him' and a secretary who does. Alternatively, he'll be divorced and wary of commitment, which precludes anything to do with single parents.

I wish I had the nerve for a one-night stand. But if I did, the kids would probably wake up and come stumbling in to see why 'Mummy's making funny noises'.

I could let my mother take the kids overnight, but that means planning ahead. The whole concept of the one-night stand is of disorganised spontaneity: the mumbled exchange in the shared taxi home, something inexplicable happening between the offer of coffee and the boiling of a kettle, that 'shit, am I wearing my new white Sloggis today or the ones with the broken elastic trailing around my upper thigh like one of those rabid tentacles out of *Aliens*?' train of thought, his garlic breath so unbearable that I have to nip back into the kitchen ('I'll just check that kettle') for some pepperoni so that my halitosis is at least on a level footing with his.

Then the horror of the next morning, waking up next to someone whose name you can barely remember and whose hairy armpits announce their presence long before you find the strength to open your eyes.

Maybe I'm getting old. I just didn't know it would happen so soon.

I hate confessions. So when Tricksy says she has a confession to make, I stiffen instinctively. I can tell by her expression that she interprets this as a sign of encouragement. 'I knew I could confide in you, Zoë,' she enthuses.

She turned up earlier than I expected, catching me in the car park. We walked in together, shoulder to shoulder. It felt like one of those first suffragette marches Victorian women might have undertaken, especially since the twenty-odd paces from door to bar feel like several miles on a good day, every male head in the place turning to stare. Today, it's Tricksy they are staring at.

The local players have got used to me in a resigned

sort of way, like people who get used to living with cancer. I know that's what they think, that bit by bit I'm chipping away at their traditions, corrupting the healthy red cells of an all-male establishment with my pink bootees. But that's their problem, not mine. I'm not going to disappear under the weight of their hostility. I'm here to stay and there's nothing they can do about it. Ya-boo. I've shied away from open confrontation in the past, but with Tricksy beside me suddenly I'm much braver, less inclined to give way. I even feel taller. Not quite Sylvie proportions, but I have no aspirations to giraffedom.

I realise Tricksy's expecting me to guess her confession. Suddenly, I'm back in Disney's *101 Dalmatians*, watching *What's My Crime?* I screw my face up in what I hope is a suggestion of intense concentration. 'You're not pregnant, are you?'

Brief baffled silence. 'Of course not. All I meant was that I haven't picked up my cue since the last tournament. Actually,' she continues, 'I haven't practised for months. The Leicestershire tournament was meant to be my last one. I've been thinking of knocking it on the head. To be honest, I've been pig-sick of the world circuit lately. Practice, practice, practice. And nothing to show for it but a few points on a ranking list and a hefty overdraft.'

How did this woman get so boring? Does she practise in front of a live audience?

She laughs, clearly oblivious to my nonplussed silence. 'Then . . . I met you. We had a real laugh in the bar, didn't we? That's what it's all about for me. I love the game, but I'm never going to set the world on fire, am I? Snooker's just fun now. A weekend away from boring old reality.' Tricksy shrugs. 'I suppose us lower-ranked players have got to stick together. I mean, there's no point us taking ourselves seriously, is there? We've got no hope of being World Champions.'

I narrow my eyes.

'Anyway,' she continues, smiling. 'I just wanted to warn you that I haven't practised for ages. I'm probably rusty as hell. You'll beat me with one hand tied behind your back. Honestly, just now I can't seem to pot a ball unless it's sitting right over the pocket.'

She slides her case up on to the snooker table and opens it. The expensive two-piece screws together with an expert flick of the wrist. 'So be gentle with me, okay?'

Tricksy wins the first frame 86–12.

Be gentle with me? Come on! I watch her set the balls up again, chalking my tip in what I hope passes for a professional touch. I can practically *smell* the men at the bar staring at us. Bob is over in the corner of the bar, apparently fascinated by tonight's episode of *Coronation Street* but watching us through the glass partition every time I glance up. He's got a huge grin on his face which I suspect has nothing to do with the fact that Deidre has just slapped Ken Barlow across the face. This is my home club. I'm showing myself up. Bob is loving it.

'I thought you said you were rusty?'

'I *am* rusty! I can't believe how badly I'm playing.'

Sure. That last 35 break was a fluke, a mere slip of the cue. The only too inclusive remark about *us lower-ranked players* is still smarting. I see the crafty cocked-hat-double-and-back-to-safety shot, but I take the more difficult long red with the promise of a black afterwards. I'm going for the jugular.

The next tournament is in Romford, stamping-ground for such legendary gods of the baize as Steve Davis, Ronnie O'Sullivan, Steve Ebden and occasionally the ill-fated Jimmy White, whenever he wanders over from Wimbledon for a quick doubles match with the lads. It's a place with a reputation. I feel it as soon as I pull up opposite the club, staring at the smoked-glass windows and flashy door buzzer and camera system. This is undisputed Matchroom territory.

Suddenly, I'm aware of my own nothingness again. A tiny almost unnoticeable cog in a vast machine of bright wheeling mechanisms. I can be replaced. I am not essential to life on the world circuit. I get my cue out of the back, noticing for the first time how sweaty my palms have become. This is what it's like to be dispensable. It's not a comfortable sensation.

When I walk in, Sylvie, the world's first snooker-playing giraffe, is towering over the bar, ordering herself an iced tea. The way she says 'iced tea' makes me laugh, nose wrinkled for the final syllable, her expression one of painful bemusement at the vagaries of the English language. She must have been shoe-horned into those black trousers, they're so tight, and the green silk blouse has a rather less than discreet YSL label on the breast pocket; Yves St Laurent, if I'm not mistaken. I'm impressed. I hate myself for being impressed, but I can't help it.

I crane my neck to look up at her. 'Hello again.'

There is no flicker of recognition in her eyes, but she half-smiles, nodding in my direction as she takes the offending glass of iced tea back to her table, sniffing at it suspiciously as if the English version is not quite up to her Finnish standards. This is the point at which normal people would dismiss her as a potential friend, but there's something horribly fascinating about her superiority. Is there a line we cross somewhere that differentiates us from the rank and file of humanity and catapults us into the outer hemisphere where the only suitable companions are other equally meteoric achievers? Or maybe some people are born arseholes, and simply grow bigger. I find myself excusing her: a father who beat her, an alcoholic mother, too many or too few siblings to curb that relentless egotism, a series of unhappy relationships that have left her an empty shell, devoid of emotion and all those other requisites for a useful social life. But at the back of my mind, there's this nagging awareness that I'm simply not 'important' enough to be acknowledged by the likes of Sylvie. Maybe, equal to the arsehole situation, some people are born small and just get smaller.

Tricksy is already installed at a table near the bar. 'Yoohoo!' she calls, waving her arm frantically.

Out of the corner of my eye I see Sylvie raise a disapproving eyebrow in our direction, and I cringe inwardly. But at least Tricksy talks. She smiles. She even makes the effort to wave her arm when she sees me. She isn't the Finnish answer to Cliff Richard's 'crying, talking, sleeping, walking, *living doll*'.

I get my coke and walk over. 'Hi.'

'Hi,' Tricksy says cheerfully.

'Been practising?'

'Hardly touched my cue.' She's lying.

'Me neither.' Two can play at that game.

'Well, it's only snooker. Not life and death.' More lies.

'Have they done the draw?'

'Not yet.'

'Where do I sign in?'

'I've already done it for you. What are friends for? Here, grab a pew.' She moves up one, patting the now empty seat beside her. Her friends stir their coffees, nodding at me. 'This is Zoë, everyone. Do you know Bo? You know Katie, don't you? And Katie Number Two.'

The two Katies giggle, as if at some private joke.

'Hi.' I nod at them. 'Hi.'

Okay, it's not much of a conversation, but it's better than that dismissive half-smile I received from the unfeasibly tall Sylvie. These are mates; mates speak to you, or at the very least acknowledge that you have arrived, even if the best some of them can do is offer you a weak smile over a cup of coffee. But I get this sinking feeling that I've unwittingly stumbled into the 'losers' corner', and that after a few months of their company, I too will be stirring my coffee with that look of half-apprehension, half-sheer-bloody-terror, waiting for the draw to be called.

I glance over at Sylvie. She's reading a magazine, totally cool, undisturbed by the chaotic drift of tableless cue-laden refugees all around her. Doesn't she care who she draws? Here I am, with butterflies starting in my stomach and a strange pressing sensation in my bladder that no amount of trips to the toilet can alleviate, all because my opponent is sitting out there somewhere, faceless, unknown, and because unknown, still undefeated. It's a sobering thought, and one that has incalculable effects on the nervous system. I feel it, these others feel it, but Sylvie . . . Sylvie looks as though she's waiting for a manicure, iced tea poised delicately in her hand.

'Dinosaur cool. Old-time style.'

'Sorry?' Tricksy emerges from a mouthful of toast.

'Sylvie. She reminds me of Greta Garbo.'

'Was Garbo a redhead?'

'Different hair, same style.'

Tricksy frowns. 'I thought Garbo had shorter hair than that.'

'Not *hair*style,' I explain patiently. 'Poise, finesse, charisma . . . good old-fashioned James Dean *style*.'

'Oh, *style*!' She nods, then frowns again. 'Really? If you ask me, I think she's a bitch.'

The others giggle, this time more loudly. This is

obviously a popular opinion. Looking at it like that, Tricksy is probably right. Sylvie's behaviour does resemble that of the stereotypical bitch. Maybe my internal wires are getting crossed. Maybe splitting up with a long-term partner has the same after-effects as a bang on the head: sudden confusion, a poor perspective on events, the misjudgment of distances. Maybe I'm so anxious to achieve, to do something I'm proud of, that I've pinned my hopes on the first shooting star I've seen, without making the necessary calculations to get there.

My desire to conform struggles weakly with my instincts. 'Is she?'

'A bitch?' Katie Number One interrupts, eyes shining. I notice her white dress shirt for the first time. On the left-hand side, above the pocket, she's had it embroidered in pink ... actually *embroidered* ... with the words 'Katie Number One'. This is the height of depravity. I try not to stare, but my eyes keep coming back to it. It's like one of those awful stickers that London East End couples always seem to have across the top of their windscreens: ROGER & SHARON. ROGER, of course, is always inevitably stuck over the *driver's* side. 'Dead right she's a bitch. I played her at the last tournament. She beat me by about three million points, then just shook my hand and walked away. Like it meant nothing. Nothing at all.'

'And when she wins tournaments, they say she doesn't even bat an eyelid. Just sits there in her seat like nothing's happened,' Bo adds, finishing her coffee with a flourish. Bo's one of those girls in her late teens who hasn't entirely decided which fashion wave to go with, and has compromised by wearing a splash of everything.

'She doesn't even shake hands with the loser?'

Katie Number Two hesitates, obviously torn between the name-blackening lie and the rather more conventional truth. 'Well, yes, she does,' she admits. 'But only afterwards.'

'In the bar?'

Katie wriggles reluctantly. 'No, when the game's over.' She struggles to gather some ammunition. 'But that's not the point. The point is . . . well . . . You can always tell how *cold* Sylvie is about the whole thing.'

I'm not convinced.

'That's right.' Tricksy finishes her mouthful of toast. 'She's *cold*. There's no other description for her.'

'She could never be a mother,' Bo adds serenely, patting her stomach.

I notice her loose smock-style top for the first time. Pregnant? At her age? Bo can't be more than nineteen. I thought teenagers nowadays knew everything there was to know about contraception. Still, it happened to me. I gesture towards her slight bump. 'Are you . . . ?' Then I hesitate, uncertain. It's never wise to come straight out and ask, even with a massive hint in the conversation like that. Nine times out of ten, the average 'pregnant' woman turns out to be simply overweight. By leaving the word unspoken, it's easier to bluff if it turns out to be a misunderstanding.

But Bo nods proudly. Her bead-plaited hair jingles. 'Three months gone. It's only just showing.' She leans back in her seat so that the two Katies and Tricksy can admire her new shape. The loose multi-coloured top suits her colouring and she has a glowing sheen to her skin that I should have recognised earlier as the radiance of pregnancy.

I'm tempted to ask if she's in a relationship of any kind, but force myself not to. It's none of my business. Bo's a nice girl, and she seems happy enough. I decide to play it safe and stick to the more obvious and non-offensive territory of snooker talk. 'Doesn't the bump get in your way when you're cueing?'

'Nah. Not big enough yet.'

Katie Number One (unmistakably 'Katie Number One' in that personalised shirt, which is presumably the point) hoots. 'It'll get in the way more when it's *born*!'

Laughter all round.

The draw interrupts this conversation and soon afterwards we're drifting apart, silently taking our cues to our allotted tables, not looking at anyone in particular. It's all part of getting psyched-up for the match, I suppose. Friends disappear like faces into a crowd, blurred, indistinct from each other. I concentrate on the beating of my heart, the dark print of the carpet under my feet, even the smooth rail of each table as I pass.

This is what I'm here for. Confrontation. The sickening sense of being forced to lay my cards on the table, whatever my hand. No time left to check that dodgy pull-back or put in a few last practice break-off shots. This is it. Death or glory. I haven't drawn Sylvie, a player I could lose to without embarrassment. I've drawn some unknown name out of the hat, a player I could probably beat if I put my mind to it, and who's all the more terrifying because of it.

Someone once said that people aren't afraid of failure, they're actually afraid of success. If you win, you have to win again the next time. And the opponents get harder and harder to beat, all the way up the ladder. It's so much easier to keep facing the same players, losing at the same level, until you've got your patter sorted out into well-rehearsed excuses, that sense of failure so thoroughly absorbed into your psyche that losing no longer feels like failure, but success. Congratulations! You lost, but you're becoming admirably adept at losing. Almost an old hand. Failure is *so* much more comfortable to live with than success.

So no excuses this time. No excuses. *Fuck it*. No excuses.

'Again?'

I pretend to be fascinated by my lunch, pushing a charred piece of Chicken Tikka Masala under the polite camouflage of a lettuce leaf. The pub is a nice one, down a cul-de-sac just off the High Street and usually quiet at lunch-times, which is why my mother likes it, but the cooking leaves a great deal to be desired.

'That's twice now, Zoë. I thought you said you were good,' my mother continues, frowning down at her lunch.

'Thanks, Mum. Why don't you just give me a paper cut and pour lemon juice on it? I mean, how easy do you think it is?' I shake my head at her. 'Did you think I could just walk in there and start winning tournaments?'

'It happens.'

Not to me. Why does she always have to be so exasperating? Forget men. Forget bosses. Forget the Inland Revenue. The ultimate conflict relationship a woman can have is with her own mother. I grit my teeth, exercising admirable restraint. 'You don't know what you're talking about.'

'Well, maybe not, but I do know that I'm the one lumbered with your kids whenever you go away.' My mother frowns at her fork, poised in mid-air with a piece of chicken suspended delicately from one prong, then puts it down abruptly to stare at me. Her tone is accusing. 'It is snooker you're playing, isn't it? You're not dumping the kids on me so you can gallivant around the countryside with some new man you've found? I hope that's not it.'

God give me strength. Ever since Adrian left, she's been fretting about my love life. It's a complicated issue to explain, but my mother thinks that if I get involved with another man, I'll want to marry him eventually. And if I want to marry him, I'll need a wedding, and a reception, and a honeymoon etc. It's not my feelings that concern her, you understand, it's the financial implications. She's just booked another session at the anti-cellulite clinic for next month. If I marry again, my mother probably suspects the money involved will result in orange-peel thighs, a sagging bottom and slacks with elasticated waists. That's a vision of hell she can't live with. 'Of course I'm playing snooker, Mum.'

'After the way your father's been behaving, nothing anyone in this family does could surprise me.'

'He's still seeing that Sharon woman?'

She makes a face at her chicken. 'He's not even pretending any more. Out to all hours with the little tart. Thinks he's eighteen again. He's got no consideration for my feelings.'

'It'll pass. It always does.'

My mother seems less assured than usual. 'Maybe. Let's get back to this snooker business. You have to admit it, Zoë . . . all this practice, and what have you achieved? Two first-round knock-outs?' She shakes her head at me and pushes her plate aside. 'I couldn't eat that. It was burnt. Was yours burnt? Mine was, all along the top. Excuse me? Hello?' The landlady pauses, cleaning the deserted table two down from ours. She looks up at my mother very slowly, as if already offended. 'Excuse me, but this chicken is burnt. I can't eat it. And neither can my daughter.'

I excuse myself, disappearing into the ladies as rapidly as possible. But I know she's right. The chicken *was* burnt and I *do* have nothing to show for my endless practice. Maybe I am my father's daughter after all, because my excuses are beginning to wear thin, even to myself. It looks like a choice between two equally hard roads: giving up snooker altogether or taking it much more seriously. I look in the mirror for a moment, washing my hands. Tough choice.

3

It's accepted wisdom. Never stand if you can sit, never sit if you can lie down, and never let your opponent break off if *you've* won the toss. Not only have you given away your first advantage, but regardless of whether or not you would have messed up the shot, you have just told your opponent one vital and destructive thing about yourself: you're a sissie. You don't believe in yourself. You're more concerned with how he/she plays than with your own abilities. You are apparently unable to play this simplest of bread-and-butter shots: clipping the penultimate red with just enough 'zing' (somewhere between top and running side) to bring that white ball off the top cushion, off two side cushions and back behind the green, or yellow for a left-hander. Getting it to nestle gently on the cushion behind the green is optimum, but not necessary unless playing Stephen Hendry.

I am not playing Stephen Hendry. I bring that white back as though on a long piece of elastic, leaving it neatly behind the green. Beyond me, in the semi-darkness, I can hear a rustle of approval from the watching lads.

'Not bad, Zoë,' says Bob grudgingly. 'But you could have put it closer to the rail, if you'd tried.'

Bloody hell. 'I'm not playing Stephen Hendry.'

'You're not playing anyone. This is a practice routine. And what's practice for?'

Here we go again. 'Learning to play our best.'

'Right. Learning to play your best.' He cradles his pint to his chest, pursing his lips up as he focuses on the white ball as if trying to memorise its position. 'Now try that again, and this time I want to see it touching the back rail. Not near it, or beside it, or behind the brown, or on the side cushion, but actually *touching* the back rail.'

I comply, easing off the throttle a little and adding just a wider touch of right-hand side. Come on, my beauty. Easy, girl, easy . . . no hurry. The white pulls off the side cushion at roughly the correct angle, then paces itself gently until it reaches the back cushion, finally coming to rest about half an inch off the rail.

Put that in your pipe and smoke it. Bob walks around to get a closer look. He eyeballs the white from all angles, then crouches down, gripping the rail with his slightly arthritic knuckles, squeezing his eyes to a narrow pillarbox slit. Eventually, he raises himself. His face is vaguely reminiscent of one of those Pekinese dogs that old women carry about in their arms: mouth, nose, eyes and forehead all concertinaed into one, breath held as if concentrating fiercely, his bald head sweating under the lights. 'Mmmmm,' he grunts, exhaling as he nods in my direction. 'Still not touching, but it'll do.'

Steady on with the praise there. I might get bigheaded: 'Again?'

Bob shakes his head, disappearing briefly into his pint glass. When he emerges, face flushed with exertion, he gives a loud belch. 'Move over. Let one of the lads have a go. Come on, Nick! Show her how it's *really* done.'

Nick is about twelve, small for his age, and has to stand on a beer crate for some shots. He grins half-apologetically at me, then gets down and plays the shot superbly. If only I'd started younger, born with a cue in my hand and a father who took me down the club at weekends, I too might be able to nurse the white delicately round the angles like that. Okay, I can play that shot exactly the same way as Nick, but it's always a struggle. I don't just look at the shot, get down and play it. I have some natural ability, but the rest of my game is sheer dog-stupid technique: stand like this, hold the cue like that, hit the ball again and again. That's not talent. That's brainwashing.

Bobs nods. 'Fantastic. Spot-on, Nick, spot-on.' He pats the young lad on his back. 'Raz? You're up next.'

Raz brushes past me, giving me a leering half-smile as I automatically pull myself closer to the wall. He's nineteen and works behind the bar, serving drinks to his under-age mates every weekend in return for the odd fiver. He only gets away with this because he's Bet's nephew. After all, she's the owner, and with Bet, family is family, whatever they may get up to. Okay, Raz is a pretty good player, by club standards, but he's too cocky with it. He puts money on his own performance in matches, then fluffs the final black under pressure, claiming his tip was dodgy or someone moved when he was on the shot. He's the sort who looks at women as if imagining you naked. He makes my skin crawl.

Raz plays his shot. The white finds that elusive back cushion, then bounces off slightly, leaving him half an inch away. It's nice to see I'm not the only one who can fail at this exercise. But half an inch. Half a bloody inch. Is that *all* I'm lacking?

'Brilliant, Raz! That was almost perfect. Good lad.'

Well, maybe not. I'm starting to suspect that, in Bob's eyes, I'm lacking something rather more substantial than half an inch of ball control. But what did I expect from these guys? This is Snooker According to Bob, and women don't even feature in the small print.

Two weeks later, I'm back on the road. Supertramp's 'Logical Song' is on the radio, the sun is shining and it's early Sunday morning so there aren't many cars about. I haven't had enough sleep but my mind is working overtime. *Won't you please please tell me what we've learnt?* I put my foot on the accelerator. I've got twenty quid in my pocket and a cue on the back seat. This is the one. *I know it sounds absurd.* This is D-Day. I'm going to win. *Please tell me who I am.* Maybe not the tournament, but my first-round match at least. Win. Win. Win. *Radical, fanatical.* I have to concentrate on that. Play it one shot at a time. Do just enough to win and no more. Adopt a chess-player's approach to the game: strategic, calm, logical. *Di-di-di-di-di-di-digital*. This time, I can definitely feel it. I'm going to win.

I pull into the Hertfordshire club car park. A black Saab cuts in front of me and slots swiftly into the last available parking space. Irritated, I tap the wheel, watching the driver through narrowed eyes as he gets out, sauntering round to check that the back doors are locked. He doesn't look like the sort of guy you'd expect to see behind the wheel of an expensive car like that. He's about six foot, unshaven, with a black leather jacket, camouflage trousers and what appear to be army boots. I change my mind about winding the window down and giving him a piece of my mind. He doesn't look like a very approachable type. The last thing I want to do is get into an argument, and end up too stressed-out to play properly. With some effort, I put him from my mind, backing the car out of the car park. No problem. I can look for a space on the road. My own fault for turning up late.

When I come back through the car park, the man is still there.

He's lit a cigarette and is bending down to stare into the car next to him. Bloody hell, he's not going to break in, is he? As I pass him, he straightens, looking directly at me. Up close, he's really quite attractive, with short dark hair and dark eyes, although his gaze is intimidating. I make a mental note of the make and number plate of the car he's inspecting, wondering whether I ought to mention it to the Tournament Controller or the club manager.

He's seen me now. He knows which car I'm in. He probably saw my cue. He knows I'm going to be in the club all day. Plenty of time to break a side window and nick the radio, or take a few tyres off for good measure. Maybe even steal the car. I glance back at my old Ford Escort, resting its front tyres exhaustedly against the pavement. No, too unlikely. The radio's worth more than the car.

'Where was he? I'm parked near the door. Was he anywhere near there?' Predictably, Tricksy is only interested in her own car's safety. As I give her the glad tidings, she sits up in her seat and peers through the smoked-glass windows of the club. 'I can't see anyone out there now, Zoë. Are you sure you didn't imagine him?'

Do I look as though I hallucinate on a regular basis? 'Yes, I'm sure,' I reply wearily. 'Shouldn't I mention it to someone? It was a Probe, I think, one of those flashy top-of-the-range Fords. Maybe it's the club manager's car. Must be someone with money.'

'A Probe? What was the number plate?'

I drop my keys on the table, glancing round for the Tournament Controller. 'One of those personalised jobs . . . 147 something.'

Tricksy looks up at me with widening eyes, like Bambi in the forest-fire scene. 'You're kidding? That's Sylvie's car . . . you know, *the Bitch*!' She hesitates, then shrugs. 'Leave it. She can afford a new one. Probably has it insured up to the eyeballs anyway. Serves her right for driving such a flash car. Bound to attract thieves.'

I hesitate. I haven't signed in yet and, if I miss the draw, I'll have wasted my time coming down here for the day. If only I'd turned up five minutes earlier, I'd never have seen that man and I wouldn't be standing here now, wondering whether to listen to my conscience or let it drop. 'I'll go and sign in. Then I can tell the Tournament Controller at the same time.'

I know from bitter experience that honesty is not always the best policy, but it seems rather mean-spirited to turn a blind eye simply because it involves someone who might deserve a bit of bad luck for once. *There but for the grace of God*, I remind myself. Besides, being the ice-maiden of ladies' snooker doesn't mean she deserves to have her car nicked. It just means she's suffering from what my father would call a 'character deficiency'. Or maybe her coldness derives from the basic fact that English is not her first language. I know I can hold my own in French, by virtue of having had it drilled into me from an early age, but being my usual charming self in a foreign language would be difficult, if not impossible. Something is always lost in the translation. For all I know, Sylvie may be the Finnish equivalent of a stand-up comic. But I doubt it.

As luck would have it, Sylvie is standing behind the Tournament Controller, sipping delicately at her usual iced tea. I know for a fact that she's seeded through to the third round this time, because the entries are so high: while waiting to play, she's gone for the dead-casual look, black jeans and T-shirt. I have to admit that she looks almost approachable like this. The designer silk shirts obviously have a lot to answer for.

I hesitate. I've always had an enormous chip on my shoulder about authority figures, an in-built prejudice which probably dates back to the first time my father took my rattle away, and which generally extends to head teachers, traffic wardens, airport security men and middle-aged business men with mobile phones. It's that infuriating sense that someone has a hold over you, either in terms of money or petty bureaucracy. Sylvie, with her air of easy arrogance, her designer clothes and that almost edible sports car outside, seems to fall into the same category. Old habits die hard, and I find myself baulking at the idea of helping one of them out. I fight the impulse to walk away without saying anything, my guilty conscience stronger than my dislike for successful smart-arses.

'Hello again,' I eventually say, catching her eye over the unmarked draw sheet. She meets my eyes for a moment, half-smiles, then looks away. I sign my name on the list, exchanging a few cheerful words with the Tournament Controller, then look up at Sylvie again. 'Is that your Probe in the car park?'

Sylvie stiffens. One eyebrow rises in a startling impersonation of *Star Trek*'s Spock. 'It is,' she replies coldly, grammatically correct as always.

Bloody hell, is this worth it? Go ahead, get your car stolen. What do I care? My feet are itching to turn in the opposite direction. 'There's some bloke hanging around out there, looking at it.'

She shrugs. 'So?'

'Well, I thought he might be trying to steal it. I don't know what it's like in Finland, but in this country we tend to worry when we see blokes like that peering in through car windows.'

'Oh.' The iced tea is deposited carefully on the table. One manicured fingernail is examined for defects, then dismissed as perfectly normal. 'I see.'

Don't get too excited. Jesus, most people would think potential car theft was just slightly more interesting than this. Warranting maybe a glance towards the door or possibly even a passing comment on warped values in our modern-day society. Not this cool 'what do you want me to do about it, buster?' stance, this apparently total nonchalance in the face of an imminent insurance claim. 'Shouldn't you have a quick look? Check it's okay?'

'What does this man look like?'

What difference does that make? Visions of myself completing one of those police Identikit profiles flash through my head, accompanied by a sinking feeling that she knows exactly who this man is, that she's far too cool about the whole situation for there to be any other explanation. 'Nearly six foot. Stubbly chin, short dark hair, leather jacket. Big boots . . . the sort you get from an army surplus store. Drives a black Saab. Badly.'

Sylvie is smiling, a lopsided smile that confirms my suspicions. 'I thought so. He's a fan of mine. A big fan.'

Tessa, the Tournament Controller, looks up from the draw sheet with a concerned expression. 'Not again, Sylvie. I thought you'd been on to the police about him?'

'They can't do anything unless he does. There's no law that covers sports fans. He can follow me anywhere he likes, and there's nothing I can do about it.'

I'm appalled. 'He follows you *everywhere*?'

'Not everywhere. I can still go to the ladies on my own.'

I almost blink. Is this humour? Humour from the Finnish equivalent of John Major? It can't be true, but yes, I see a smile hovering over her lips as she picks up her iced tea again. Sylvie smiles. Sylvie cracks jokes. Sylvie bears some vague resemblance to the human race.

'So he won't steal the car? Even as a souvenir?'

Sylvie's eyes flicker. 'He doesn't want a souvenir,' she says casually. She tucks a loose strand of hair behind her ear, looking away as if no longer interested in the conversation. 'He wants me.'

I'm just coming out of the ladies, wondering whether the already damp green hand towel they've provided for today's tournament is going to be replaced at some point or whether we'll be spending the rest of the day wiping our hands on our trousers, when the draw is called. I stop wondering about Sylvie and her mystery fan, and start panicking about my match. I have to win today. If I don't win today, I can't justify playing any more.

Tricksy, finishing her coffee near the bar, gives a brief shriek as our names are called together. 'You and me!' she says excitedly as I stroll over to collect my cue, my face as nonchalant as I can manage under the circumstances. I suppose it had to happen some time, but since Tricksy only recently hammered me at my home club, I had hoped for a longer stay of execution. 'Katie One is playing Katie Two, we're playing each other, and Bo's got old . . . what's her name?'

Patiently, I follow her pointing finger. 'Edna.'

'Edna,' she nods. 'Third time this year! Lucky cow. I wish I could get one of the biddies for a change. Sweet old dears, but they can't pot to save their lives. Edna's seventy-three, you know. At that age, you'd think she'd need a licence to cue.' Tricksy smiles slyly in my direction, picking up her cue case and motioning for me to walk ahead of her to the table. Her tone is deliberately innocent. 'Age before beauty.'

Sticks and stones . . .

'You've lost all your first-round matches so far, haven't you?'

May break my bones. I'd like to break all yours, mate. 'Mmmm.'

'Such a pity. It drags you down, that sort of thing. You get into a vicious circle and then you can't win anything, not even a raffle.'

We reach the table. I unpack my cue, wiping it down meticulously before chalking the tip. I can still hear

Tricksy's voice, but now it seems to be coming from a great distance, blotted out by the sudden necessity for concentration. It's like going into a trance. Ignore her. Focus on the game. For the next few hours, nothing else matters.

I study the tip. It slopes gently down on all sides, a tiny green mushroom, deceptively firm to the touch. Somehow, I know that it will repel all boarders like a pirate ship, bouncing effortlessly off the white with the *élan* of a Springbok.

As with tyres on a car, the tip is our first contact with the world and therefore the most vital. It must be nurtured into its optimum shape, religiously maintained, and discarded only when its relationship with the brass ferrule has become too close for comfort.

Choosing a tip is no easy task. Faced with a box of these pale, slightly rounded, communion tablets, it would be easy to assume that they were all the same. Nothing could be further from the truth. Each individual tip has its own unique personality. Pressed lightly with a finger, one may be too hard at the centre. Another too springy. A third might be too soft. The perfect tip is relative. Some players prefer the rock-hard to the more yielding, others go for something with plenty of bounce. As for myself, I like a tip which can be filed down almost to the knuckle: hard, but not so hard that it can't dig deep enough into the ball for a screw shot or something with plenty of side. This one is perfect. It was a little unresponsive at first, but now it's been 'played in' and is kissing the balls like a professional.

The referee catches the glint of a coin for us. We shake hands. I break off. Tricksy plays safe. I play safe. Tricksy plays safe. I play safe. It can't last.

The opening she leaves me is not easy, but I take it on. First blood is vital. Like a birth horoscope, first blood sets a lasting trend for the match. Played badly, this stun-down-red-for-black could leave a gaping hole in my armour. Played well, it could win me the frame, if only in terms of mental one-upmanship. Played superbly, it should give me that orgasmic rush of adrenalin necessary to win the match, putting me in an unassailable position from which to storm the citadel and take no prisoners.

I play it averagely. The red goes down. The white runs on too far, leaving me a clip-and-run safety on the black, but the deed is done. Tricksy knows I mean business. She messes up the next safety, leaving me in again, and this time I manage a fifteen break. It may not be earth-shattering stuff, but it's quite enough to put the squeeze on Tricksy. She comes back with a few good reds, but colours elude her like butterflies, always just out of reach. I scrape another twenty-odd points under my fingernails, tucking a black away here, a pink there, rolling the brown off its spot and into a waiting pocket.

Tricksy says nothing, but her face is pale and determined. She grinds chalk on to the unbending tip as though already apportioning blame. Her mouth moves silently, in words of prayer or possibly blasphemy. Her next shot confirms my suspicions. She is rallying. The red flies up into the top left-hand pocket, and she drops down on the black with the vengeance of angels, pulling neatly back off the pot for her next red. A second black follows, not even touching the sides of the pocket. These aren't a few lucky shots strung together like cheap souvenir worry beads. This isn't damage-control. This is a break.

I lose the frame. It's so unexpected, I feel as though someone has just whipped my entrails out and wrapped them round a tree. Silently, I retire to my corner while the referee sets up the balls again, watching those hypnotic white gloves move against the backdrop of the baize. Fuck. Fuck. Fuck. I sip my now cold coffee. Examine my nails minutely. Glance over at the next table with feigned interest. Pretend to stifle a yawn while the referee adjusts the score board.

What sort of player lets a frame slip through her fingers like that? Where was it, that fatal error? Probably the last red, taken on too cockily after the pocket-pace brown. Trying to smash it in like a schoolgirl. Jawing the red. I left that table wide open. I did everything but hand Tricksy a gold-leaf invitation to win. Ignored the easier but less flashy red into the middle. Wanker. I deserve to lose this, armed only with the table technique of Pee-Wee Herman and the dizzying intellect of a canary. If I don't pull my finger out . . .

'Me to break this time, isn't it?' Tricksy says cheerfully, not waiting for a reply before she gets down to play the shot. She has the jaunty step of the recently reprieved. I want to knock the wind out of her like a punchbag. I want to steamroller her out of existence. But I don't move. Tricksy nods down at the shot she's just played, clearly satisfied, then strolls back to her seat. She picks up her drink, smiling to herself. 'Cheers.'

I walk to the head of the table. It stretches away in front of me like the pitch at Wembley, glittering and full of strange promise. I can see my face in every ball, a dazzle of lights catching their curved surfaces like the sun on a host of satellite dishes. She's left me a long shot. I could play the clip-and-run safety with an outside chance of kissing the black and leaving the white in the pack for her. Or I could go for the kill. There's a red out on its own, flirtatiously near the pocket. But no easy black. The pink would go, but I'd have to pull back sharply from the pot, maybe screwing six inches or more. At this distance and with my technique, it's a suicidal shot. But glorious if successful.

Three guesses what shot I select, and two don't count.

Screwing the ball is one of the hardest shots to master. It's a shot of strange contradictions. You drive the white forward, and after contact with the object ball, it hesitates for one breathless second, then spins backwards like a woman on the rebound. It's an impressive shot. Even a short-distance screw looks like it needs power, and lots of it. The further away the object ball, the more you feel you have to thrash the white. But the secret is . . . gather round . . . the secret of a screw shot is *control*. Some will tell you it's all in the wrist. And as long as the wrist doesn't move from the vertical, that's okay. But a screw shot needs more than just wrist, it needs acceleration and braking at the same time. You must come into the white parallel to the cloth, never hit down on it. That merely 'bounces' the screw and dissipates its backward motion. The power has to be stroked into the shot, not forced. Like a lover, you must seduce the ball into screwing back towards you. It won't accept rough treatment. And the longer the stroke (the further you move through the white), the more effective the screwback.

'Good shot, Zoë!'

I half-smile at Tricksy's grudging acknowledgment. I've left myself almost a full-ball contact on the pink. It requires stunning back-down for that red at the bottom of the pack. After that, I'll need some sort of half-ball shot on the black to spin me sharply into the pack and loosen the other reds.

It's under control. The frame is mine. I have it in my hand. I go through the drill. Square into the shot, using the cue as a pointer. One one-thousand, two one-thousand, three. Hesitate at the pull-back. Full throttle into the white but keeping my cool, never letting my head rise with the shot. Waiting for the drop before moving. Only belatedly remembering the follow-through, and checking my cue against the length of the cloth after the shot. I've marked a faint red ring around my cue where the follow-through should reach to, and there's a thin piece of Sellotape at the butt end where my hand should grip for optimum control.

Bob scoffed at me for using what he calls 'visual aids', but it's working so far.

Another ball drops. I move round mechanically for the black. The pattern on the carpet is a guideline, a tightrope, where the faintest hesitation could be fatal: I follow it with my eyes all the way round to the other side, chalking my cue, replacing the chalk in its belt-pouch, counting silently to myself as I get down to the shot.

I win the frame.

Don't let it throw you. Okay, that's one down but there's two more to go. It's best of five for the first round. I haven't won yet, I've simply pulled even. Ease up on the over-confidence. She's watching me. Keep that poker-face blank. This tip is fascinating. Totally engrossing. It needs a little chalk though, here on the edge. Maybe more shape. I get my file out of my case. It's something to do. Takes my mind off the next frame. The score line. I file down on the tip, gentle, almost surgical. She's too cool, too unconcerned. We're level again. I'm playing well. *Why isn't she worried?* It must be a front. Tricksy's worried. She must be. She just isn't going to let me see that. Take it slowly. One ball at a time. Still something kicking the cue out to the left on long shots. Not the shoulder, that's falling fine. Maybe the wrist, which really means the grip. Too tight. Strangling the cue means a chain reaction is taking place: pushing the wrist to one side, knocking the arm out of kilter, raising the shoulder and eventually the head. Disaster. Loosen the grip.

'My break?'

When does the slight incline become a hill, and more importantly, when does the hill become a mountain? The game is like a tiger, with me in its jaws. I'm fighting back, of course, but it's grindingly slow progress and there's blood on my hands. Unfortunately, I can't tell whose blood yet.

We get to the final frame, holding two frames apiece.

I'm stretched so thin it feels as though the sun could shine straight through me. Tension is singing in my ears, and it isn't a cheerful tune. Tricksy looks reasonably composed, but now and then I catch a strained look on her face that tells me she's feeling something similar. This is what we're here for. This strangely controlled war of nerves. The elegant death-throes of two players who would rather agree to amputation without anaesthetic than show fear. Striding boldly into the deadliest of mental struggles, armed with only a cue and the courage to use it. Captain Kirk was wrong; the final frontier is not space, but snooker.

The last black is almost an anti-climax. I win the match long before we get to that; about forty points beforehand in fact. Tricksy stuns white behind brown for a killing snooker. I calculate the angles with the speed of a Nobel Prize winner, taking the white off three cushions to cannon what remains of the pack. As luck would have it, one red shoots off at a tangent, clipping the black free from the cushion and dropping into the left-hand pocket. I scoop up the black, run on for an easy red, come back for the black again, then take the narrow path back up to baulk for a near-impossible-to-get-out-of snooker behind the green.

'Shot . . .' Tricksy murmurs, tapping the table with one reluctant finger. She's fucked and she knows it. After her abortive attempt to escape from baulk, the free-ball situation comes as no surprise to either of us. I'm well ahead, and although the points are still there on the table for her to collect, we both know that it's not going to happen. Tricksy is all played out. She's pulling up on the shot, striking off-centre. Her cue action is weakening by the minute. With snooker, it's all in the mind. You can't win if you don't believe you can, however many opportunities to win you're handed. It's as simple as that.

'Well played.' Suddenly, Tricksy's shaking my hand and packing her cue away without another word. I'm through to the next round. I've won. I've beaten Tricksy. It feels strange, walking away with the winner's sheet in my hand, knowing that it's my name instead of hers on the top line.

I turn back briefly, worried that there's been a mistake, that we forgot something, played too many frames or too few. Then across the room, I catch Sylvie's eye. She's waiting to play her first match, dressed now in tournament gear, black trousers and severe white blouse, the pink bow-tie her only concession to femininity. She's seen the result sheet in my hand. I raise it slightly, almost a salute, and Sylvie smiles. For one glorious moment, my lifelong obsession with failure is forgotten. I won. The *loser* won.

Nothing good lasts for ever, which is exactly the point Jehovah's Witnesses try to make during their door-to-door sales pitch. Most people being born optimists though, few Jehovah's Witnesses get any further than the door.

But in the case of a lucky flush in snooker, it's only too true. I struggle with my next-round opponent, a young Belgian ranked somewhere in the twenties, blessed with a cue action that would make Steve Davis blink. Okay, she let me in once or twice, or possibly about fifteen times a frame, but whatever it was that helped me beat Tricksy has disappeared like morning dew. Soaked straight back into me.

'Lost your second-round match, did you?' Tricksy asks pointedly as I return to the alcove seat, where she has been making a tower out of empty beer bottles. She nods towards it wearily. 'Fancy a beer?'

'I thought I'd watch some of the other matches. Pick up some tips.'

'Ha!'

In a bad mood? I prop my case up in front of hers. 'Want to come along? Sylvie's on table three. It's near the bar.'

'Sylvie? Ha!'

'Not keen?' What's the matter? Had a taste of your own medicine? I glance briefly over at table three. Sylvie's just getting down to break off again. By the scoreboard, it looks like being the fourth frame, so it must be a tough match. I thought she would have won it by now. 'Okay. You watch my cue?'

She doesn't look up from her beer tower. 'Uhuh.'

Like anything else that demands talent and technique, losing is an art. Some people lose 'better' than others. Tricksy is clearly not a good loser. Fair enough, I'm never exactly overjoyed to walk away empty-handed, but I tend to blame myself rather than my opponent. This may result in a stomach ulcer ten years from now, but right now it feels like the only sporting thing to do.

Snooker is a game which is associated not only with saturation coverage on BBC 2, but also with what might be called 'gentleman-like conduct'. It's no longer politically correct to say something like that on late-night chat shows, but it's a term which is still freely used in the clubs. Now that I've had a chance to get used to the circuit, I've started to believe in good conduct, both on and off the table. Apart from the sinking feeling that you've made a fool of yourself by mouthing off about an opponent, it does nothing for the image of snooker. Especially for women, who still have everything to prove. Okay, give them two fingers, but do it in your head. You have to smile and smile and curse them inwardly. A lucky cunt is a lucky cunt, there's no argument there, but keeping it all inside is part of the game.

On this occasion, it's me who's the lucky cunt, and it feels great. I may have lost my second-round match, but what the hell, I've earned myself two points and a place on the ranking list. So I forgive Tricksy her monosyllabic attitude and head over to watch the final frames of Sylvie's match.

Sylvie is standing near the table, her chin propped delicately on one hand, her face lost in shadows. I don't recognise her opponent. Whoever she is, she's playing well and seems to have taken two frames off Sylvie already. From the scoreboard, Sylvie is down two frames to one, and the other girl is at the table, taking on a long blue with what appears to be utter confidence. She's a stocky woman in her late twenties, bleached-blonde hair tied up in a bun, with one of those irritating magnetic chalk clips hanging from her belt.

She misses and Sylvie steps in almost immediately, springing out of the darkness like a *deus ex machina*. A loose red shoots into a pocket, the abandoned blue also falls victim, then Sylvie knuckles down to a small but convincing break. When the other girl comes back to the table, she finds herself thirty-two points behind and trussed up turkey-style behind the green.

Good players are like automatic gearboxes. They move up and down a gear according to the situation, never doing anything too flashy or too dangerous, just chipping away at a lead until they're on top of the situation. They know better than to waste vital energy on an early round match, which may be needed later when they pull out all the stops for a quarter or semi-final. The opponent threatened, Sylvie reacted, but only enough to stamp her authority on the other woman's mind. Prevent the match from slipping away. That one frame deficit is not going to grow any larger. Sylvie has hit her stride now. Her opponent must have played at least one other match to get to this round. Sylvie, being a top seed, has to step in and contain the damage from a cold start. Not easy unless you've got your shit together. Sylvie clearly has *her* shit well under control.

Watching Sylvie play is like watching a master craftsman (oh bloody hell . . . crafts*person*) doing his/her thing and doing it to the best of their ability. Everything is done with a confidence born from long hours of practice. It's awe-inspiring, almost mesmerisingly so. It's a beautiful thing to watch. And while I watch, something else strikes me, something odd, that has its roots in who I am and where I've come from. What on earth is a woman like me, pushing thirty, a mother of two, and until recently a housewife and general dogsbody, doing in a place like this?

How did it happen? One day I was cleaning the cooker, the next I was cleaning up on a snooker table. It's almost surreal. You know how you get into this life situation, and you just know *that's it*, that's how it's meant to be from now on, you're stuck like that for the rest of your life and you might as well give up those childish dreams and aspirations, and the night-sweats that have their origins in the fairly justified fear that life has passed you by, and then suddenly, quite without warning, you're free of it. Unshackled. Homeward bound.

That's how it feels, watching Sylvie play and knowing that I have two world-ranking points to my name. I'm a fully fledged woman snooker player and there's absolutely nothing anyone can do about it, not my mother, not my father, not my erstwhile partner, not even my children. I'm here at last. But do I really belong here, or am I just kidding myself? After all, there are different levels of belonging. If I can't improve my game, I will never merit anything better than a dismissive glance from the likes of Sylvie.

4

I wake up this morning to the sound of rain against the windows, and suddenly remember Kevin, that strange little guy who first taught me how to hold a cue. Today would definitely be a raincoat day for him. His parting shot echoes through my head as I get dressed: *'Don't let the bastards grind you down.'* What did he know that I didn't? Apart from the fact that rain is depressing.

Actually, I'm more of a Clark Gable type myself, enjoying the feel of rain against my skin, never taking an umbrella out with me when the skies darken but physically urging it to fall, leaning back into a cloudburst like a Mid-West American farmer after months of drought. There is no greater secret pleasure for me than to sit in a window seat at night when it's raining, push the window open just wide enough for me to wet one wrist under the downpour, and turn the lights off so that all I can see is rain, glinting off oncoming headlights. It's the opposite of sun-worshipping, except for the tactile hedonism both obsessions share, that sensation of being alone and open to the elements. They say rain lovers are manic depressives. That may have been true of Kevin, whose mood shifted abruptly every time the skies opened, but for me rain acts as a catalyst for so many other, deeper, more complex emotions and memories that sometimes seem to have happened in another life, a different time.

I look in on the kids. Jemima is already dressed, but Tom is lost somewhere in the depths of his over-large Picasso-style smock-top, fumbling around the room like a headless ghost.

'Hurry up,' I remind him briskly. 'You've got early assembly this morning.'

Okay, it's a lie, but he knows what I mean. Tom doesn't actually have a formal assembly yet, he's still too young for anything but splashing paint around at kindergarten, but his teachers do encourage the kids to form a circle, holding hands and murmuring prayers, before the budding Rembrandts hit their easels. Jemima, however, has been late for assembly three days running.

I have to make a real effort to get out of bed these days. Even when I go to bed early, I can't sleep. So when I wake up, I'm still so tired that I tend to turn over and forget about everything. Fortunately, Jemima has different ideas and is usually first at the bedroom door whenever her newly found skill of telling the time allows her to accuse me of over-sleeping.

When I pick up the pile of post by the front door, and flick through the bills, I see the envelope immediately: the World Championship entry form that I've been waiting for. Jesus, this is it. The big one. Double-ranking points, and double the normal entry fee too: *'World Championships Qualifiers in Brighton'*.

It's a whole week, not a weekend like the other tournaments. How the hell am I going to manage that? My mother won't be impressed. 'Not again, Zoë,' she said last time. 'I'm too old to be doing this every month. At my age, weekends are for spending at dinner parties or the health club, not looking after kids.'

But I can't miss this one. My first World Championships, coming up just as I've started to show some potential on the circuit. It would be madness to skip it. But the bank will probably disagree with me there. I've been more in the red this month than the Russians. Perhaps I can borrow the money.

'How much?' my mother gasps. 'You've got to be kidding. I've told you before, go out and get a job.'

'I will, Mum.' Just not yet. There's too much at stake to spend valuable practice time in some nine-to-five position, slogging my guts out over a photocopier instead of a snooker table. Where's the glory in that? If I get a job now, I might as well trade in my cue for a personal pension plan, and file my dreams away under P for Pointless.

I could be a great player, I'm sure of it. I just need a little more time to prove it, and a lot more money to afford those basic necessities of life, like tournament entry fees, accommodation and petrol expenses, and the odd luxury item such as a cue extension or one of those fiddly plastic whatnots you stick on the end of the rest, for reaching awkward balls along the cushion.

'I'm going to start taking some evening courses soon. I promise.' Okay, this is a fib, but only from a certain point of view. After all, 'soon' is a fairly elastic term which may mean 'next week' to her, but actually means 'next year' to me. I throw in some complicated technical jargon to throw her off the scent. 'I need to get some more qualifications. An IT course, or maybe something in Windows.'

There's a note of suspicion in her voice. 'Well, okay, but a loan is out of the question at the moment. Maybe next month.'

That will be too late. After she's hung up, I stare out of the kitchen window, cradling the dead phone in my hand. Rain is streaming down the glass. I need to lay my hands on at least fifty quid, preferably by the end of this week. My chances of paying it back are slim, almost as slim as my childhood hopes of joining a travelling circus, although a good performance at the World might leave enough for me to cover my hotel bill, and still honour my debts. I've heard the prize money there is much higher than at the usual run-of-the-mill tournaments. But the way things have been going recently, I'd need to take the World title itself just to break even. Christ, how much harder can it get, this snooker-playing business? I've had easier car crashes.

Outside on the ledge, a few struggling geraniums are bunched together in the windowbox Adrian bought, drenched under the onslaught of rain. When did I last see Kevin? It must be at least six years now. That old snooker club above the furniture store closed down about the same time, and I've never seen him in my home club. Where does a guy like Kevin hang out? Adrian might know, but I don't want to bring him into this. It's already enough of a mess without tangling the reins even further.

If I could find Kevin, he might be impressed with how my game has improved, and lend me the money in order to see his former protégée succeed. That sounds calculating, almost callous, but I'm in a fix here and snooker demands everything, absolutely everything. At this point, I think I'd crawl through mud and barbed wire in order to enter the World Championships.

Besides, Kevin was always flush, one of those men who still live with their mothers well past thirty, and who hold down some dull predictable post in local government from leaving school right the way through to collecting a pension. Okay, yes, precisely the sort of man my mother would have preferred to see me settle down with. Safe, dependable, a solid earner. But Adrian came along instead, with his secret collection of Ella Fitzgerald recordings, and his passion for pistachio ice cream. It wasn't much of an improvement on the Kevins of this world, but it was *different*, and at nineteen, anything different is fascinating, almost compulsively so.

I make a few phone calls. Sure enough, Kevin is still working in local government. I agree to meet him tonight at the club, mentally crossing my fingers in the hope that my mother will agree to babysit.

The kids have both recovered from their bout of gastric flu, and it's only Tom who's any trouble at the moment. He does have a tendency to overlook his need for the toilet until it's too late to take action. My mother has made some tenuous connection between Tom's forgetfulness and my desire to play snooker, which causes enormous rows whenever I go back to collect them, but it seems worth the trouble.

So when I put the phone down, I'm bursting with sudden excitement and grinning like a schoolgirl. Kevin sounded surprised but pleased to hear from me, and obviously impressed that I'm playing again. I can feel it. The World Championships are within my grasp, and I'd be a runner if only I could persuade some crazy fool to back me. I reckon Kevin fits the bill nicely.

They call love the tender trap, overlooking snooker as the next best thing to that breathless anticipation and loss of limb control which traditionally accompany the start of a love affair. For me, even walking innocently into a snooker club brings on cold sweats. I suppose it's an association of place with experience. The same phenomenon can be seen at work in any dentist's surgery, where you never know whether you'll be walking out with a smile on your face or a numb jaw. In snooker, the rewards may be greater, but so are the pressures. It's not simply that luck plays a part in any win or loss, although that does provide some explanation for the strange inner tension which makes one leg feel shorter than the other until after the match, it's also that you're walking naked into battle, armed with only a cue. Team-sport players have an easier time of it. They can blame someone else for their own failure, and that individual burden of guilt and inadequacy must seem much lighter when shared by eleven beefy lads. In snooker, you stand alone under the spotlight. You have to be geared up for success, but prepared to bleed.

Kevin knows this. He must do, because when he arrives at the club, he gives me a brief tight hug and looks down at my cue case, crossing himself. 'You did it. You really did it. A woman . . . in snooker.' He glances around the club, no doubt noticing the shadows lengthening as we move closer to the table. 'How are this bunch taking it? Badly, I expect. Not a brain between the lot of them. But some good players nevertheless. You learning much from them?'

Chance would be a fine thing. I slide the case up on to the table rail, opening it and taking out the cue. The two halves click neatly together like the final pieces of a jigsaw puzzle. 'No one will play me.'

'Ha!' Kevin gives a twisted smile. 'Typical.'

'Bob gives me some coaching now and then. But I'm considered bad luck round here. I put them off their game.'

'I bet you do.'

I glance at Kevin, but he's still smiling. Here is an

ally at last, someone I can turn to *in extremis*. Feeling the muscles in my shoulders and back slowly begin to unbunch, I realise what an enormous weight I've been carrying around for the past few months, that sense of battling against an intractable force, as if I've been walking into a high wind.

Kevin runs a hand nostalgically over my cue. 'So you kept it. I wasn't sure you would.'

'I never thanked you for sending it. I should have done.'

'Doesn't matter. I never used it myself . . . it was too short for me. It's possibly a bit too long for you.' He measures it against my shoulder. 'See? You need to lose a couple of inches. Otherwise you'll always be overstretching for the follow-through. Any good cue doctor would tell you the same. Either that, or you have to move your hand position further up the butt. You've marked it in the wrong place for your height. All you need to do is worry about where you're hitting the ball . . . and the next thing you know is, the cue's all over the place and you haven't got a hope in hell of hitting dead centre.'

I move my hand further along the butt, trying out a shot with the new position. It feels strange, but certainly the cue seems to be more under control. 'That's brilliant!'

Jeez, it's amazing what one small tip can do for your game. I'd wondered why it was so hard to keep my cueing accurate under pressure. Tonight, I'll move that piece of Sellotape further up and use it as a guide to my new hand position. 'But now I feel a bit cramped on the shot, rather like Quasimodo.'

Kevin leans over the table, pushing my bridge hand further up towards the tip. 'Just adjust your other hand . . . to keep the distance even. And spread your legs more, Zoë. Who taught you to stand like that? Your feet are practically on top of each other. How can you expect to stay still in that position? One push and you'd be over.'

I stare down at my feet, perplexed. 'Who's going to push me?'

'I am,' he says shortly, giving me a sharp nudge in the ribs.

I sway, and the cue moves with me.

'See?' Kevin strokes his chin, thinking hard. He hasn't even bothered to take his raincoat off, he's so absorbed with my stance. I'd forgotten his little trick of playing with his lighter while he thinks, turning it over and over in one hand, flicking it deftly through his fingers, over his knuckles and back on to his palm. 'The stance is vital. Get that right and you're half-way there. You're facing the shot, that's good, but somewhere between your waist and your feet, you've gone all cock-eyed.' He chews on his lower lip. 'Your knees! Look at your knees!'

I squint down through the narrow gap between my body and the cushion rail. This man's passion for the game, for getting the details right, is unnerving. 'What about them?'

'They're wrong, woman, they're wrong!' He seizes

one of my knees in a firm grasp and pushes it apart from the other. I can sense, rather than see, how all the heads in the room have turned towards us. I feel like a prize exhibit, something freakish to be prodded and stared at. Kevin bends again and straightens my other knee impatiently. 'I showed you before how to stand, first time you played. Something wrong with your memory?'

'Kevin, that was years ago. Besides, Bob said . . .'

'Sod Bob! What does he know? I'm telling you now, and that's what I say . . . knees further apart and that one straighter. It'll buckle under pressure the way you've got it at the moment. Steadiness. That's the key. Steadiness.'

The key. Gotcha. I sigh, then play the white that he puts in front of me. Already I can feel the difference. The cue is working smoothly, no longer at drift under my elbow. My whole body keeps still on the shot, not just from the waist up, but feet, knees, back, shoulders, arm, head. The whole frame is working as a unit.

'Better?' Kevin stands back to admire his handiwork. 'It's a knock-on effect, you see. Everything affects everything else.'

He speaks to me as if I were a six-year-old. I suppose that in comparison to his expertise I'm a mere babe in arms. Back in the late eighties, when we saw Kevin so regularly, he never discussed his past with me or Adrian, and we never liked to ask, wondering whether he was just one of those club players who like to assume an authority within the game that they've never really possessed. But Kevin's not like that, I can see it now, having had ample time to study Bob and the other 'good' players who hang around the club. He's a bona fide expert. The romantic in me decides there must be a mystery here, something shady in his past that he never talks about. I'll probably never know the truth but maybe I don't want to know. The mystery is more appealing.

Carefully, Kevin adjusts the fingers of my bridge hand. 'One little mistake in the stance, and the whole thing can crumble. If you've got your cue hand in the wrong position, you'll probably start hitting off-centre . . . pulling the shot to the left for example. If you're reasonably intelligent, you'll notice that after a while, but you won't know why you're doing it. So you automatically compensate by cueing to the right instead. In order to do that, you may have to move slightly . . . change where your feet go, for instance, or lean into the shot. That compounds the problem, makes it worse. Before you know it, you're putting all sorts of side on the ball that you never intended. After a while, you get so used to it that you don't notice what you're doing. Some players do it all their lives, then complain because they can't hit a plain ball shot when they need to.' He nods at me seriously. 'It's all inter-related. Watch the basics and the advanced technique will take care of itself.'

What a star. How on earth have I managed without Kevin? I try not to reveal how pathetically grateful I am, hoping he will interpret my starry-eyed look as being the result of too many hours spent working under overhead lighting. 'Thanks. I promise I won't forget.' I kiss him on the cheek, self-consciously aware that all eyes in the club are on us. 'Don't look now, but I think we have an audience.'

Kevin grins, pleased but obviously embarrassed by my peck on the cheek. Shrugging off his raincoat, he slides his own cue out of the soft leather-look case. 'Who cares? We've got work to do. When did you say the World Championships are being staged?'

This is it. I feel awful, but I know I have to ask him. There's no other way that I can see of getting there. I cross my fingers behind my back. 'The Qualifiers are on this month. But I've got a problem.'

'Yeah, your game sucks.'

I attempt a smile and fail miserably. Fuck it, why is asking for money so bloody difficult? If only I'd kept in touch. 'No, it's . . . er . . . actually, it's the entry fee for the World. I can't cover it.' There. It's done now. Too late to take it back.

Kevin doesn't look up at me, chalking his tip studiously. 'And you're wondering whether I'll lend it to you?'

Well, this is unexpected. Maybe the man is psychic after all. 'Mmmm. Sort of. The thing is . . .'

'You can't repay me.'

I shake my head silently, watching him. Please say yes. Please please say yes. This is the most important thing that's happened to me since I discovered contraception. If you don't say yes, I might as well crawl back under the bedclothes and not come out until I'm a granny. That's how important this is.

He hesitates. 'How much?'

'Fifty would help.'

'I'll let you have a hundred,' he says, then blinks as I descend on him. 'No more kissing! My ticker won't take it. I'll lend you the money . . . or rather, let you have it on perpetual loan . . . on one condition.'

Here come the terms. 'Yes?'

'You bloody well come back with a few more ranking points under your belt! Ninety-sixth in the world? What sort of ranking is that?'

'Mummy? Doesn't Daddy love us any more?'

This is the question all single mothers dread.

I look down at Tom, trying to decide how to answer. His small sticky hand is tightly clasped in mine as we cross the road towards the car. Beside us, Jemima skips cheerfully, her blonde plaits bobbing on her shoulders. In her multi-coloured anorak and with a lurid pink knapsack on her back, she looks like Heidi on acid. She is seven years old, going on seventeen. She already terrifies me. But Tom is only just coming up to five, and still babyish, with his round uncomplicated face now looking up at me questioningly as we get to the pavement.

I side-step a teenager with a ghettoblaster, smiling down at Tom in a rather forced manner. Secretly, I hope he can't hear me above the music. 'Of course he does. He moved out because Mummy and Daddy decided it was for the best, darling.'

Jemima has found the car and is pulling at the door handles. 'They didn't do sex any more, stupid!'

I freeze, then stare down into my bag fixedly, pretending to root for the car keys. Do I pretend not to have heard that, or should I challenge Jemmy about it? It's probably something she's picked up at school. Kids seem to be growing up so quickly, they're barely out of nappies before they're dating. I didn't even know what sex was until I was about fourteen, and even then the idea was all a bit hazy and unbelievable. Still, maybe that was why I got pregnant so young. Perhaps it's better to be up-front about the whole thing, and hope your children can avoid making the same mistakes you made.

I smile tentatively at Jemima. 'Did you have a big lunch?'

'Not really. Sausages, onions, gravy, mash, peas. Double helpings of rhubarb crumble and custard.'

Tom nods. 'Bangers,' he ventures. 'And orange.'

'You have orange every day, stupid!' Jemima points out.

Tom sticks his bottom lip out, allowing me to strap him into his seat without protest, staring mulishly at Jemima. He looks aggrieved. 'Orange,' he repeats at last.

'You like orange squash, don't you?' I murmur supportively, sliding into the front seat and adjusting the mirror so I can see Tom's face.

He nods again. 'Orange,' he says, with enthusiastic emphasis.

Jemima laughs, making a choking sound. 'Baby!'
'Orange!'
'Baby! Baby! Baby!'
'Orange! Orange! Orange!'

I shut myself off from their slanging match. It's easy once you acquire the habit, like being a switchboard operator who can talk calmly while all around you telephones are insistently ringing, or living near Heathrow and not being woken by aeroplanes passing overhead, not even Concorde taking off. Familiarity breeds contempt, or in this case, selective deafness. It's simply a question of practice.

Practice! I feel guilty immediately. I only managed an hour on the snooker table this afternoon. I know this week will be difficult. It's Tom's birthday on Friday. He'll be expecting the works: cake, party, presents, balloons. I've invited a few of his school friends over, and their mothers, but it feels more like a trip to the dentist than a fifth birthday party.

None of the other mothers sees eye to eye with me, not on the subject of playing snooker anyway. A few of them are impressed by my newly acquired world-ranking. One mother even stops me in the street sometimes, to ask how the snooker's going. She plays pool with her husband, so it's only natural she should take an interest. But generally speaking, they all look on me with the same mixture of pity and disgust I could imagine them feeling for some drug addict or old drunk, found urinating in the gutters. I have to admit it. In the eyes of the other mothers,

I have become what my mother would call *persona non grata*.

'Are you going out again tonight? To play snooker?' Jemima asks me suddenly,

I glance over my shoulder at her. There's a note in her voice that disturbs me. Her pale face watches me fixedly. Not knowing what to say, I look back at the road, hating myself.

'Granny ... is granny coming over?' Tom asks excitedly.

Now I feel even worse. Tom's beginning to associate his mother's absences with his granny. What are the future implications of this association? Will he grow up to be one of these men who can only date older women? Or will he be imprisoned in later years for attacking women outside snooker clubs? It would be all my fault. I'm an unfit mother. I can see it now, splashed across the front page of *The Sunday Sport*: Pervert Blames Snooker Mum For Warping His Cue.

Perhaps I shouldn't go out tonight.

I had been planning to hit the club for about eight, once they were firmly tucked up in bed, leaving my mother to do the honours if either of them woke up. Tomorrow is out of the question as far as practice is concerned. I had wanted to do some heavy-duty practice in order to make up for my absence tomorrow. Players can't afford to slacken up before a big tournament. Kevin is always hammering that point home, reminding me of the times I've gone in ill-prepared and lost because of it.

But Jemima's narrowed eyes are still on my face. She's old enough now to know where I'm going and why. I try to remember what it felt like to be seven, but fail miserably. I can remember bits and pieces of my early life, but not how I thought or felt or what I imagined. Except for one occasion, checking under the bed for monsters after watching a particularly horrifying episode of Dr Who. I also remember hiding behind the sofa every week while the Dr Who titles came up. Even the music scared me. Actually, I still get shudders when I hear it now. I'm not sure what that says about my emotional adjustment to being an adult, but it can't be normal.

Jemima is rather more bomb-proof than I was at that age, but that's no reason to assume she can't be hurt. I feel awful. Now what? Do I admit I'm going out and see her face fall? Do I smooth it all over with some reassurance which isn't true, and then slip away tonight once she's asleep? The third option is even less appealing. I could ring my mother and cancel. I could stay in tonight and amuse myself by watching endless repeats of *The Bill* on UK Gold.

'Well?' Jemima insists, straining against the seat belt as she leans forward.

That note of vulnerability in her voice gets me right under the rib-cage. I suddenly realise what people mean when they describe themselves as being 'torn apart'. But at the same time, it's not just a tearing sensation, it's also an awareness of shrinking, of getting smaller and smaller in the driver's seat until I'm just a tiny pair of hands turning the wheel and a barely visible face looking up into the mirror.

I force myself to sound in control. 'Sit back, you'll hurt yourself if I have to stop suddenly. What's all this fuss about? I often play snooker in the evenings. You've never complained before.' The traffic lights ahead have just turned to red. Irritably, I slam the gear-lever into second with a crunch and feel the car shudder slowly to a halt. The longed-for escape of the practice session is already disappearing. I hate the way Jemmy's staring at me in silent accusation. 'All right. I won't go this time. We can have fish fingers for tea.'

'And orange,' Tom adds firmly, beaming.

The birthday party. It's almost a horror sub-genre in itself. I remember now why I hated birthday parties as a child. Someone always says something awful about your outfit, and the next thing you know you're in tears under the kitchen table or in the airing cupboard or, years later, out on the veranda kissing some ugly fuckwit you can't stand but who at least has the good sense, or the good manners, not to tell you that your 'little black dress' makes you look like the Michelin man.

Jemima comes dashing past me in the hall, just as I'm helping five-year-old Daniel unbutton his coat. She is crying.

'Hey!' I straighten up. At that moment, there's a loud crash from the kitchen and a squeal of laughter. Either the sandwiches or the hot sausage rolls have just completed a backward somersault with pike off the kitchen table. I glance frantically in the direction of the kitchen, then back at Jemima, now running up the stairs with one hand over her face. 'What's the matter?'

'I . . . hate . . . you!' she yells almost incoherently and disappears with a bang into her bedroom. Subsequent bangs indicate that either she is taking her wrath out on the bunk beds or is constructing some form of barricade to prevent my entry.

Oh God. It must be the dress. I had persuaded her not to wear her jeans, saying that birthday celebrations deserved party dresses rather than her typically casual approach to clothes. I had then dug out her last party dress, hardly worn and now rather too small for her, but still (I foolishly thought) respectable for parties with its cute pink flounces and full lace at the collar.

I pat little Daniel on the head. He stares up at me from under a mass of golden curls, cheerfully fascinated. 'That was Tom's sister. Tom's sister is crying,' he observes candidly.

'Yes, and so will you be if you miss any more of the party. Tom's in the kitchen with your other little friends.' I chuck his coat disrespectfully on to the growing pile of miniature duffles and anoraks. 'Run along and join them. And tell Tom not to throw any more food on the floor, there's a good boy.'

Jemima, as expected, refuses to open the door. It does lock but I took the key away months ago, and the fact that I can't open it even when I put my shoulder firmly against the wood indicates a barricade of some sort. 'Open this door immediately!'

'Go away!'

'What's the matter?'

'It's all your fault.'

Naturally. Whose else? 'Why don't you tell me what this is all about, Jemmy, and then maybe I can sort something out.'

More muffled invectives. Then a short tearful silence. 'Mickey says I look fat.'

I knew it. Why on earth did I insist she wore that dress? I must be turning into my mother. I've been watching myself for signs of this happening for years, and it seems that the inevitable has happened. I am forcing my daughter to wear creations fit only for low-budget remakes of Pollyanna. I have now officially become my mother. 'Mickey who?'

'Mickey from three doors down.'

'Hey, where's my brave little girl gone? I thought you were going to be my right-hand man at this party, not go all weepy on me.' I take a deep breath and cross my fingers behind my back. 'Don't listen to that stupid boy, Jemmy. You look lovely.'

'No, I don't.'

'Yes, you do.'

'No I don't!' she screams, then dissolves into howling tears again. 'I hate you! I hate you!'

I stand there for a moment, remembering similar episodes in my past. The memories seem to lift like curtains and, for a moment, I see myself at eleven years old, standing rebelliously on the porch of a neighbour's house, dressed in some appalling yellow smock for a Christmas party, with my hair in pigtails and my teeth clamped tightly in a hideous iron brace.

The door in my mind opens to reveal a charming Christmas scene, with a glittering tree, children running and shrieking, coloured tinsel hanging from the ceiling, and Cynthia, a large raw-boned girl in dungarees (very fashionable at the time, though I can't imagine why) who stood there and laughed at my yellow smock for a good five minutes before slamming the door shut in my face. Afterwards, as I recall, she told a friend: 'Nobody comes to one of my parties dressed as a cheese.'

It was a great line, but I hated my mother for that indignity. She had inherited the smock from a friend whose daughter (luckily for her) had grown out of it, and she had insisted I wear it at least once. Cynthia's Christmas party was the memorable outing for that dress, and here I am now, handing on similar misery to my daughter.

'I'm sorry I made you wear it,' I say quietly through the door. 'Look, why don't you change out of that dress? Put your jeans on, and that blue shirt Granny bought you. Then come down and join the party. I thought you were braver than this. I thought you were almost grown-up.'

Gradually, Jemima's sobbing subsides, and then I hear the creaks and sniffs as she slides down from her top bunk and starts stripping off the loathed pink dress. I can't quite recall why I insisted she wore it, but it seems a massively stupid thing to have done. Tentatively, I tap on the door again. 'What have you put in front of the door?'

Pause. 'The wardrobe.'

I stare at the blank door in front of me, then smile at the thought of her lugging the huge mirrored wardrobe from one side of the room to the other. 'Really?'

There's silence, then I can hear a muffled giggling. 'Really.'

'Well,' I say lightly, hesitating at the top of the stairs. 'You really must be strong, after all. I hope you can move it back again, otherwise you're going to miss the best bit of the party.'

'A magician?' Jemmy asks idly, not bothering to hide her distaste.

'Nope.' I start going downstairs, but slowly, listening for any sign of reaction. 'Pizza Express should be delivering any minute now.'

Her sudden squeal and hurried movement is reassuring. The young bounce back quickly, unlike adults, who can't be lured away from deep emotional distress like that even by the undoubted delights of a twelve-inch double-crust Hawaiian pizza. Although it's true that food can sometimes prove to be a satisfactory diversion from some adult problems, as long as the traditional fridge-raiding binge of double-chocolate fudge cake and Häagen-Dazs ice cream doesn't end in guilty self-flagellation and a fortnight of carrot juice. Unfortunately, speaking from personal experience, it usually does.

Okay, I have averted a minor tragedy today, but how long until another one appears on the horizon? Jemima is growing up so fast, and I can't always be there for her, not with the World Championships coming up soon and a dozen five-year-olds dancing round a pile of broken plates in my kitchen.

As I pass the hall mirror, I stop suddenly and frown at my reflection, confused. Is that pale, strained-looking woman really me? I peer closer, ignoring the shrieks from the kitchen for a few seconds. A wrinkle! This can't be happening. Two wrinkles? No. I pull at my skin with one tentative finger, stretching it tight. They're fine lines, that's all. Laughter lines. First wrinkles don't hit in your late twenties. They're strictly reserved for professional thirty-somethings heading into forty, the ones who wear tartan mini-skirts with opaque black tights, put their hair up in tightly coiled chignon styles and take their lap-tops everywhere, even to the beach. My mother has wrinkles – it's the number one obsession in her life – but I simply don't believe that I come into the wrinkle category yet.

'Mummy?'

I look down at Tom who has come out of the kitchen and is tugging at my sleeve. 'Have you made a mess in there, Tom?'

He nods cheerfully. 'Is it time for pizza yet?'

'Not yet, darling. Go and take your friends out into the garden while I clear up.'

I allow him to drag me into the kitchen by my sleeve. I'm not sure whether to call the police or a psychiatrist.

I think I may be on the verge of a nervous breakdown. My pine-effect kitchen looks like the scene of a road traffic accident. There's tomato ketchup on the walls and mutilated slices of ham underfoot. A dozen pairs of eyes follow me round the room as I stoop to retrieve the sauce-covered offerings from the lino. I pile them up near the bin like a collection of flabby pink insoles, then wipe my hands on a dish-cloth and look around the kitchen accusingly. 'Okay. Who's been playing with the ketchup?'

Total silence.

'I guess you won't want any pizza then.'

One small boy scrambles out of my recently installed vegetable carousel, uttering a spine-chilling Red Indian war-cry and threatening me with a carrot: 'Pizza now! Or prepare to die, pale face!'

From upstairs, I can hear Jemima moving the wardrobe back in a series of long dragging noises and sudden thuds. I ought to check she's not hurting herself. I put my hands in the air. 'I surrender, Chief Little-Big-Carrot. Now out into the garden, you noisy lot. I'll call you when the pizza van arrives.'

They rush out shrieking and whooping. The doorbell rings. It's too early for Pizza Express. I know it will probably be Jason's mother, turning up for her obligatory cup of tea. She will probably be closely followed by a small number of other mothers, all eager to exchange gossip over cups of tea or the odd glass of wine. How wonderful. Two hours of 'mummy and baby' talk. I can hardly wait.

It's moments like these when I could cheerfully hang myself.

Some days later, tired but apprehensive, I pull up outside a B&B in Brighton, wishing Kevin could have come down with me but knowing that it's all up to me now. This is not just another town, another tournament. This is the holy of holies. This is where they separate the women from the girls. This is where it all hangs on the first-round draw. This is the World Championships. This is my personal definition of hell.

I've agreed to meet Tricksy in the club bar at seven o'clock. It's only five now, so I wander round for a couple of hours, trying not to look lost. I don't know what it is about the World Championships Qualifiers that provokes this sense of emotional turmoil, but it feels as though I'm inches away from a defining moment, the sort of moment that you either fumble or fix for ever. I don't have the faintest clue which way I'm going to swing, but my stomach hurts as though I've just gone down thirty floors in a high-speed elevator and my head is pounding.

I walk through the busy streets in a daydream. I know I'm gazing around the place with the stunned expression of a seagull who's just swallowed a packet of condoms, but I can't seem to snap out of it. My first-round match is at ten o'clock tomorrow morning, and I'm terrified.

Brighton is an uneasy mix of the Victorians and the

late twentieth century. On the one hand, you have the beautifully restored piers with their iron legs knee-high in salt water and history, and on the other hand, you have high-tec nightspots, laser discos, gay clubs and theme bars. Existing somewhere in between these two extremes is the perennial sweep of the sea and the striking white unreality of the Brighton Pavilion. The sea has an excuse for being there. The Pavilion, however, looks like something a Martian with a bizarre sense of humour might have dropped into the middle of town, having nicked it from India sometime early in the nineteenth century and eventually grown tired of carrying it round in his spaceship. No other explanation for its presence seems plausible.

The sea air slaps me in the face. I'd forgotten how bright the sea can be, with the sun swinging above it like some enormous naked bulb, burning a double image into my eyeballs. A sharp wind blows me down on to the seafront. I find one of those old-fashioned benches enclosed by a wall and a roof, facing the sea, and sink down with my eyes closed. I can hear the tide, breaking mechanically on the shingle. I can hear a seagull overhead, screaming at nothing in particular, then fading out over the pier in a long series of manic cackles. I can hear the faint grind of traffic behind me, muffled by the high dull walls surrounding the bench. I can hear the deranged whistling of the wind along the seafront. I can hear voices. Voices. Getting louder. More familiar.

I sit up, looking along the promenade. Who the hell

is that? Then I see her. It's Sylvie. She's walking along the seafront towards me, about a few hundred yards away, talking to a man, her head bent. I know that fierce fast voice, each word clipped but unmistakably hers.

Curiously, I'm pleased to see her. The top seeds don't need to arrive for another day or two, so Sylvie is here early, no doubt enjoying a few days of sea and sand with her boyfriend. And who can blame her? If I was involved with anyone, and didn't have kids, that's exactly what I'd be doing.

The cold wind strengthens. I pop my hands in my pockets, hunching into my coat. One part of me knows that Sylvie is a bitch, the sort of player who only talks to you if you're in the top ten, and cuts you dead if you're cannon-fodder, ranked somewhere in the hundreds, and fit only for the likes of Sylvie to cut her teeth on in the early rounds. I ought to hate her. If I had any guts, I'd hate her. But one small sneaking part of me admires her aloofness, respects that brand of single-mindedness that gets her to the final of so many tournaments.

It's a strange world, snooker. Once you're at the table, it doesn't matter if you're a brain surgeon or a factory worker. Your world ranking is all that matters, and you get treated accordingly. In the top ten, you're a god. Ten to twenty meets with grudging respect. Twenty to fifty gets you the occasional nod. Anywhere beyond fifty, you're a nobody. In women's snooker, the only exception to this is when a player has taken time out, to get married or have a baby, and returns at a lower ranking than they used to possess. Those lucky ones get admitted to the ranks of the top players without the actual ranking to prove it.

I'm not bitter about that. Like everyone else, I accept it as part of the game. In fact, it's only at times like these that I question the validity of the system. I know, for instance, that I can't nip over to Sylvie now, or even give her a cheerful wave. I know her, but I don't *know* her. She would probably be horrified to be greeted like that by a low-ranked player. The ranking system jars uneasily with the outside world. Those stifling rules don't seem to apply out here, in the cold bright sunshine of the 'real world'. But Sylvie may still think they do. She may not see the disparity between that world and this one. All she will see is some anonymous nobody embarrassing her in front of her boyfriend. She probably doesn't even remember my name.

Sylvie and her man come closer. They are going to pass right in front of my hiding place. If she glances sideways, she'll see me. Suddenly, it's me who's embarrassed. I'm wearing ancient tatty jeans and jumper, my old black anorak with the fraying edges, and worse, these clapped-out trainers with holes at the toes and laces that don't match. I'm not wearing any make-up. I don't even think I had time to brush my hair before leaving the B&B. I wasn't thinking about my appearance. I just wanted to get out into the fresh air before going to the snooker club for my final practice.

Sylvie, of course, is impeccably dressed. Her red hair lifts elegantly on the wind, revealing delicate silver earrings. The long black coat ends in smart dark green trousers, a sharp crease running down the front of each leg, immaculate black boots completing the picture. Her subtle make-up reminds me of the pages of *Cosmopolitan*, high cheek-bones underscored by a faint but expensive-looking blush.

But I'm glad to see I'm not the only woman who has trouble with her boyfriends. From the taut line of her mouth, and the brief angry gestures of her hands, Sylvie is arguing with him about something. Women don't talk to strangers like that. Not unless they've just nipped in front of us at the delicatessen counter. Anyway, they look like a couple. I can't see his face, because his head is bent towards her, but I can see he's wearing an expensive suit. The blue patterned tie flapping over one shoulder in the wind looks like it's made of silk. He says something to her sharply, then lifts his head and looks out to sea. His expression is tense, his eyes very dark.

I stiffen, recognising him. It's the guy I saw hanging around in the club car park that time. The one who follows her everywhere. Her shadow. He may look totally different in the expensive suit, but I'd recognise him anywhere. Those eyes give it away. Sylvie said he was pestering her. So why on earth is she walking along Brighton seafront with him?

You know those moments when you feel this incredible urge to rush in and save someone from total disaster, but can't make your mind up, remembering all those other occasions when you did precisely that and got slapped back for it? Well, this is how I feel, watching

Sylvie with that creep. She can't seriously want him around. Maybe he's been waiting for a chance like this, to find her alone and unprotected, then pounced, knowing she can't defend herself. Maybe he's steering her towards his car at this very moment, planning to abduct her. Sylvie may not even realise the danger she's in. 'Sylvie!'

She stops dead and turns towards me with an impatient frown, obviously not recognising me. Bloody wonderful. If only I'd kept my mouth shut. Another second and they would have passed me by. But no, I had to show myself up again. I'm getting used to looking like a wanker, it's almost a hobby of mine.

I get up awkwardly from the bench. 'Sorry. I just . . .' then tail off, not really knowing what I was going to say.

Sylvie stares at me in sudden recognition, then looks back at the man. I can't work out if the expression on her face is one of relief, or irritation, or just plain surprise. Whichever it is, I still wish the ground would open up and swallow me. But I'm not going to be able to escape. Astonishingly, Sylvie towers across the seafront towards me, holding out her hands. With her high-heeled black suede boots, she looks even more like a giraffe compared to my pathetic five foot one. The husky accent seems more marked, as though she's reverting to Finnishness under stress, but she's smiling at me in a friendly enough way. I'm immediately suspicious. Sylvie *never* smiles at people like that. 'How lovely to see you. Are you down here for the tournament? I was just thinking of doing some practice. Shall we go to the club together?'

Well, at least I don't have to worry about one of them being mad. Quite clearly, Sylvie has flipped. She manages to maintain one of the world's most perfect monosyllabic relationships with me over a period of some months, then blows the whole set-up in under ten seconds. I'm gaping, but there doesn't seem to be much I can do about it.

The man stays where he is, clutching the iron railings of the seafront, but his face is furious. 'Sylvie!' he calls after her, in true Heathcliff fashion, but she ignores him. Nothing unusual there. She ignores most people.

But he's obviously not giving up. He comes over, and Sylvie visibly shrinks. There's definitely something going on between these two. He then gives me what's obviously intended to be a quick threatening look, and stares silently at Sylvie for a few moments. When he eventually speaks, his voice is strained but English. No Finn, this one. Actually, with those rugged looks and the expensive suit, he's doing a fairly good impersonation of Pierce Brosnan in *Goldeneye*. 'Don't think this finishes it, Sylvie.' I narrow his accent down to the North London area. 'I don't give up that easily.'

When she makes no comment, he turns on his heel and heads back along the seafront, taking long angry strides. I wish Adrian could have made dramatic exits like that, but the most I ever got out of Adrian was a slammed door and a half-eaten pizza.

Sylvie drops my hands. 'Thanks,' she says huskily.

'Zoë, is it? He was making a real nuisance of himself, Zoë. I was beginning to think I would never get rid of him.'

'You should call the police next time.'

She gives me a shaky smile. Why have I never noticed before that her teeth are slightly crooked? There's something comforting about that imperfection. Sylvie's beginning to look less like Barbie and more like a human being. Unfortunately, her powers of reasoning appear to be on a level with anyone who's ever written a thriller where the girl goes *up* the stairs in an unlit house to the bedroom where she suspects the madman who just killed her lover is now waiting with an axe. 'There's no point calling the police. What could they do?'

'You could get a court injunction.'

But Sylvie shakes her head. She seems strangely oblivious to the dangers involved. She hasn't even turned to watch him walk away. There's something very fishy about the whole business.

'You can't just let some strange man follow you round like that, Sylvie. He might hurt you one day.'

Sylvie laughs bitterly. 'He's already done that,' she says, looking down at me with a sudden uncomfortable directness. 'He's my husband.'

5

God, I love this game. Being there. Doing it. Listening to gossip. Passing it on. Sylvie's revelations about her estranged husband are par for the course on a world circuit where you never know what's going to happen next. At the end of the day, the only thing that really matters is the game. Putting everything on the line for the sake of some dubious piece of paper that allows you the right to another shot at the title. Who cares who's sleeping with whom? Who cares about the financial and emotional cost of the game? Who cares about the dreary B&B you're shacked up in, complete with leaking radiator, an impressive colony of moulds in the shower, and mysterious damp patches on the bed? Who cares about the strange looks you get when you walk down the street, cradling a world-class cue you needed a mortgage to afford? After all, it only takes one great shot to make up for all the shit.

I'm not surprised by Sylvie's complex love-life. Snooker is a form of insanity. It's not in the nervous-breakdown category, nothing sudden or shocking, like stripping off in the middle of a board meeting or falling in love with Mike Oldfield's 'Tubular Bells' and playing it at top volume on Sunday mornings. It's a gradual slide into obsessive behaviour, and more difficult to handle socially when you're a woman. Being crazy about snooker is almost *expected* of a man. But, as a woman player, life becomes very complicated if you want to avoid losing your boyfriend or husband. It calls for ingenuity.

Lets's face it, playing snooker as a woman is almost like having an affair behind your spouse's back. You know the sort of thing. Making far-fetched excuses about where you're going for the weekend. Booking tables in an assumed name. Sneaking into the club under cover of darkness. Explaining the shiny cue case to bemused people at bus stops: 'Snooker cue? No, I'm an aluminium sales rep in my spare time.' Or saying it's for your father when ordering snooker gadgets from puzzled shop assistants. That last is the height of indignity, but it does save awkward questions.

You know you're reclaiming your identity when subterfuge seems not only unnecessary but downright infuriating. I can still remember where I was the day I admitted to being a snooker player. It's little things like this that alert you to a corner having been turned, an uphill gradient successfully attempted, a respectable amount of distance having been covered.

It strikes me that Sylvie's husband looks exactly the sort of man who wouldn't be able to handle his wife's success. I'm guessing here, because Sylvie didn't care to elaborate on the situation. But I have my suspicions. As women players, and therefore sporting freaks to most citizens, we've all been there. It takes courage to stand up and admit it in public: 'I'm Zoë and I'm a full-time snooker player.'

It's as easy as that. Honest.

I knew I shouldn't have taken up snooker. I'm just no fucking good at it. Here I am, well into the third frame, twenty-seven points down, with a potential thirty-five on the table. Rebecca from the West Midlands took the first two, and if I lose this one, I only have one frame left in which to snatch a victory from the jaws of certain death. It's a familiar story for me, but not one I particularly wanted to repeat in my first-round match at the World Championships.

I can almost see my consolation prize hanging there above the table: an entry into the World Plate competition, specially designed for those morons who go out in the first few rounds. Only very sad people are proud of winning the World Plate. I didn't plan on being one of that number this week, but it may yet happen if I don't pull my finger out.

Rebecca from the West Midlands is only seventeen, but boy, can she play hard-ball. It's like watching Bam-Bam armed with a snooker cue. Her glossy chestnut pony-tail bounces violently around the table. 'Hey, referee, can we have a speed-gun on table twelve?' Does she realise we need this white for the next frame?

In this situation, playing someone who could out-pot

you even if the table was the size of the known universe, which unfortunately it isn't, there are three options available to you: a) you speed up; b) you slow down; c) you play your own game regardless of theirs.

Okay, c) is clearly the best option, but there are some advantages to a strategic combination of a) and b), with c) lurking somewhere in the background until needed. Firstly, if taking a beating at the hands of a younger opponent, it makes you feel so much better to get up and slam some outrageous pot down the full length of the table. It also helps if the ball goes in. Secondly, nothing rattles a fast player more thoroughly than playing someone who appears to be geriatric. Taking ten minutes to play a simple stun shot would irritate even Father Time. You can't make procrastination too obvious, of course. There are limits, and a warning for slow play will get you nowhere.

Successful ploys for breaking a faster opponent's rhythm include a coughing fit, for which much water and back-slapping are required, a loose tip, for the securing of, or a sudden knee injury which makes progress round the table painfully slow. I'm not advocating poor sportsmanship, you understand. None of these should be put into action while an opponent is on the shot. But snooker's a game of the mind as much as the wrist. You just have to learn to keep it within the rules.

It takes a strong personality to stick to option c). Let's face it, how many of us can play our own game under pressure? If your opponent knocks in a fifty-odd break, you're going to be affected. There's no question. If you're streets ahead, your cue action improves, your game comes together, you start making pots you'd usually miss under pressure.

Everything can change during the course of a game. It's a sliding scale, up one minute, down the next. To learn *not* to react is the hardest thing in the world. Sure, you have to close up when the scoreline's tight but you're ahead. Equally, you have to go for your shots when the pressure's on to make the points. But it's a question of extremes. To make those frequent minute adjustments necessary for an even-handed approach is beyond everyone but the best players. At the end of the day, all I want is that five-second glory shot, and sod the percentages. I guess that's why I'm only ranked ninety-sixth in the world. The other ninety-five are obviously much smarter than I am.

But not today. Today is different. Today, I want to win. I don't care what it takes, I just want to walk away from this table with the winner's slip in my hand. If that means ignoring Rebecca the Rocket here, or forgetting everything I know about flashy right-hand spin shots, or blocking everything out until all I can see are the four rails of the table, then so be it. But today I am not going to lose.

Only twenty points in it. I lay a careful snooker behind the brown.

Rebecca misses the blue by inches. She walks away from the table reluctantly, looking back over her shoulder as I move in for the kill. Her sudden and curious resemblance to Miss Piggy, at the point of having her sexual advances turned down by Kermit for the umpteenth time, suggests to me that Rebecca from the West Midlands is squealing silently behind that icy façade of disinterest.

This is it. This is it. Keep calm.

I scrape the frame up under my fingernails like dirt.

Rebecca charges off to the toilets with the air of a young vulture, deprived of her prey for the time being. In first-round matches, there are no interval breaks. You take your opportunity to escape to the toilet when the need arises, though there is an unspoken rule that biological needs should not be excessive. The mid-match point in these situations is rather like an unofficial 'half-time'. Players queue for the toilets or nip to the bar or smoke furiously at the table, depending on a player's normal reaction to stress. Rebecca is clearly of the 'toilet' school of thought.

No doubt she will be exchanging bitchy comments about me in the ladies; communal meeting-place and venue for those vital in-between-frame pyscho-therapy sessions, where players either shred toilet paper to appease their aggression or make vicious comments about their opponents to whomever else happens to be in there. Any hostile silence you encounter in the ladies is usually down to both players being in there at once, which means a dignified silence must be kept at all costs, and any toilet paper shredding is to be done noiselessly, behind closed cubicle doors.

'How's it going?' Tricksy whispers in passing. A small piece of white toilet paper attached to her shoe indicates the successful accomplishment of her 'half-time' mission.

'So-so. Yours?'

'So-so.'

'Know how you feel.'

'See you later then,' she hisses, heading off to her own table.

By the time Rebecca comes back, I have it all under control. I am not going to do anything rash. I will not take that long blue on. Given two reds, I will play the sensible one first. When there are no pots on, I shall simply play safe. The tighter, the better. There are no prizes for second place, as unimaginative television commentators are always telling us. It may not be a game of two halves, but it's certainly a game of two players, and I'm the one who's going to win today. Tomorrow I can lose big time. I don't care about tomorrow. I don't even care about making a big break. Breaks don't win matches, they only win frames. All I care about today is making Rebecca from the West Midlands suffer.

'She's what?'

'Married,' I repeat wearily. How did I get into this conversation?

I settle back on my bar stool, taking a final drag on the

post-match cigarette Tricksy offered me. I don't really smoke, but winning always seems to call for something out of the ordinary. In the absence of a fat cigar, this will have to do.

Sylvie never actually said *don't tell anyone*, but if she wanted everyone to know, she would hardly have kept her failed marriage a secret for so long. I must be the only player on the circuit who knows about him. Correction. The only *low*-ranked player on the circuit who knows about him. I can't believe she hasn't told her cronies, that bunch of short-haired, Doc Martened, skeletal women in Naf Naf jackets who hang on her every word.

Tricksy is still incredulous. 'To that creep? Was that all she said?'

'She didn't want to talk about it. And maybe he's not a creep,' I say, trying to keep my voice down. The bar is crowded and I don't want anyone to overhear our conversation.

'Of course he's a creep. She must be mad.'

'Sylvie would hardly have married a creep, would she?'

'Sometimes you don't know they're creeps until it's too late.'

This is fair enough. 'Okay. Let's say he was fine when she married him, but the stress of the marriage breaking down has turned him into a . . . creep-like person . . . from the outside.'

'Why are you defending him?' Tricksy puts down her half-pint of lager and gives me a strange look.

Behind her, someone is playing the bandit and the coins drop, giving me a few moments of noise in which to collect my thoughts.

Am I defending him? I guess I am. 'I don't know. Maybe he just didn't look like a creep when I saw him with her.' Maybe people only look like creeps when you think they're behaving in a creepy fashion. After all, it's pretty creepy to follow a strange woman around the country. But she isn't strange, not to him. 'I don't even think they're divorced.'

'She's a dark horse.'

'So's he.'

Tricksy stares at me suddenly. 'Do you fancy him?'

'What?'

'You fancy him, don't you?'

'I do not!'

'Ooooh. You fancy the creep!'

'He's not a creep. And I don't.'

'Liar!'

This is too much. 'Piss off.'

'Ahah!' Tricksy points at me in mock accusation. 'Why are you getting so upset, then? Liar!'

'Think what you like.'

'I shall,' she says firmly. 'Maybe I'll tell Sylvie. She could off-load the creep on to you, Zoë. Solve all her problems.'

'Don't you dare!'

Tricksy laughs at my expression. 'Okay, okay. I won't tell her. But you've got to admit, it's a funny thought . . . you and the creep!'

'Get lost.' It's at times like these that I try to remember why I started hanging round with Tricksy, and whether it's all worth the effort. Me and the creep. I feel a surge of irritation. She's even got me calling him the creep. He's probably a nice bloke when you get to know him, though I know I'm using 'nice' in a slightly ironical sense there. He's certainly good-looking, but I know that comment is strictly off-limits now. Tricksy would immediately pounce on it and use it against me in future conversations.

'What's his name, anyway?'

'I don't know,' I say truthfully.

'You didn't ask what his name was? You're useless!'

I decide to change the subject. 'When's your next match?'

This has the desired effect. Her face lights up. Tricksy is very proud of having won her first-round match, although the fact that she was playing a sixty-year-old woman with arthritis would appear to have been a deciding factor in the outcome. I have wisely not commented on this though, knowing Trickys's temper to be somewhat volatile.

'Half an hour. How about yours?'

'Not until two o'clock.' I can't help grinning. Okay, I dispatched Rebecca of the West Midlands with some difficulty, but the final score is all that matters. In the end, her potting skills couldn't make up for her lack of ball control. The fact that I struggled for twenty minutes to pot the pink in that last frame has no bearing whatsoever on the result. Thankfully. Unlike

Zen philosophy, how you get there is not as important as the destination itself.

Now I'm up against a player ranked in the thirties, some apparently deranged woman with a toddler and a lime-green striped shirt. She looks, rather disconcertingly, like a walking spearmint. I keep bumping into her in the bar. Her name is Peg, and she's got one of those disapproving faces that always remind me of my mother. But that's okay. We both know we're playing each other in the next round, so eye contact is at a minimum.

Tricksy belts off to the toilets to fix her make-up and spend the obligatory three minutes alone in a cubicle, chanting to herself, or whatever it is she does in there before every match. I stay in the bar, keeping an eye on her cue.

Sylvie is somewhere in the large crowd of girls down at the far end, playing cards and making such a racket that a referee pokes his head through the door every few minutes and tells them to shut up. I don't look in her direction too often. I don't want to catch her eye and be reminded of Tricksy's ridiculous insinuations. If he's not good enough for Sylvie, why on earth should he be good enough for me?

You know those magazine articles where some degenerate twice-divorced hack undergoing counselling for alcoholism tells you why you should be living a fuller life, and then proceeds to show you how it's done by listing 'fulfilling' hobbies and pastimes that can help you achieve this? Well, there's something very satisfying about being able to turn the page and settle, far more comfortably, into an advertisement feature for bikini-line waxing.

Snooker has done this for me. I no longer feel 'unfulfilled'. I no longer turn off the television in self-disgust, wondering how I can develop a more rounded personality. I often feel extremely pissed off with the programme line-up, but that's a different matter. In snooker, you are never alone. Sometimes you wish you were, given some of the sadder people on the circuit, but it's never a dull existence. Snooker is a living, breathing entity, rather like a tree; as a player, your only concern is how far up the branches you can get, and whether the other birds are going to end up shitting on you.

Today, though, life up in the trees is wonderful. The baize has never looked so green. The hours of practice are paying off. In my head, I can hear Kevin's voice: 'Easy does it. No need to hurry.'

I love Kevin. I love my cue. I love this game. I even love Peg, my opponent in this match. Her toddler escapes from the bar at intervals, calling 'Mummy! Mummy!' in a penetrating voice, and she shoos him gently back in to his dad, returning to the table all flustered and apologetic. I don't mind because I'm winning. She could be old Mother Hubbard for all I care, and invite dozens of her darling little children to perch on the table in between frames. It wouldn't bother me. I am spilling over with generosity. I am hitting the ball dead centre. Not even sex feels better than this. Well, loosely speaking.

Tricksy meets me coming back from the table, clutching my winner's slip as triumphantly as a winning Lottery Ticket. She looks at it gloomily. 'Did you win?'

'Certainly did.'

'I lost.'

I can afford to be generous. 'Unlucky.'

'Mmm.' Tricksy pulls angrily at her orange blouse. 'This bloody shirt's meant to be lucky.'

'It can't be lucky every time.'

Pointing out the obvious has never worked with Tricksy. She scowls at me. 'Very funny. I'll see you later. I'm going back to change.'

'Okay.' I pause. She looks rather more upset than usual. Something more sympathetic sounding is obviously required of me. 'You okay?'

'Okayish.'

I nod. That seems fair, under the circumstances. 'Okay.'

'See you later, then.'

'Yeah, see you.'

This conversation would be fairly normal after a lost match, if it wasn't for the one-sided bitterness. It's a strange sensation, not losing my second-round match. I know how Tricksy feels, though maybe not, since she's never gone further in a tournament than I have, except, of course, for that now memorable occasion when I beat her.

For the first time, I sense a yawning abyss ahead of us, although only the faintest signs of it may be showing at the moment. Players of a certain rank tend to stick together. When you get 'promoted', your set of friends has an unsettling tendency to change, throwing you higher and higher up the game until you meet the magic circle of the top ten. Very few people make it that far. There are exceptions to this phenomenon, of course, but those who refuse to allow it to happen don't command the same respect as those who willingly accept their fate.

I like Tricksy. She's a mate. Do I really want to leave her behind?

It's at this point that I realise how ridiculous I'm being. All I've done is win one more match than Tricksy in the World Championships. To be honest, I don't anticipate getting any further. I'll be playing a seeded player in the next round, and my chances of getting past her are probably lower than my chances of being awarded an OBE. Which are pretty damn slim, let's face it.

I'm not leaving Tricksy behind, I've just pissed her off by winning. Tomorrow, I'll probably be back in that dreary losers' corner with all my other mates in the above-fifty ranking bracket. It's a grim thought, but it brings me down to earth fairly sharply. That's one of the problems with snooker. You get so used to visualising the next shot, you start thinking that everything in life works like that. Maybe it does, in a way. After all, it's only after you 'visualise' the tax inspectors on your doorstep that you start to panic, root out your tax form and fill it in. But you can take the art of visualisation too far, sliding from the first flush of match success to the World title in one fluid movement. If you get delusions of grandeur, and start treating your friends like rungs on a ladder, sooner or later you're going to put your foot out, and find nothing but fresh air.

So, in spite of having possibly the most important match of my life next morning, I find myself in the bar that night with half a dozen 'losers', playing poker, and getting horrendously drunk. I can't actually play cards. This is simply my attempt at showing solidarity. Maths was never my strong point and once you've had several double vodka and cokes, the queen starts to look remarkably like the king, and mistakes happen. But I pretend to play, losing, naturally, but trying to join in with the spirit of things. The last thing I want to do is get all serious on them and withdraw into some ivory tower like Sylvie does before a big match. Okay, that's probably why she wins, but it just doesn't feel like my style.

Sometimes, you get to a point in your life where you can't pretend any more to be something you're not. It might work in the club, with the men who don't know what I get up to on the circuit, and only know I'm a world-ranked player, but it won't work here. These people know who I am. And I know who they are. It's a sad but strangely comforting feeling, being among failures and knowing you belong.

★ ★ ★

Bo groans. 'I'm out.'

'Good. Give me another card.'

'Shit. Is this twenty-one or twenty-two?' I peer down at my cards, blinking.

'Can't you count?'

'If you can't add up, how the hell d'you play snooker?'

'Easy. I use my fingers.'

Roars of laughter. 'I can believe that!'

'Whose round is it?'

'Yours.'

I stagger to the bar, still laughing. 'Same again, please.'

'Nice young ladies, aren't you?' the barman says drily, looking over my shoulder at the other girls, fighting over whose turn it is to deal and doing a fairly good impression of that curious brand of male football fan who throws a burning roll of toilet-paper over the pitch *before* kick-off. 'You're making more noise than the locals.'

'Good. How much for the drinks?'

He's in his forties, wearing one of those awful v-neck jerseys that show off the sweat stains under his arms, and tartan golfing trousers that are too tight for his over-developed rump. I watch with bated breath as he bends over for a bottle of Newcastle Brown, half-expecting them to split open and reveal grubby boxer shorts emblazoned with the Superman logo.

Why is it, when women enjoy themselves, it's always

men like this who feel the need to criticise? They spend their entire lives acting like hormonally-challenged minors with a serious Biactol habit and the IQ rating of a Bargain Basement face flannel, but are the first to point an accusing finger at the opposite sex if the little darlings look like they're having a better time than is allowed under Section Fifteen of the Boring Bastards Act of 1970, when the sixties officially closed and 'decent' women were told to remove all floral hair adornments, come off the pill, and return to the kitchen.

Bollocks to that. I pay for the drinks and grab a bottle of Budweiser by its scrawny neck, wishing it was the barman. 'Why don't you come over and join us?' I ask sweetly. 'We're about to play strip poker and we need a good laugh.'

'Piss off,' he snarls.

'My pleasure.'

I'm drunk, and I know it. But it's a free country, or so the government would have us believe. I'm not going to be made to feel embarrassed about my behaviour by some middle-aged penis-to-forehead transplant victim with a fetish for golfing outfits.

My head hurts. Actually, 'hurts' is not the right word for the sensation I'm currently experiencing. 'Hurts' could win the Understatement of the Year Award as far as this hangover is concerned. When did I last drink that much? Long before the kids came along and put a stop to those late-night binge sessions with the girls, that's for certain. Long, long before I became a white-wine-spritzer-and-heavy-on-the-spritz-sort-of-gal. I'd forgotten the peculiar chemical imbalance that results from an ill-advised over-consumption of lager, especially when combined with a late-night-early-morning – *sod it* – actually-almost-dawn session with the girls.

But what the hell. You only play third-round matches in the World Championships once. Or you do if you play as badly as I'm likely to this morning, what with a twenty-one gun salute going off in my head at regular intervals. It's not a pleasant sensation. I'll be lucky if I can see the table, let alone the balls, through these squinting, puffed-up miniature pink blancmanges that are passing for my eyes this morning.

'You look awful.'

Thanks, Tricksy. State the obvious, why don't you?

'I told you not to have that last drink,' she continues, helping me over the club threshold with the solicitous air of a boy scout helping an ailing granny across the road. 'It's a classic case of one too many.'

'Shut up.'

Apparently undeterred by my tight-lipped reply, Tricksy peers into my narrowed blood-shot eyes and pats my hand, which today seems to have developed a sudden case of Parkinson's disease. 'I've got my lucky shirt back at the B&B. You look like you need some extra help this morning.' She smiles, clearly not noticing my gritted teeth. 'You're about my size. I could nip back and get it.'

'No thanks.' I'd rather play snooker in a gorilla suit

last worn by a large sweaty man with a contagious rash. I smile back at her though, feeling a terrible pain shoot through my head as the corners of my mouth twitch into an uncomfortable imitation of cheerfulness. 'I'll be fine.'

'Well . . . I suppose that *is* quite a flashy new outfit. Buy it somewhere special?'

What do you think, Einstein? I lean my cue up against the bar and look round the club. My stomach is performing an Auld Lang Syne jig with my bowels, and they're both scoring *nulle points* in the audience-appreciation bracket. 'What, this old thing?' I manage to say modestly, running a hand over the fine green silk of my blouse to indicate its subtle yet infinitely expensive and exclusive texture. 'I can't quite recall.'

'Drink?'

'Of course I did,' I snap.

'No . . . do you want a drink?' Tricksy opens her purse as gingerly as though it were a post-Christmas credit-card statement. 'Coke, tea, or coffee?'

That bad, is it? I've still got some of Kevin's loan in my pocket. 'Why don't you let me buy the round? I'll get you a lager, if you like. You're not playing this morning.'

'Well, thank you very much indeed for reminding me of that! I might have forgotten if you hadn't pointed it out to me.'

I wince. 'Sorry. That was thoughtless.' You never remind a player who's out of the tournament of their ability-to-drink status. It's too humiliating. 'Coffee?'

'Nah. I'll have half a pint of lager. It's half-ten, after all . . . almost lunch-time.'

'Very nearly afternoon.'

'It is, isn't it?' Tricksy bites her lip. 'Should I have a pint, then?'

'Go for it.'

'Okay.' She leans decisively towards the barman. The grumpy old bastard from last night appears to have disappeared. The barman this morning is much younger, sporting a Keanu Reeves hairstyle and a wit so sharp he could probably open bottles with it. He's wearing one of those multi-coloured waistcoats like the ones Tom Cruise eased himself into in *Cocktail*. Tricksy eyes him appreciatively. 'One coffee and a pint of lager, please.'

'Coming up,' he murmurs. 'Like you. Up and coming.'

Tricksy giggles. 'You like meeting women snooker players?'

'Oh yes, but especially the new talent.'

I think I'm going to puke. *Where* is my only question. I can't reach his flies from here, so that's one down. I look at him nauseously. What a creep.

Someone taps me on the shoulder. 'Hi.'

I turn. It's Sylvie. 'Hi,' I say uncertainly.

'Nice blouse.'

'Thanks.'

'So . . . through to the third round!'

'Yeah, amazing huh?'

'No, not at all.' Her husky accent and irritatingly

shiny red hair have caught the attention of the leering Tom Cruise look-alike behind the bar, but she seems oblivious to his gaze. 'You deserve it.'

Groan. I hate compliments. I never know how to take them. Do I look arrogant by saying 'Thank you' or do I pretend to blush and say modestly, 'No, really, it was a complete fluke'? I can't get used to this slick pat-on-the-back atmosphere of the better players; it's like being in the masons. 'Who are you playing today?'

'Oh . . .' She shrugs. 'No one.'

'What, you're out?'

I must have sounded shocked. Sylvie laughs delicately, raising her eyebrows in that gesture of haughty disbelief which I'm almost getting used to. 'No, of course not. I meant . . . no one difficult.'

Nothing like a touch of cheerful arrogance, is there?

She continues. 'I shouldn't have any trouble until I get to the semis. Then, it's just a question of finding the . . .' She pauses, clearly searching for the right expression, a little frown on her forehead.

'Loo?' Tricksy suggests rather too brightly.

I shoot her a look, then turn back to Sylvie. 'Chink in the armour?'

'Exactly.' Sylvie nods. 'The chink . . . it's very important.'

'Couldn't have put it better myself,' the barman says slickly, handing over my coffee with a smirk. 'I'm never happy until I find the chink.'

Charming. Sylvie ignores him. She touches my shoulder very lightly. 'Well, good luck.'

I smile awkwardly. 'You too.'

She walks away. Tricksy watches her with the expression of a barracuda, deprived of its breakfast. 'She makes me sick. *"No one difficult . . ."*' She parodies Sylvie's voice and dismissive gesture. 'Silly cow.'

I'm not sure I agree. It sounds harsh, that attitude towards other players, but at least Sylvie knows who she is and where she's going. She knows her own worth. She's also having terrible husband trouble, which, in my eyes, makes up for a lot. I should know, I've been there myself with Adrian. Okay, we were never married, and Adrian didn't exactly follow me round with the pleading eyes of a half-starved spaniel, but the break-up of a relationship is always traumatic, whatever the circumstances. Sylvie has got her shit together though. She's not going to let her marriage-from-hell interfere with her plans for the future. I'm beginning to think that's what life's all about. Finding out what you're best at, and not letting anyone else stop you making the most of it. That's certainly what snooker's about. Attitude, attitude and more attitude. Though being reasonably handy with a cue helps.

I grit my teeth. If Sylvie can do it, so can I. What difference is there between us but attitude? Okay, maybe she has a teensy weensy bit more natural talent than I have. But sod it, I'm going to go flat out today. Hangover or no hangover. I'm going to pretend my head's not thumping, and I'm going to pot well, concentrate, and play each frame as if it were the last.

★ ★ ★

There's nothing like a shitty hour or two on the table to make you feel like hanging yourself from the nearest cue rack. Man problems have nothing on snooker for sheer quality of depression and angst. Finding yourself several frames down at the interval in a World Championship match is far, far worse than finding your man in bed with another woman. Okay, finding him in bed with another *man* may just have the edge there, but common or garden penile wanderings are almost non-events compared with the gut-wrenching agony of facing defeat on a snooker table.

It's not that I'm a bad loser, although I'm suspicious I may be soon. It's just the sheer waste of it all. You work; you slave; you sweat blood and tears and any other bodily secretions that seem likely to be involved in a game of snooker; you lose all your old friends; you gain really strange new ones; your man decamps with the only working hi-fi system in the house; you struggle day after day to bring up your kids in a reasonably normal fashion, telling them bedtime stories about Stephen Hendry's World Championship matches or that fantastic last black which won you a place in the second round; you dig yourself deeper and deeper into financial shit until you could fertilise a whole garden of roses with it, and what happens? You manoeuvre yourself cunningly into a losing situation, and then you rot there, wondering what the hell went wrong.

I stomp off to the bar during the interval. I'm tempted to order a couple of large whisky-and-cokes, then play the rest of the match cross-eyed but cheerful.

But the grumpy old git barman is back, dragging his unfeasibly large backside through the bar hatch as I approach. He sees my scowl and smiles. 'Losing?'

'Not exactly.'

'Coffee, then?'

I open my mouth to say 'whisky', shut it again, think of Kevin, then nod my head reluctantly. 'Black, no sugar.'

'Bad head?'

Is he laughing? My eyes narrow on his ugly striped shirt, then rise to his bloated, unshaven face, leering at me with its non-designer stubble and its quivering bulbous nose, pitted with blackheads like a malignant strawberry. 'I'm fine, thank you very much. I like black coffee. It puts hairs on my chest.'

'Now, why would a nice young lady want hairs on her chest?' He dumps the coffee on the bar, looking me over with an unpleasant smile. 'Not a dyke, are you?'

'I could be tempted to become one,' I say sharply. 'If I spent much more time in your company.'

'Ha bloody ha.'

I take a tentative sip of the black coffee. Unlike its unwashed maker, it smells great. What is it about strong black coffee that zips you up a notch or five and kicks all the shit out of your system? Black coffee is a drink with attitude. I'm usually a tea-with-everything sort of person, but this situation calls for something with more body than Arnold Schwarzenegger. Unsweetened black coffee hits the spot perfectly.

He's still watching me, lounging on the bar like

an overgrown slug. 'Lots of them are, you know. Dykes.'

I almost choke on my coffee.

He reaches over and pats me on the back. 'Too hot?'

'How the hell do you work that out?'

'Stands to reason, doesn't it?' he sneers, looking along the room. 'Women . . . playing snooker? Got to be something wrong with them.' He stares down with undisguised lust at the semi-transparent material of my green blouse, unbuttoned to just above my cleavage, of which I have always been justly proud but which I now wish I had left covered up this morning. 'Not you, of course. Nothing wrong with you . . . I can see that from where I'm standing.'

Ugh. 'How fascinating. You must be a psychologist.'

'Snooker's a man's game. I don't mind you girls having a go from time to time. In fact,' he leers again, apparently missing my expression of disgust, 'it's a turn-on, seeing a girl bent over the table of a Saturday night. But all this World Championships stuff . . . it's nothing but a joke. Girls can't play snooker.'

'Well, thanks for the insight.'

'You know what the cues are for, don't you?' he calls after me, still eager to impress. 'It's penis-envy!'

Wonderful. Of all the snooker clubs in all the country, I had to walk into his.

'Problem?' The referee asks me quietly as I sidle back up to the table. He is looking curiously back down towards the bar. I hope he didn't catch too much of that conversation. I can already sense many eyes on me from all over the room.

'Nothing I can't handle.' I flash him a smile. Not all men feel the same as that Neanderthal behind the bar. Some of them, like this guy, give up their spare time to referee these women's matches. I know we don't have enough cashola in the bank to pay them a fat fee like the men do, but they turn up every time just the same, happy to do their bit for ladies' snooker. 'Just some prat at the bar who probably doesn't know one end of a cue from the other.'

He nods. 'Okay. It's your break.'

My break? Have I really been gone ten minutes? I had been planning an impromptu trip to the toilets, but it looks like Greasy Slugman at the bar has cost me that luxury by keeping me talking. Ah, well. No pee for the almost defeated.

My opponent, Susan, a petite well-spoken blonde from Guildford, has been sitting there waiting for me all through the interval. Despite having the youthful appearance of a toddler, she must have the iron bladder control of a Buckingham Palace sentry. I've seen her sip her way delicately through an entire jug of iced water over the past hour or so, yet she's making no move to the ladies. Maybe she's wearing incontinence pants, or at the very least, a nappy. Maybe she's got one of those special plastic bags, with tube attached. Maybe she's not really drinking the water, maybe she has a tiny pot-plant hidden just behind her left molar which she's been secretly watering throughout the match. Maybe she'll actually produce it at the end of the match, and present it, flowering freely, to the loser. A.k.a. me. Or maybe I'm just gradually cracking up, getting more and more mentally unbalanced as the match slips further away.

Get a grip. What is it, a three-frame difference? An hour and a half, tops. It's nothing. It's an omnibus edition of *Coronation Street*. It's a cheap flight to Paris from Manchester Airport. It's a Raquel Welch fitness video. I can do this.

It's amazing what a fluke can do for your confidence. It's like tripping over in the street on your way to a party, ripping your new Control-Top tights from ankle to thigh, but finding a fifty-pound note in the gutter as you're struggling to your feet. Tights, *shmights*. A fifty-pound note makes up for a whole drawer full of ruined black nylons, twenty per cent Lycra or not.

Susan is smirking at her recently arrived boyfriend during the next frame, when the white she has just struck clips a red it was clearly not intended to make contact with, bounces gently off a colour and drops straight into a pocket. Her smile disappears abruptly. The boyfriend shakes his head disapprovingly, which reduces her to a quivering blonde mass of aspic, and she sinks back into her chair with a defeated expression.

She's left me a rather inviting pink over the top left-hand pocket, the reds wide open, and the knowledge that her mental state has just shrunk to that of a three-year-old whose favourite toy has been taken away. I pot a red, sink the pink, sizzle another red into the middle, slash down confidently for the black, and then I'm away, rattling her playpen with a vengeance.

The old magic is back. I can feel it tingling in my cue arm like a bad attack of shingles. I'm getting cocky, but not so much that it's dangerous. I play a couple of flashy shots, even one of those left-handed roll-in pots along the side cushion. *Howzat?* I soon take it down to a two-frame deficit, then only one frame, and suddenly we're even Stephens, as they love to say in the commentary box. Now there's nothing between us but air.

Susan goes to the table. She shakes her head at an easy red. Then she fumbles a stun shot even my youngest could play. This is crunch-time. Her eyes have clouded over. She looks suspiciously like she's going to cry; indignity of indignities in women's snooker. Her bladder control has gone completely; she scuttles off to the loo at least three times in one half-hour stretch, getting a warning from the referee and a few supercilious glances from her boyfriend, who, judging from his tight-lipped look, is struggling to keep within the no-coaching rule. I know this 'boyfriend watching the game' scenario back to front, side to side, and any other position within the bounds of your imagination. He's obviously dying to give her some good old-fashioned tips of the 'I'm a man, you're a woman, and you're playing this game all wrong' variety, and hopefully show her how to turn the match back around. But, according to the rules of ladies' snooker, he's not allowed to give her any help.

In the last frame, I get down to play a crucial ball. If

I pot this pink, if I can execute this right-hand-down-hard, reverse screw with plenty of poke, pulling the white up sharp as a whip off this frighteningly long pink, and landing, *plop*, two inches away from the seductive curves of the black, I can win this match.

Most people think women don't have the killer instinct, but they do on the snooker table. It's no joke. Watch any good woman player about to sink a vital pot, and although she may shuffle her feet beforehand, cough, sniff, roll her eyes, tuck her shirt in, pull it out again, wiggle her bum, adjust her cue arm, pull up a bra strap or do any of those other irritating things people do when they're nervous on the shot, when she actually gets down to hit the ball, I can guarantee that her eyes will narrow, her breath will stop, and she will bare her teeth like a lioness. Men beware. There's no messing with us on the shot.

I stand there for a moment, chalking my cue. This is it. *This is the pot.* Get this, and you're home sweet home. That black will drop like a penny if you play this pink right.

Calmly, or at least attempting to appear calm, I examine the possibilities surrounding this shot: a) I can miss the pot entirely and leave Susan in; b) I can pot the pink and leave myself an impossible black; c) I can play the shot perfectly, pot the black, and qualify for the final stages of the World Championships.

Immediately, I'm sweating. That was the wrong thing to remind myself of at this particular moment. I'm not just playing any old shot. I'm not just winning a frame, or winning a match, or even getting some solid-ranking points under my belt: I'm playing this shot to see which of us qualifies for the quarter-finals of the World Championships. My mouth opens and shuts like a guppy's. My heart-beat is coming and going, like waves crashing erratically on a shore. Is it possible to have a heart attack in your late twenties? I'm sure I read somewhere that it's possible. Heart murmurs can go unnoticed for years. This is it. I'm having palpitations. I've got angina. *Is there a doctor in the house?* Is all this worth dying for?

I look up. There's a black film in front of my eyes. I wipe the sweat from my forehead and, as my hand comes away from my face, my vision clears. Across the dark snooker hall, Sylvie has just finished shaking hands with her opponent, who turns and scuttles off down the hall in tears, bowed over her case like a grieving widow over her husband's coffin. Sylvie is now calmly putting away her cue. I watch her in silence for what feels like centuries but is, naturally enough, only about ten seconds. Sylvie is never scared of that important last shot. Sylvie treats it like any other. That's why she wins. All my doubts and fears disappear like germs faced with Dettox. I get down and pot the balls without thinking about it.

For the next ten minutes, I stand around, grinning like an idiot, shaking hands with my tearful opponent, the referee, Tricksy, Katie, Clare, and every other unsuspecting victim who walks past my table. I put my cue away, still grinning. I'm probably doing an embarrassing imitation of the Cheshire Cat, but I'm unable to stop myself. I feel as though my mouth has become fixed in this absurd quarter-melon shape.

'Well done, you cow,' Tricksy mutters, but manages a lopsided smile. 'I suppose you won't speak to me now. You'll be far above us lowly players.'

'Don't be ridiculous.'

'You're saying that now, Zoë . . . but you just wait. One day you'll cut us dead, like that lot do.' Tricksy jerks her head dismissively in the direction of Sylvie and her clique of immaculately dressed top players, all chatting animatedly in the bar.

Through the glass partition, I can see Sylvie's head turn in my direction, and then her silvery tinkling laugh as someone whispers in her ear.

I freeze. Are they laughing at me? I can almost feel the blood beating in my temples; it's like having the percussion track of Barry Manilow's 'Copacabana' running continuously in my head. Then Sylvie looks away. She probably wasn't even looking at me. For fuck's sake, I'm getting so paranoid. This snooker world is getting smaller and smaller by the day. It's closing in on me like a set of sinister false teeth.

The referee signs the winner's slip and hands it over to me. 'Well done, Zoë,' he says, smiling as I look down at it with a numb sense of disbelief. 'Quarter-finals next, in Switzerland. Hope you've got a passport.'

I grin. 'At the moment, I wouldn't care if I had to be smuggled over the border in a giant cuckoo-clock.'

Then it hits me – *pow!* – like a fridge door in a Tom

and Jerry cartoon. My grin fades. My teeth shatter and drop out one by one, then I fall flat on my back and bluebirds twitter around my head. The finals of the World Championships are being held in Geneva. The finals are next month. It's a glitzy, glamorous, ten-day, all expenses paid trip to Switzerland, with the prospect of a world title somewhere at the end of it, but in my excitement at qualifying, I've forgotten one itsy, bitsy, oooh, barely significant detail . . . who the hell's going to look after my kids?

6

'No way!'

'Ten days, that's all,' I plead with Adrian. We're outside the discount store where he works, and from the way he keeps glancing at his watch, he's got a lunch appointment that's more important than continuing this conversation. 'It's the chance of a lifetime for me, otherwise I wouldn't ask.'

'Listen to yourself, Zoë. This snooker crap is all out of perspective. It isn't a job. It's a game.' He taps his filofax. 'Some of us have a living to make.'

'At lunch-time?'

He adjusts his new tie self-consciously. 'I'm meeting a colleague.'

'What's her name?' When he shoots me a filthy look, I realise I'm approaching this all wrong. 'Adrian, please. Take the kids. I know it's a massive favour, but I'll think of a way to pay you back.'

'How do you expect me to work *and* look after kids? I've only just been promoted here. I can't take any time off.'

Desperate, I launch my secret weapon. 'But you're their father.'

'Yes, and if I can't work six days a week, I can't afford to pay maintenance for them. So why don't you open your eyes and face reality? This dream of going to the World Championships is pointless. Totally bloody pointless. You're a mother, Zoë, and your place is at home.' Adrian walks off angrily, the ankles of his suit flapping in the wind like a flag at half-mast. Within seconds, a young blonde in a raincoat comes dashing out of the store, calling his name, and Adrian waits for her at the corner of the street. He doesn't look at me again. They walk off together towards the High Street, arm in arm.

So that's the new Ms Right. I was wondering what she looked like. Heading back towards my car, I pull my coat closer against the wind. I suppose it is unreasonable to expect Adrian to take ten days off when he's still settling in to a new position at the store. And it *would* be difficult for him to juggle his new responsibilities with getting the kids to school every day, and arranging for someone to pick them up afterwards until he got out of work. Besides, he was never any good at cooking, even with a microwave. What would they eat? Fish and chips every night? No, Adrian is out of the question.

What am I saying? Am I deranged? Am I finally two reds short of a snooker ball set? The father of my children has just refused to look after them while I'm playing the World Championships, no less, and I've nodded my head and agreed with him. I need help.

Urgently. My brain is a leaking colander. I have no nails left and my knee-joints are aching from constant practice. I have a first-class air ticket to Geneva for the World Championships, two kids, and no method of escape.

There's no point even asking my mother to look after them. Last time I asked, she slammed the phone down so hard I thought I might lose the hearing in my right ear. Besides, she and Dad appear to be on the verge of splitting up. She's losing patience with his behaviour over Sharon. I can't say I blame her. I suppose it's important that my mum and dad sort this out, but it still leaves me without anyone to look after the kids.

Now I know how it feels to be Cinderella, in her pre-pumpkin stage. I've got an invitation to the ball, but about as much chance of going to Geneva next month as Adrian has of winning an award for charm.

Actually, Adrian can be quite pleasant at times. As far as I'm aware, he still gives up his seat on the bus to little old ladies or women with buggies. Let me explain. At school, Jemmy has a friend called Emily. Emily has a mother called Sandra. And Sandra, hearing of my troubles on the junior school grapevine, drops round on Tuesday to say that she can take the kids while I go to Geneva.

Sandra looks okay, the sort of woman who regularly cooks fish fingers and baked beans, takes her kids to the park, tucks them up, reads them interesting bedtime stories and always, *always*, walks them to school every morning and back every afternoon. In other words, she's not like me.

'Are you sure it's okay?'

Sandra nods. 'Hey, don't worry about it. Us mothers have got to stick together.' She smiles down at the kids. 'We're vegetarians, though. Can little Jemima and Tom cope with that?'

No fish fingers. Okay. Strike that and substitute green-lentil rissoles. 'They'll eat anything.'

Sandra has bleach-blonde hair down to her shoulders. She has Levi button-fly jeans. She belongs to the Neighbourhood Watch scheme. She bakes carrot cake for school fund-raising events. She has a social conscience. So, I reckon I can trust her with my kids. The only drawback, in fact, is that she watches *EastEnders* rather than *Coronation Street*. This disturbs my psychic balance, but hopefully the kids will be in bed by the time this perverted activity takes place, so I think I can square it with my conscience if I'm only leaving the kids with her for ten days. What's that? Five episodes, tops. Under the circumstances, it's a risk I'm prepared to take.

I look at the kids. 'You'll be staying with Mrs Bottomley next month. Just for ten days.' Jemima lolls in her seat, unconcernedly. Tom mashes his ham sandwich into the table with cheerful fingers, not looking up at me. No alarm there so far. 'Is that okay?'

'Do you have Nintendo?' Jemima asks Sandra directly.

'Uhuh,' Sandra nods. She lifts her head and winks at me with one of those nauseating 'aren't kids cute?' expressions. 'I'm sure Emily's big brother will let you play on it. He even has some of the latest games.'

'Kung-fu?'

'I think so.'

Jemmy shrugs. 'Cool.'

Don't you just hate it when another mother impresses your kid more than you do? I smile wanly at Sandra. 'You've made a new friend there.'

When Sandra bends her head to give Jemmy a dazzling smile, I suddenly realise that the woman's teeth are perfect. They look like shining pieces of chewing gum in a row. She must practically live in the dentist's chair. Then she flicks her hair back, lifting Tom and giving him a swift cuddle. 'We're all going to be great friends, aren't we?'

At bedtime, Jemmy redeems herself in my eyes. 'Are we really going to stay with that woman?' she says as I bend over the bed, tucking her in with the guilt and fervour only a mother can feel who's abandoning her children in order to play a game of snooker.

'Don't you want to?' I ask anxiously. I pinch her arm playfully, pretending to admire the muscles. 'A brave little girl like you, not wanting to stay away from home for a few nights!'

Jemmy shrugs. 'I don't *really* mind,' she says slowly, then yawns. Her incredibly long lashes flutter against her cheek for a moment, then the huge eyes open again sleepily and fix on my face. 'But she's not going to do much more of that kissing and cuddling, is she?'

That's my girl!

I'm in the snooker club the following week, when Kevin comes out of the bar and gives me a wink. He's been talking to a grey-suited man in there for half an hour. I've been practising long blues as ordered and my cue arm is aching, so I don't feel particularly like smiling back at him. 'Cheer up, Zoë. I'd like you to meet Mr Parker. He owns the Parker's Pump & Shoe Company, down at Longfield.'

We shake hands.

Kevin nods. 'Mr Parker's interested in your career. He's been sponsoring one of your local players here, a lad called Raz, but now he wants something with more . . . international appeal.'

'To raise the profile of the company,' the man says helpfully, taking a cigar out of his pocket and lighting it. The smoke from his cigar floats thickly under the snooker lights. He has a pair of black leather shoes so shiny I can almost see the club reflected in them. He has one of those high domed foreheads where his greying hair has evidently decided to retire from active service, and thick-rimmed glasses which catch the light whenever he turns his head. 'Raz is a good player. But he's a bit of a troublemaker, if you know what I mean.'

I couldn't have put it better myself. Raz has never been my favourite person, and news of his latest fracas has obviously reached Mr Parker's ears: some young lad foolishly accused Raz of fiddling the scoreboard. Raz, never one to hang about, immediately headbutted him. Such a smooth operator. I'm warming to Mr Parker.

Kevin starts pulling reds out of the top pocket and rolling them on to the baize. He's grinning, which is an unusual thing for Kevin to do, so I'm both amused and mystified. 'Show us some magic, Zoë.'

I'm feeling all out of rabbits today, but this could mean the difference between playing full-time snooker and just scraping by with the odd hour here or there. I roll my shoulder painfully in its socket. It's still aching after those long straight blues. As Kevin bends to get the colours out of the pockets, I pretend to help him, keeping my voice low. 'You could have chosen a better day. I'm knackered.'

'Just do your best.'

'And what exactly will this deal involve?' I glance at Mr Parker. 'He's not the sort of sponsor who's likely to take a personal interest in me, is he? A *highly* personal interest?'

'You don't have to sleep with him, for God's sake. But you may have to play the World Championships wearing a shirt with Parker's Pump & Shoe Company written across it.'

I shrug. 'I can live with that.'

'Okay. Now pot some balls. And make it look good.'

'Don't I always?'

'Do you expect me to answer that?'

Mr Parker coughs politely. I expect he does a lot of that, smoking those expensive cigars. 'Everything all right? I can always come back another day.'

'No, Mr Parker,' Kevin says, walking towards him, and there's a steely note in his voice as he looks back at me. 'Zoë's very keen to show you what she can do. Aren't you, Zoë?'

'As mustard,' I snap back. But, to be honest, I'm more than a little bit nervous about this. My hand's aching from those long blues Kevin told me to work on. The long straight blue is a shot of notorious difficulty. It's easy as piss if you're cueing straight, but all you have to do is take your eye off the ball for a second, or lose concentration, or start getting down to the shot too quickly, and your cue arm goes out of kilter, you put side on the ball without meaning to, and you miss the pot. One inch, half an inch. It makes no difference in snooker. You don't get any points for 'near' misses. A missed pot is a missed pot, however well you played it. So practising those long straight shots for anything over ten minutes is highly stressful. And now I'm supposed to show Mr Parker some 'magic'.

'Why not show Mr Parker the line-up?'

I can think of a dozen reasons why not, but I suspect Kevin won't be amused by a refusal. The line-up is a standard practice routine for professionals. Most good amateurs use it as well, because it teaches a player not only potting, but ball control. Ball control is the single most important technical ability once you're at the table. You can be a brilliant potter, but even natural ability runs out of steam eventually. Under pressure, potting becomes ten times harder. In a match, it's much better to place the white as near to your next intended ball as possible, because as sure as eggs are eggs, if you leave it to chance, chance will turn round and give you a smart kick up the arse.

Kevin first showed me the line-up when we used to play together in the old days, when Adrian was still around and I didn't really know one end of a cue from the other. It brought my game on so rapidly that I fell in love with the routine, and wouldn't dream of spending an hour on the table without running through it at least once.

The line-up is simple. You line all the reds up in a straight line lengthways down the table, from the black spot to just beyond the blue, keeping the colours spotted as usual. Two reds go below the black. Five reds in between black and pink. Six reds in between pink and blue. Two reds after the blue. Some beginners put four reds after the blue, and none before the black. Those first two reds before the black are the hardest, because too steep or too shallow an angle sends the white careering into the other balls, and that's forbidden. The white must not touch any ball other than the ball you're about to smack into the back of the pocket. If you miss a pot, or hit another ball by mistake, you stop, replace *all* the balls (yes, even the ones you've potted correctly) and start again from the beginning. It's a tough exercise, but played well, it's as close to heaven as anyone can get in a practice session.

The line-up separates the players from the non-players. Each pot is a pressure-shot, the ball control required is immense, and the rules are demanding.

Luckily, Mr Parker doesn't know the rules.

'Ooops.' I skid into a red after stunning down off the pink. Kevin coughs and looks away. I act casual and pot the now loose red, dropping gently down on to a half-ball black. That's better. I like it when the table looks neat. It gives me a warm glowing sensation inside which I have sometimes mistaken for indigestion.

'Good shot,' Mr Parker murmurs with every sign of appreciation. 'Not bad, this girlfriend of yours.'

For the first time, Kevin looks embarrassed. His face is slightly pink. He shuffles his feet. 'She's not my girlfriend.'

Mr Parker glances sharply at Kevin, then at me, and smiles. He looks down at the glowing end of his cigar. 'Is he a good coach, Zoë?'

I manage to stifle my own smile, chalking my cue assiduously. I get down on the shot, concentrating hard on a long narrow-angle blue up into the yellow pocket. It *thwacks* the back of the pocket at a satisfying speed. The white twirls elegantly on the spot for a second, reacts to the backspin I've applied, sliding sideways half an inch under the force of its own momentum, then halts abruptly like a conscientious driver at a red light. 'He's great. But I'd play a lot better if I could afford more practice time.'

'Really?' He raises his eyebrows, clearly impressed by my party-piece shot. 'Well, we'd better arrange that immediately then. Send a run-down of average monthly figures to my office, and when I've made a decision, I'll let you know how much sponsorship you'll be looking at. But there are a few ground rules before we go any further. I expect good press coverage for my money. Every time you win something or get interviewed, I want my company's name mentioned.'

Don't worry. When it happens, you'll be the first to know.

'And if there's any bad press, I withdraw my support. As I did with Raz.' He waves a hand at me, smiling. 'But I'm sure there won't be. I doubt that you'll be starting any brawls during your matches. Lady snooker players. Can't get a much cleaner image than that, can you?'

Mr Parker clearly doesn't know much about the ladies' game.

Three days later, the phone rings. It's Sylvie, asking me round to her place the night before we fly out to Geneva. I'm torn between acting cool about this sudden attention from one of the top players (hey, I get these invitations all the time) and gratefully gushing down the phone at her. I decide not to gush. I've found in the past that this merely indicates desperation on the part of the gusher, and turns most people off faster than you can say 'brown' and 'nose'.

Luckily, I soon realise that *not* gushing was a wise move. As I suspected, this will not be the start of a lifelong friendship. Sylvie has an ulterior motive for inviting me to a sleep-over. Almost as soon as I arrive at her flat, she forces me on to a kitchen stool and puts a steaming mug of coffee in front of me. 'Have you told anyone I'm married?' When I shake my head, she looks astonished. 'Really?'

'It's none of my business. Besides, I don't want to interfere.'

This, of course, is a lie. Some situations call for honesty and some for tact. This is one which requires not only tact, but a little white lie as well. I don't see the harm in it. Did she really expect me *not* to pass on salacious gossip about a major player?

Sylvie looks different off the circuit. I'm used to seeing her in severe white blouses, or those expensive silk creations that some exotic clothes company sponsors her to wear. In pale green jeans and a loose T-shirt, Sylvie looks almost human. She sits on the high kitchen stool opposite me, swinging her feet in soft brown Hush-Puppies, sipping her coffee contemplatively. 'You haven't even told your friend . . . what's her name?'

'Tricksy.' I shake my head with the utter conviction and steady gaze of someone who knows they're lying their arse off. 'Absolutely not.'

'I would have told her. You must be very . . . honest.'

'Oh, I am.'

'Okay,' Sylvie says in a stilted voice, still looking away. She puts her coffee cup down on the table and stares into it moodily, leaning on one hand. The fine red hair falls over her forehead, and she shakes her head slightly with an irritated gesture, looking sideways at me. 'I do want to tell you. I have to tell someone. I just . . .' She breaks off, looking swiftly away.

I put my cup of coffee down next to hers, very gently, so as not to disturb her train of thought. Then I lean back and grip the edge of my kitchen stool in anticipation. I hope she's going to tell me all the gory details. But these torturous affairs of the heart can be so difficult to follow, especially when relayed in a Finnish accent. And I'm slightly suspicious of her motives. Why tell *me*? Sylvie's got friends on the circuit. She always hangs round with the same bunch of girls, most of them top-ranking players. The only feasible reason I can think of for her confiding in me is that I'm so far from the top that she reckons there's no chance of the story spreading. If she discussed personal problems with any of her cronies, the news would probably be all round the circuit by the next tournament.

Then something happens which scares the shit out of me. Sylvie bursts into tears. I've never been terribly adept at these situations, but I manage a fumbled pat on her back and a few murmured words of sympathy. This seems to do the trick. Sylvie soon brightens, reaching into her back pocket for a tissue and dabbing at her eyes. She must be wearing some fucking brilliant waterproof mascara. If I did this, I'd look like a suicidal panda within twenty seconds. I'm on the point of asking her which brand she uses, when she sits up straight and takes a deep breath, as if about to plunge into a swimming pool.

'Sorry,' she says, smiling weakly at me. 'I've never

spoken about this to anyone, except my mother, and she's . . .'

Fresh tears. I suspect that 'dead' was the word she couldn't produce. I manage another pat on the back, this time with a sort of combined rub/circular patting motion thrown in. It's funny. You know how you get these fixed impressions of people, and never waver from them, unless something like this happens to prove your instincts wrong? Well, I always had Sylvie pegged as a hard nut. Cold. Self-sufficient. Completely humourless. A cross between Spock ('What is "emotion", Captain?') and a Passport Control official. Certainly, Sylvie's the last person I expected to see burst into floods of tears.

'What's his name?' As she looks up at me through bleary bloodshot eyes, I give her what I hope is an encouraging smile. 'Your husband?'

'Matt.'

'Okay. So, why did you break up?'

Her back stiffens, and for one awful moment, I'm suspicious that we're back to square one, and Sylvie's going to start bawling again. But no. Her head comes up slowly. 'My . . . sister . . .' she says eventually, through gritted teeth.

Now we're getting somewhere. I nod, pushing my lukewarm coffee cup away before she dribbles into it. 'Your sister.' I fetch a fresh tissue from the Kleenex box near her state-of-the-art halogen cooker and microwave combi, fearing another tidal wave. 'I'm guessing this has something to do with your sister?'

'I found him and Kristin in bed together.'

It's one of those moments when you wish you had some incredibly witty or thoughtful or constructive comment to make, but come away from your mental reservoir empty-handed. 'Oh shit.'

Sylvie stares damply into space. 'I'd been out all evening. They probably thought I was going to stay out all night . . . I often do, when a practice session goes on too late for me to bother driving home. I go to a motel or something. But that night . . .' She pauses, shredding her tissue vehemently. 'I heard them before I saw them. He always makes this funny little noise . . . you know, like a horse.' Sylvie waves her hand in a suitably disgusted gesture. 'And I walked in and saw them together . . . with her on top . . . it was awful . . .'

I'm beginning to think I had a pretty good break-up with Adrian. At least nothing like that happened to us. 'Are you getting a divorce?'

'I don't know . . .' Sylvie sighs, sitting up straighter. She picks up her cup of coffee, takes an unwary sip and almost spits it out. 'Ugh. Cold. Want another?'

'Thanks. So you still love him?'

Sylvie smiles wearily, filling the round chrome kettle. Her shiny carnation-pink nails loom like huge distorted claws in its reflective surface. 'I wish I could hate him, Zoë. I really do. But Matt's such a charming bastard. So persuasive. So believable.' She laughs bitterly. 'He even claims he still loves me. That he doesn't know why he did it. If it wasn't so awful, it would be funny.'

Well, it sounded like a good excuse to me. It's not uncommon for me to do similar things without knowing why I did them. Still, believing him isn't *my* problem. 'And your sister?'

Sylvie laughs, then freezes up, staring down into the bright reflective kettle surface. The water starts hissing gently as the element inside heats up. Eventually, she shrugs. 'I just walked away. I haven't seen her since.'

Long silence. 'Kristin's younger than you?'

'By six years.'

'And all this took place in Finland?'

'I wanted to stay near my mother. She'd been ill for a long time. Matt didn't like it, of course. We met in London, you see. In Regent's Park. I got knocked over by some kid on a skateboard . . . Matt helped me up, bought me a coffee and a packet of Elastoplast.' She smiles. 'He was very sweet.'

Hard to imagine. But I nod sympathetically.

Sylvie measures the coffee into the cups with an air of precision. 'We agreed to meet again whenever I was in London, which was quite often. The season started, and before I knew what was happening, we were seeing each other every month. We got engaged. He came over to Finland and met my parents. We got married. End of story.'

'And your parents didn't mind him not being Finnish?'

She shakes her head. 'My father's Irish.'

'Really?' Embarrassingly, my voice comes out as a squeak.

'The red hair doesn't give it away, then?'

'I hadn't thought about it.'

She almost smiles. The kettle is bubbling noisily. She waits beside it, one hand poised. 'Anyway, we got a house over there. I commuted to play snooker. Matt got a job in a local art gallery – he specialises in organising exhibitions – but he was never happy, I think. Always itching to get back to London, where the real money was.' Her face hardens. 'And then Kristin came home from college.'

Students. They're the worst. Hormones racing about like Formula One Drivers, looking for the chequered flag. Still, having had an opportunity to view Matt at first hand in Brighton, I can see why Kristin was tempted. Come to that, given half a chance, I'd be fairly tempted too. Not that I'd get an offer from someone like Matt. With those looks, he must be used to women swarming all over him. 'And she didn't try to contact you after you left?'

Sylvie makes a harsh noise under her breath. The kettle comes rapidly to the boil. As it clicks off, she grabs the handle and pours the steaming hot water into the cups as though she were involved in a time and motion study. I notice that her Finnish accent is only really pronounced when she's angry. 'What could Kristin possibly say to me that would make it okay between the two of us? After what she did with my husband? I never want to speak to that woman again. I hope she rots in hell.'

7

I had no idea what municipal hygiene really meant until I came to Geneva. It's the cleanest city I've ever seen, although I believe Vancouver runs it a close second. Not that I have much to measure it against. I travelled around Europe occasionally as a teenager, lugged about on foreign holidays by my parents, but since I got involved in the *fin de siècle* baby boom, it's been the odd excursion to Southend that's kept the colour in my cheeks.

'Une chambre avec douche?' the blonde receptionist asks politely, keying my details into the computer as I nod mutely.

The hotel lobby is covered in white tiles floors. The walls are made up of speckled mirrors. Even the huge exotic pot plants are real.

'C'est chambre 547,' she continues, sliding the plastic key-card across the counter with the surreptitious air of a spy handing over secret documents. 'Bienvenue à Genève!'

Play snooker and see the world. It's an alien concept

to me. For women, playing snooker doesn't usually qualify as 'travelling'. You may get to visit different places every month, but the most you see is the inside of a snooker club or the inside of a hotel room or, if you're lucky enough to break down, the cheerful green banks of a motorway. Forget what they tell you about the glamour of snooker. Even the top male players spend more time on the table than at the side of the swimming pool. After all, no pain, no gain. There's no room in this game for pleasure-seekers. Not that the women have the option of pleasure-seeking, not on our prize money. If you win a tournament in the ladies' game, with the possible exception of the World Championships, you'll be lucky if you can afford a Strawberry Mivvi and the bus fare home.

So why carry on? Not simply because we're suckers, though there is that. We play because we love the bloody game, with all its stomach-heaving ups and downs, its petty squabbles in the toilets, those moments of utter triumph when the last black trickles into the pocket and you know you've whipped her like egg-white.

Sylvie barely spoke to me on the plane. But what did I expect? Automatic friendship for life? Get real. In snooker, friendship is a cut-throat business. You're judged as a player by who you sit with, who you talk to, where you hang out after matches, not just by how well you play. Sylvie's not about to make conversation with someone of my lowly ranking. I may have qualified for the quarter-finals of the World Championships, but my only reward will be a grudging nod across the bar from the 'top' players. They can't entirely afford to ignore me, but their finely tuned social antennae tell them that this is my one and only shot at stardom. And they're possibly right. By the end of these Championships, I may have revealed myself as just another also-ran.

I'm swimming in the hotel pool at 7 a.m. the next morning (black and white swimsuit, £19.99, courtesy of Dorothy Perkins; goggles, 200 Swiss francs, on loan from the Health Club receptionist) when a dark head surfaces near me. It's a man and he appears to be looking at me.

I stare back at him, bleary-eyed, through the goggles. (I haven't quite got the hang of them. I know it's meant to help if you spit on the plastic glass – ugh! – and then wash them in the water before putting them on, but it never seems to work for me. I just end up peering out through two saliva-stained igloo holes.)

Then his hand snakes out and pulls at my shoulder. I nearly capsize, not being terribly adept at treading water in the deep end, and struggle to escape. I open my mouth to yell, but all I get is a mouthful of sanitised pool water. It tastes like a cross between mouthwash and urine. Okay, I've never actually tasted urine, but this is how I imagine it would taste if mixed with mouthwash.

I push him away and fight my way to the side with one arm flailing around in the water like an octopus's tentacle and the other waving in the air to attract the attention of the lifeguards. I feel aggrieved as well as alarmed. This is too posh a hotel for clients to get attacked by perverts first thing in the morning. I didn't even know they had perverts in Switzerland.

'Calm down, for God's sake!'

I know that voice. I stop flailing, grab the side, and pull off my goggles. It's Sylvie's estranged husband, Matt. I stare, spitting out a mouthful of pool water which narrowly misses his face. How does this bloke do it? Every time I turn round, there he is. 'You nearly gave me a heart attack, you bastard.'

'Sorry,' he replies, mildly enough. He treads water beside me, bobbing up and down like a sleek-headed seal. His shoulders are muscular and bronzed. This man is obviously no stranger to winter sun. 'I didn't mean to startle you. You remember me, don't you?'

I nod, getting a better grip on the wall. 'I know who you are. I'm Zoë.'

He smiles. Immediately, I know why so many women fall for his charm. If I'm not careful I could be one of them. 'I just want to have a word with you, Zoë. About Sylvie.'

Sylvie. *Of course.* Well, I reckon I can stop fluttering my eyelashes in his direction now. For one crazy melt-in-the-mouth moment, I thought he was here to chat me up. But let's face it. What man in his right mind would look twice at me when he's married to a stunner like Sylvie? The absolute cow. 'Couldn't you have waited until I was *out* of the pool?'

'I thought you might walk away.'

'I might swim away. That could be just as effective.'

Matt gives me another of his charming smiles. I practically need Ray-Bans. But I remind myself that this man is a creep. He slept with Sylvie's sister as soon as her back was turned. He's a bastard. He has no scruples. Unfortunately, he also happens to have an uncanny resemblance to Michelangelo's David. 'I want her back, Zoë. I need to explain what happened. And I know you're her friend . . . I remember you from Brighton . . . you could persuade her to see me, to give me another chance.'

My wet hair is clinging to my head. I wring it out with one hand, watching him. Okay, I'm a total pushover, but what the hell. I don't often have the chance to be a total pushover, so I may as well make the most of it. 'I'm in Room 547. How about calling in after breakfast? I've got the first session of my quarter-final tonight, but I could spare you half an hour before practice.'

I want to add 'How are you at back rubs?' but leave it, figuring he's not that desperate. Anyway, it's been so long, if I did get lucky, I probably wouldn't be able to remember what goes where, or why. It's a sobering thought.

Why is it that the mere sniff of a man can tempt a celibate woman like myself to forget everything, *everything*, in pursuit of that elusive testosterone? Under the heading of Men, of course, there are many categories, and not all of them come into the 'tempting' bracket.

Matt is the sort who would be filed under F for Fucking Gorgeous, but cross-referenced under A for Already Partially Taken, with the footnote Possibly a Snake. Needless to say, I disregard the last two entries and concentrate on the F part. The Fs are always more interesting.

I should, in theory, be practising. They've set up a couple of tables downstairs in the 'Ballroom', and the rota has me down for a ten o'clock start. But as soon as he knocks on the door, my dedication vanishes, leaving me with an oestrogen haze where my ambition was. Not that I'm likely to get sex. But one can dream.

I make us both some coffee, and stand drinking it in the middle of the room, not wanting to sit down because my figure looks so much better in a totally vertical or horizontal position. Sitting down, I suspect I look like Baba Papa, the squidgy TV character.

Matt perches on the edge of the bed like a recalcitrant schoolboy, staring down into his cup with a morose expression. 'Has Sylvie told you anything about me?'

'Enough.'

He looks up then, wary. 'About Kristin?'

I've heard so much about Sylvie's sister that I almost feel I know her. As Matt clearly does, in the biblical sense at least. 'Especially about her.'

'Oh.' He sips his coffee. 'It was a terrible mistake. But Kristin's not like Sylvie. She's fun to be with. She's got a great sense of humour. She always laughs at my jokes.'

'And Sylvie didn't?'

Matt looks at me with a 'Who are you trying to

kid?' expression on his face. I notice he's got this cute thing he does with his hair, flicking it back whenever it drops on to his forehead. Okay, maybe it's a little too stage-managed to be 'cute'. But it's effective, nevertheless. 'You know what I mean. Sylvie's not like other girls. That's why I married her in the first place.'

'You still love her?'

'Of course,' Matt says quickly. Rather too quickly in my opinion.

'But you slept with Kristin.'

He puts his cup down on the floor jerkily, spilling a little coffee on to the carpet. 'Sorry.' He prods the stain with his shoe. 'I told you, Kristin was a mistake. Sylvie was never around, and I needed someone to be there for me. I know it sounds unbelievable, but I didn't do it for the sex.'

Jeez. What a sacrifice it must have been, taking his clothes off for another woman when all he wanted was a little understanding. 'Have you told her this?'

'Who, Sylvie? I've tried, but she won't listen to me.'

'So where do I come in?'

Matt comes over and takes my hand. He looks into my eyes. It's one of those moments when you can smell the bullshit coming, but the bull is so charismatic, you end up not caring about the shit. 'Tell her I'm here, Zoë. Break it to her gently. The last thing I want is for her to get upset and lose the Championships. But I'm going mad without her. I can't sleep, I can't eat. All I can think about is her.'

What an insult. You're holding *my* hand, and all you can think about is Sylvie? My earlier vision, of the two of us making mad passionate love under the stars, fades away over the Alps. He's got coffee breath, anyway. I smile sweetly and extricate my fingers. 'I'll see what I can do.'

'Matt's *here*? He must be mad,' Sylvie says flatly, looking around the bar as if expecting to see him there. 'No. I don't want to see him.'

Wonderful news. Her heart is hardened towards him. There can be no question of a reconciliation. I immediately conjure up billowing curtains, a steamy satin-lined bed, Matt stripping off his tight Levis under the shimmering elegance of an Alpine moon.

'I think . . .' Sylvie adds, looking at me uncertainly. She chews delicately on a strand of red hair. 'Maybe I should see him. Since he's come all this way.'

'Oh, don't let that worry you. He can probably afford it,' I say blithely.

'Mmm. You're right. He does get a good salary from that art gallery,' Sylvie says, crossing her ridiculously long legs and leaning back in her seat. She removes the umbrella from her cocktail, tosses it across the table and raises her glass. I'm impressed. Sylvie's beginning to act more and more like a human being. At the moment, she's *almost* spontaneous. 'Fuck Matt. Here's to my future without him. I know it sounds awful, but whenever I think about Matt, all I see is him and my sister, naked, on that waterbed.'

Waterbed? In Finland? Doesn't it freeze up in winter?

She drinks, then twirls the *frappé* ice with her finger. 'It was the worst moment of my life. I shall never forgive him for that.'

Poor Matt. It doesn't look like Sylvie's going to have him back. Now, don't get me wrong. I'm not interested in stealing someone else's property. In my experience, that's the very worst way to get a man. It's one of those bloody irritating pieces of 'good advice' your mother gives you, which you ignore, and which then turns out to be true *with a vengeance*. You feel guilty, he feels guilty, and his former loved one ends up running you both over in her car or breaking in at night and scattering steel tacks over your bathroom floor. (This really happened to a friend of mine. Not recommended for people with flat feet or tack-coloured lino.) But Matt's the only man I've had near my bedroom for years, and if Sylvie really doesn't want him, it seems only fair to let me have second refusal.

I play the most miserable opening session of my career. Actually, it's the only opening session of my career. Usually my snooker frames are like sex: all over before I can blink, a bad opening position, a worse second one, leaving me breathless but frustrated by the end of the third. This time, I get a reprieve. The over-night interval guarantees a fresh start in the morning.

I'm three-one down by the time we clock off. I'm playing the under-age Wondergirl, Florrie. Every time she pots a ball, the spectators cheer, probably more for her fifteen-year-old complexion than her talent. I'm just beginning to feel like the forgotten woman when the referee calls a halt, shakes both our hands, and invites us to come back the following morning for the concluding session. I go back to my room, change out of my incredibly unflattering Parker's Pump & Shoe Company shirt, and head straight down to the bar.

Matt's in there, drowning his sorrows. 'Drink?'

He orders some unpronounceable Swiss liqueur. By the taste of the vile stuff, it's made from fermented goat droppings, but he appears to be enjoying it, so I knock it back in one and feel myself turning a horrid shade of green.

'Good, huh?'

I can hardly breathe. Does he expect me to reply?

'Have another. These liqueurs always taste better once you've acquired a taste for them.'

I smile through my nausea. 'Fine.'

He orders two more. 'So, Sylvie won't see me. Do you think she'll change her mind?'

'I doubt it, but she might. Who can tell?'

'Women!' he mutters, then glances swiftly at me. 'Sorry. I didn't mean . . .'

'That's okay.' I'm used to the stupidity of men. Besides, I'm not here for his conversational skills. If I was, I'd have been better off talking to the fan-tailed goldfish in the hotel lobby tank. They probably have more than one topic of conversation, unlike Matt, whose mind does seem to dwell rather obsessively on

Sylvie. Can't he see he has a willing sex-starved creature in front of him? Maybe I should have worn something with a plunging neckline, but the most revealing thing in my suitcase is this perfect-for-all-occasions black dress. Sadly, it's a scoop neck and it falls sedately to just below my knees. So far, he hasn't even glanced at it.

Matt fishes a wallet out of his back pocket, rummages through it briefly, then produces a card. He hands it over. 'If Sylvie says anything about coming back to me . . . just ring that number. Any time. You can reach me at the other number most evenings.'

I glance at the card. A North London address. I knew I'd pinned that accent down accurately. 'Sure thing.'

He stares broodingly into his liqueur glass, then drains it. 'She's a heartless bitch. I'm probably well shot of her.' He grunts. 'Kristin's got bigger tits than her anyway.'

Charming. This is clearly not a man who knows how to differentiate between breast size and personality. I glance surreptitiously down at my own reasonable allowance. Not exactly Pamela Anderson, but not Twiggy either. I've passed for a woman in most situations. I knew I should have brought something with a lower neckline. I glance at Matt before taking another tentative sip at my liqueur. He's right. It doesn't taste like fermented goat droppings second time round. Now it smells like melting tarmac, and tastes even worse.

Is Matt really worth all this? I could be having a quiet night in my room, watching subtitled re-runs of *Dallas*, with JR dubbed into Swiss French so that he sounds strangely like Pinocchio's father. I caught a glimpse of it on my way down to the bar. It looked like thrilling stuff.

Suddenly, Matt puts his arm round my shoulders and squeezes hard. 'I hate this place, Zoë. I've decided to fly back to London tomorrow. There's a flight at noon.' Another tight squeeze. Is it my imagination or is it a more meaningful squeeze this time? 'Why don't we grab a bottle of champagne, go up to my room, and celebrate?'

No, it wasn't my imagination. He's a prat, but I'm tempted. It's been so long since I had sex, I'm not even sure whether this is an appalling chat-up line or I'm simply out of touch with current trends. 'Celebrate what?'

'Your match.'

'I'm losing.'

'Oh.' He swiftly downs his liqueur. It's obviously having the desired effect. He's slurring his words now. 'Well, why not celebrate being an attractive woman in a glamorous foreign city?'

Okay. I'm a sad person. I need a serious reality check. But for a moment here, I actually believe him. Correction: I allow myself to believe him. Matt's drunk, or at least that seems the only logical explanation. Fully clothed, I can just about hold my own with the more glamorous of my sex. But let's face it, I'm not Page Three material. I've had two children. My stomach looks like a relief map of the Himalayas. Once bra-less, my tits point south within three minutes. Matt's too attractive to be this desperate for sex without being just a teensy bit drunk. He's on the rebound. He needs a little TLC. Sylvie won't give it to him, and Kristin, damn her vital statistics, isn't on hand to soothe his troubled penis.

I promise myself that I'll be embarrassed about this tomorrow, but not tonight. Tonight, I shall believe every word Matt says, even if he gets carried away and compares me to Bo Derek. Fuck it. Why not? Sylvie doesn't need to know. She's out with a couple of her cronies tonight, trying some Japanese restaurant the receptionist recommended. Right now, she's probably sitting on the floor, barefoot, half-way through a mouthful of sushi. 'Okay,' I hear myself saying. 'But I'd rather we went up to my room, if that's all right with you.'

He smiles slowly. 'No problem. No problem at all.'

God, don't you hate that I've-just-scored-and-aren't-I-a-fucking-stud expression on a man's face when you eventually say yes? Briskly, I burst his bubble. 'I assume you've got some Durex?'

Matt looks taken aback by my bluntness, then swallows. This is clearly not the line he had anticipated. Have I made a blunder? I read *Cosmopolitan*. I read *New Woman*. I even watch late-night chat-shows on Sky occasionally. I know protection is a woman's responsibility as much as a man's these days. Clearly Matt is unaware of these developments in male-female relationships. No doubt I was supposed to melt tenderly into his arms, undistracted by such ugly realities as contraception . . . or possibly he just expected me to cross my fingers at the appropriate moment and put my trust in the rhythm method.

But Matt rallies. He nods dumbly, patting the back pockets of his jeans with a guilty expression. 'Er . . .' He glances over at the men's toilets, then back at me. 'Give me a minute, will you?'

As we head up in the lifts, I'm struck by a sudden thought. Once you've wrestled the little sod out of its packet, do you push a condom inwards, or outwards? Fiddly bastards. Whichever way you roll it, the teat at the end always looks inside-out. In fact, the average condom makes a man's penis look like a baby's bottle. A clever design feature, no doubt dreamt up by some man with an oral sex fetish, but someone should tell him it's like eating a banana with its skin on. No danger of unwanted calories, but not something anyone in their right mind would choose to do. Sex would be great without condoms. Sadly though, I can't persuade myself to be reckless or insane enough to dispense with their services.

It occurs to me here that I'm not exactly being swept away by romance, but what the hell. Romance is over-rated. For me, casual sex is still the undiscovered country.

Next morning, I wake up beside an unfamiliar dent in the pillow, and the sound of running water. Matt's having a shower. I lie back and stretch my arms luxuriously above my head, then wince. Maybe I don't feel so good after all. There's always a price to pay for these one-night stands. Muscles are aching that I thought had atrophied long ago, my head hurts from too much champagne, and every time I think of Sylvie I feel ridiculously guilty.

I say ridiculously, because that's what it is. I didn't 'steal' her husband for the night. She dumped him – or ran off, to be more precise – and quite rightly, since she caught him humping her sister. Cutting the marital ties was a sane reaction, just as my going to bed with him last night was a sane reaction. I hadn't had sex in months and it was offered to me on a plate. What was expected of me under those circumstances? A saintly refusal?

Last night, I was dying to be reminded what it was like to have sex. And Matt certainly reminded me. To be honest, I was seriously underwhelmed. Was it really always that boring? All that pushing and shoving and shouting 'Oh, oh, oh' in a futile attempt to get him to finish. He then had the nerve to fall asleep immediately afterwards, still inserted up to his neck. I ended up squashed between his chest and the headboard, stuck for hours in what he called the Screaming Mandrake position. Before adopting the position, I asked him *why* it was called the Screaming Mandrake. Matt said he didn't know. By 6 a.m., I had a fairly accurate idea.

But full marks to Matt. He gave me the Diamond Service. He wiggled everything God intended him to wiggle. The fact that he fell asleep immediately afterwards was due, I'm sure, more to the amount of champagne he had consumed than to any lack of sexual etiquette. He did his best within the narrow perimeters of one-night-stand sex. But I just couldn't take him seriously. Half-way through the Screaming Mandrake, I suffered a fit of the giggles which, with some considerable expertise, I managed to pass off as an orgasm.

Problem is, Matt couldn't tell the difference. Okay, men aren't the most observant of creatures, especially in bed, but you'd think he could differentiate between laughter and a multiple orgasm. Even considering my Oscar-nominated performance, that's still pretty damning evidence of basic incompatibility. Okay, fine. I know I wasn't after compatibility. I was after sex. And I got it. But some evidence of sensitivity in a man wouldn't go amiss on these occasions, would it? Oh fuck it. After months of celibacy, anything's better than DIY.

Five minutes later, there's a knock at the door. I stumble off the bed, and pull on an old thigh-length T-shirt. It's Sylvie.

I'm staring. I know my mouth is open, but I can't get it to shut.

'Can I come in?' she says, then her own mouth gapes slightly as she looks over my shoulder. The bathroom door has just opened. From her expression, I guess that Matt has just walked back into the bedroom. I desperately hope, though common sense tells me that it will make little difference to the situation, that he is either partially clothed or at least wearing a towel.

'Sylvie?' Matt has obviously seen who it is. He sounds gutted. For a moment, I almost pity him, and then I remember it's me at the door, within easy reach of Sylvie's hands for any number of retributive actions on her part. Slapping, pulling hair, punching, or poking me in the eye, all leap irrevocably to mind.

'You bastard.'

But she's calm. Apart from a slight inflexion of the words, there's nothing to reveal what's going on inside her head. Okay. So much for Matt. I stand there like a statue, waiting for my turn. How can she be so calm? She can't possibly be mistaken about the situation. You'd have to be fairly dim not to put two and two together and come up with the figure for a divorce settlement.

Then she turns her head slightly, like a mannequin coming to life, and she looks directly at me. An icy shudder runs down my spine. Sylvie is not simply looking at me. She is disintegrating me. She runs her eyes slowly and painstakingly down the T-shirt, down what can be seen of my thighs, over my knobbly knees, pausing with a twitch of her eyebrow to let me know how completely unattractive she considers them, then down to my feet and back up again to my face. I shrivel under that cold laser-like stare. What sort of person does *this*? she is saying, though of course she isn't saying anything. Her mouth isn't moving, but her eyes tell me exactly what she thinks of me. It's a 'he's-a-bastard-but-he's-still-my-property-until-I-figure-out-what-to-do-with-him, you man-snatching *toad* expression. I feel as though I'm being skewered. Slowly. Painfully. But with infinite dignity on the part of the skewerer.

Then Sylvie turns and walks away.

Matt pushes past me in a second, wearing my flowery dressing-gown, and dashes down the hotel corridor after her. 'Sylvie! Wait! I can explain.' Why do men *always* say that?

Okay. Is it possible that we can pass this off as a bizarre coincidence? I don't think so. It would be over-optimistic to assume complete non-intelligence on Sylvie's part. She's not going to believe, for instance, that Matt came round early this morning to borrow a miniature milk carton, spilt it on his entire outfit and had to change into my dressing gown while he dried his shirt, jeans, underpants *and* socks with a two-speed hairdryer. This explanation could work with some people, but not Sylvie. If Matt had only kept his socks on, we might have stood a chance.

Ten minutes later, Matt comes back. 'I followed her back to her room,' he said, out of breath. 'But she wouldn't let me in.'

I flop back on the bed. 'She's going to kill me.'

'Kill *you*? What about me?' Matt shrugs out of the flowery dressing-gown, which was *so* becoming on him, and reaches for his clothes, still in the untidy pile where he'd drunkenly removed them the night before. I notice with some satisfaction that his penis is now shrivelled to the size of a chipolata. He drags his boxer shorts on, oblivious to my smile. 'Have you heard of Medusa? Well, Sylvie's worse. She doesn't just turn men to stone, she cuts off their balls first and uses them to play snooker with. How the fuck am I meant to get her back now? I've got a flight home at midday. She'll be playing until after one o'clock. And all you can think about is yourself!'

'If she's so terrible, why the hell do you want her back?'

'I don't know . . .' Matt mutters angrily. He looks down, wrestling with his shirt buttons. 'Because of who she is. What she is.'

'Because she's a great snooker player?'

'Maybe.' Matt catches my eye and flushes. 'Is that so awful?'

'Pretty much.'

He looks stung. 'You don't understand.'

'I'm beginning to.'

'It's not just that. She's intelligent. She's attractive. Her family's got money.' Matt zips up his jeans and sits on the side of the bed to fumble with his socks and shoes. 'She's everything I've ever wanted in a woman.'

'So why go round shagging other people?'

'I can't help it if women are always throwing themselves at me.'

You complete and utter bastard. I count silently to

ten. 'From what I remember of last night, it was the other way round.'

'I'm surprised you can remember anything, you were so pissed!'

'And who bought me the champagne?'

'Consider it as down-payment.'

This is the final straw. 'Get out.'

'My pleasure, sweetheart.'

After he's gone, I huddle up in the bedclothes for ages, crying my eyes out. I can't remember when I last cried like this. It's as though the flood-gates have been opened somewhere inside, and all the tears I should have cried on other occasions, those gut-wrenching, face-blotching, wish-I-could-die tears that I'd longed for so many times, are now uncontrollably forcing their way out. I didn't even cry this violently the day Adrian left.

Then I remember my match. I glance at the bedside clock through swollen eyes and realise I have only half an hour to wash my face, do my make-up, get dressed and present myself at the table for an eleven o'clock start. It's at total fuck-up moments like these that an appreciation of life's rich ironies comes in handy.

When someone falls in love with snooker, or any sport, with the possible exception of push-ha'penny and tiddlywinks, they make a pact with the devil. I'm not talking Faust here. I don't mean little red devils with flaming tridents appear and offer you eternal victory in exchange for your soul – although personally I don't think that's such a bad deal – I mean that those things which most people put first in order of importance (like parents, spouse, kids, gardening programmes, Torvill and Dean) begin to rate fairly dismally in comparison with the game. It becomes a case of 'can't stop, won't stop'. Everything else pales into insignificance before the great god, snooker.

The point I'm making is that relationships suffer. Not just close personal relationships, but the passing ones you have with local grocers or bus drivers or the woman who always seems to be walking her dog when you're out posting a letter. Most people get to know these acquaintances to a certain extent. They remember names, conversations, those little details that smooth the path when you occasionally want them to do you a favour. When you're always thinking about snooker, and I mean *always*, not only do your powers of recall go out the window, but so does your ability to strike up these conversations in the first place. And loved ones are lucky if they get an 'mmm?' from you after some lengthy monologue on their day.

But the worst thing about this, the absolute killer, is that when something happens that you simply *can't* ignore, something so appalling and earth-shattering that 'snooker-thought' gets suspended for at least half an hour, when you try to sneak back afterwards into a snooker frame of mind, you find yourself in disturbingly unfamiliar territory. Your perspective on the game has altered. Subtly, and not for ever, but enough to wreak havoc with your confidence at the time. Let's say you're crossing your living room when the lights go out. You think you know where everything is in the dark, but you never really do. Inevitably, you go sprawling over some forgotten obstacle and end up flat on your face.

Snooker's like that. Playing snooker with an emotional crisis at the forefront of your mind is akin to playing blindfolded. You don't have a cat's chance in hell of hitting a ball.

After losing my match by the dismal scoreline of six-one, I stumble up to my room, remove the now creased shirt with its naff Parker's Pump & Shoe Company logo, and take a long cool shower. The maid has obviously not bothered calling in. The shower base is still full of dark hairs, where Matt 'shed' during his shower. It's like having had a bear in your bathroom. I sluice most of the hairs away, but I still feel dirty afterwards, as if the visible reminder of his presence there has somehow removed the illicit thrill from my one-night stand and turned it into something I should be ashamed of.

Later, standing by the window and gazing down through the buildings to the blue dancing surface of Lake Geneva, I realise it's Sylvie I'm feeling guilty about, not my uncharacteristic act of promiscuity. I don't give a toss what Matt thinks of me, but I do care, passionately, about losing Sylvie's friendship. Shit. Why do I always have to take one step forward and two steps back? Let's face it, men come and go. Once you leave school, life-long girlfriends are hard to come by; and even harder to keep. I don't want to lose Sylvie's friendship. It was just beginning to show promise. And I had the impression that Sylvie liked me too. Then Matt came along and fucked the whole thing up. Literally. Matt wanted to get laid. I fell for his bullshit because I wanted to feel loved again. But maybe that's the basic difference between men and women. Women react with their hearts. Men react with their testosterone levels.

When I go back down to the dimly lit ballroom where the other quarter-finals are still being played, I look around for Matt, but he's nowhere in sight. Clearly, he wasn't lying when he said he was flying back to London today. It wouldn't have surprised me to find out that it had been a ruse to make me feel sorry for him, but for once, Matt must have been telling the truth.

Paula is sitting on the third row up of raised seating near Sylvie's table, taking notes. I think she's here as part of the committee, reporting back on each stage of the Championships. At the moment, she's the only friendly face I can see, so I might as well sit next to her. The ballroom isn't exactly crowded though. There was a full house for last night's opening sessions. But this afternoon, there's only a small gathering here, and they're mainly watching Sylvie's match. A tall elegant redhead works minor miracles at the ticket office.

Sylvie's playing Tracey, another top player. Tracey's one of the girls she hangs out with, and I don't think Tracey's even beaten her in competition. They usually meet at quarter-final or semi-final stage, but as far as I'm aware, Tracey's never won a major tournament. It's the sort of match where you would normally expect the top-dog to walk away with a relatively easy victory, but Sylvie is sitting in the shadows with a morose expression on her face. Tracey is at the table, calculating her escape from an impossible-looking snooker.

Paula looks up as I squeeze past a corpulent Swiss onlooker and his red-cheeked wife to nestle in beside her. She seems surprised to see me, leaning over with a hoarse whisper, 'I would have thought a game of snooker was the last thing you wanted to see at the moment. I heard about your match.' She raises her eyebrows at me, tutting quietly under her breath. 'Six-one . . . Quite a drubbing.'

Yes. Thank you for reminding me. I manage a sickly smile, looking down at her notepad. 'How's Sylvie doing?'

'She's playing utter crap,' Paula whispers. 'Five-three down now. Tracey's taking her to the cleaners. I don't think she's even scored yet this frame. All Tracey needs is one good break and it's all over.'

I'm staggered. An enormous sense of guilt envelops me. I've been pissing about in my room, thinking about myself as usual, while Sylvie's been dying out here on the table. And why is she playing so badly? Well, I don't need a degree in psychology to work this one out. Perhaps if I hadn't been screwing her husband last night, I could at least have turned my match around this morning, and Sylvie would have been assured of a place in the World Championship semi-finals. Instead, we're both fucked. It's all my fault. And the worst thing is, Matt wasn't even good enough in bed to warrant causing this much pain.

Gradually, my eyes adjust to the low lighting. Sylvie plays another safety shot, attempting not to pot a ball when she hopes to prevent Tracey potting one; she returns to her seat with slightly hunched shoulders. I can't see her face from this distance, but her posture speaks volumes. She settles back in her seat as if she doesn't expect to get up again for some time, and her shoulders droop as she stares down at the floor, miles away. Her cue is balanced delicately against her right knee, but she is holding on to it as though it were a life-raft. This was meant to be *her* tournament. She's been playing so steadily all season, slowly moving up through the gears towards the big one, the World Championships. And now this girl, this small dark-haired girl, sallow skin shining after hours at the table, is going to destroy everything.

It's like watching a rabbit caught in a car's headlights and knowing there's nothing you can do to stop the inevitable. There's something appalling about waiting for the death blow. There's no way she can pull it back now. Sylvie knows that. Tracey knows that too. It's written all over the girl's face as she gets down on the shot so painstakingly, making damn sure of it, but already trembling with victory, the release of tension.

I glance around at the rapt audience. This is what they've come here for, quite apart from the added novelty of seeing women players. Snooker is about confrontation. There's no escaping that fact. If you can't handle losing, you shouldn't play. I've seen friends lose before. I've lost myself, too many times to mention, so that the pain of losing has almost faded to a dull ache. I barely even registered my loss this morning. There'll be other opportunities for me. I'm sure of it. But watching Sylvie lose like this, in the quarter-finals of a World Championships she might have won under different circumstances, and knowing that I've had a hand in her failure, is worse than all those other times. I feel like an executioner.

'Looks like Tracey's got it,' Paula says, jabbing me sharply in the ribs. 'That break puts Sylvie . . . twenty-two behind . . . with only blue, pink and black left. She's got no chance.'

She's right, of course, but I don't want to believe it. 'Sylvie's won frames from this far behind. You can't give up on her yet.'

'Are you serious? She's lost it, Zoë. She's out.'

'Not yet . . . Not yet,' I murmur, willing Sylvie on.

Then Sylvie gets up, walks slowly to the table – no, *saunters* is the word I want – and rolls the pink gently across the cloth with her hand. She's smiling, holding out her hand towards Tracey, but her eyes are unnaturally bright as though she's holding back tears. The audience burst into applause. Tracey punches the air and kisses her cue religiously. I *hate* people who do that.

'There. She's conceded,' Paula says with satisfaction.

'I told you it was all over. There was never any chance Sylvie could have pulled that match back. She's done the right thing. I hate it when players piss around for ages, pretending they can still win. It's so boring.'

I know this is fair comment. Paula is absolutely right. Sylvie couldn't have won. She has done the right thing. It's an act of courtesy towards the other player. Tracey now has to steel herself for a gruelling semi-final, and the last thing she would want is to be exhausted after a long drawn-out battle with a player who can't accept the fact that they're beaten. I know all this. But it doesn't make it any easier. I wish I could turn back the clock, go back to last night in the hotel bar and tell Matt to piss off. I wish I could have spent all night chastely alone in my cold little bed, and then when Sylvie came round this morning, I could have asked her in and offered her a cup of tea. We could have chatted and then gone off to our respective matches with clear consciences and minds geared-up for battle. But I didn't tell Matt to piss off. I didn't spend the night alone. And when Sylvie came round, she went away in probably much the same state I was in after Matt left. In other words, totally fucked up emotionally.

'Where are you going?' Paula asks in surprise as I get up. 'There's another quarter-final on now, to be played to a finish.'

'I need a stiff drink.'

Paula shrugs disapprovingly. 'Suit yourself.'

I nearly bump into Sylvie on my way out. She halts in the doorway, inches away from me, cue case in hand,

and we both stare at each other for about ten seconds. Her eyes are glassy with unshed tears, but she holds herself rigidly. I realise that she's waiting for me to move out of her way. Feeling like a total shit, and knowing Sylvie probably blames me for what just happened on the table, I move awkwardly to one side to let her go first. She stalks past me, head high, her cue case held stiffly by her side.

I want to go after her and apologise. But that would only make it worse, wouldn't it? I suppose I persuade myself of this because I don't really want to go through some dire explanation-cum-apology-cum-self-justification fiasco in the lift, or outside her door, or in the hotel corridor . . . I know bloody well she wouldn't let me in her room . . . and besides, it makes sense to assume that someone who's just made the biggest balls-up of her career wouldn't want her husband's latest conquest hanging round while she's dying to creep into bed and bawl her eyes out. I've already done the creeping into bed and bawling my eyes out bit today. So I head off to the bar instead, leaving Sylvie to kick her cue case round the room, or whatever it is she intends doing to relieve a combined fit of post-match and post-husband blues.

8

Tracey won the World Championships. I spent many hazy hours in the bar. Sylvie thoroughly ignored me for the rest of the week. By the time we flew back, I had the firm impression that I was the invisible woman. But hell, the World wasn't a total disaster for me. I reached the quarter-finals. I had an all-expenses-paid trip to Switzerland. I got pissed. I got shagged. What more could one ask of a snooker tournament?

After the World Championships, I spend several months doing the usual: practising most days, trudging off to each monthly tournament and acquitting myself respectably but never with the startling brilliance I feel sure I am capable of, trying to keep up with the housework, looking after the kids and pretending to my mother that I'm still working towards some fictitious computer qualifications. This charade with my mother is necessary until I can start winning tournaments. Until that day comes, my mother will believe that snooker is a waste of time. Okay, she'll probably still think it's a waste of time, even if I do win a tournament, but

I'll feel better about admitting that I'm not studying computer languages or whatever it is they do on these adult education courses, if I've got at least one large silver trophy collecting dust on the sideboard. It's a question both of pride and self-justification.

The guys at the club are giving me a hard time at the moment. After one particular incident (that wanker Raz and his best buddy Bob ganging up on me again – Christ, they must hate women, or is it just me?), I'm almost tempted to chuck the whole thing in. Go and find an easier career for women, like becoming an astronaut or a jockey.

It happens like this. I'm in the club when Raz, the owner's nephew, looking pleased with himself, offers me a game. Now, this is unusual in itself. Most days, the men avoid me like the plague. They have two chances if they play me, and neither is particularly appealing. If they win, no one is interested in their victory because, hey, I'm a woman and everyone knows that women can't play snooker. But if they lose, it's apparently the mental and emotional equivalent of having their balls removed without anaesthetic. So the men generally go for the no-risk option. They don't play against me at all.

I'm so stunned I agree. But I soon find out why Raz wants to play me. He has a bet on the game, with Bob, who has draped his copious buttocks over one of the adjacent bar stools. The bet is not over whether I win or lose. It's more humiliating than that. Raz has bet that I won't score above thirty points against him.

Bob doesn't like me, but he clearly trusts me not to lie down and let Raz steamroller over me. He is watching me from deep inside a pint of bitter. His small darting bloodshot eyes, set above that heavy jowl, remind me of a pig. Every time Raz pots a ball, Bob even lets out a tiny squeal before plunging back into his bitter.

Raz cracks another shot down the cushion, rattles the red, and swears violently. 'That was fifty-two,' he mutters, slamming the marker along the scoreboard. He grabs up his cloth, spits on it, then rubs it down his cue, staring at me. 'Don't take all day. I don't want to lose my rhythm.'

I knock in the sitting red, stroll round for the black, sink it easily, and leave myself a nice little cut to bounce off the side cushion and back for a second black. Everything goes as planned. I put a third red down in the middle and look at the pink to take me to twenty-three points. I already have ten on the scoreboard. This shot, a just-off straight stun into the left-hand bottom pocket, will win Bob his bet. The whole situation is grating at my nerves, but this is my first opportunity in ages to play an actual game outside a tournament situation. Solo practice is all well and good, but game practice is something I desperately require if my game's going to improve.

I chalk my cue, noticing that Raz is moving round to stand right in the line of the shot. 'Can you move a couple of inches to the right? You're right in my eye line there.'

'Take the bloody shot, woman, and stop wittering.'

Raz turns impatiently to Bob. 'Typical. This is what happens when you give a woman a snooker cue . . . she can't stop talking long enough to use it.'

I grit my teeth, size up the pink, and get down on the shot. All the time, I'm aware of him standing right in front of the pocket, watching me. Then, just as I pull back to hit the white, Raz drops his cue with a loud clatter. I can't stop at this stage even though I've inadvertently glanced up. I'm committed to hitting the white now. It strikes badly off-centre, I can hear it in the contact. The pink misses the pocket by at least an inch. I stand up angrily. 'You did that deliberately.'

'Oh yeah, like I really want to damage my cue.' But he's not meeting my eyes. He stoops to pick up his cue, then examines it minutely.

'You put me off.'

'For fuck's sake, it happens all the time in here. You're only making excuses because you're such a crap player. Christ, you can't even pot a straight pink.' He puts on a mock whining voice. 'Somebody coughed. Somebody dropped their cue. Somebody nudged me. Grow up, Zoë. That's seventeen to you, and it's my shot.'

'You're a cheat.'

Raz stares at me. His face hardens. 'What did you call me?'

'You heard.' This is bravado. I glance at Bob to back me up, but of course he's grinning. He may be losing his bet, but this is still music to his ears. Zoë, the proverbial thorn in his side, is probably about to get decked by Raz, someone who doesn't give a toss if you're male, female or anything in between. If you've offended him, you get smacked in the teeth. A year ago, I wouldn't have said a word. I would have shrunk into the shadows, terrified of a possible confrontation. Things are different now. Okay, my hands may be shaking, but I'm not prepared to step back meekly and let Raz get away with it. 'Can't you win without cheating?'

'You're asking for trouble.'

'No. I'm just trying to play a decent game of snooker.'

'Decent? You can barely hold a cue.'

'Is this because I'm a woman? What exactly is your problem, Raz?'

'My problem?' He comes closer. Up close, he seems so much taller than I am, and I can see his hand twitching around the butt-end of his cue as if he's dying to give me a crack with it. His eyes are livid. 'I'll tell you what my problem is. I get this great sponsorship deal going with that bloke Parker, and then along comes Little Miss Butter-wouldn't-melt-in-my-mouth, and he takes the money away from me and gives it to you. To a fucking woman!'

Bob gets down off his stool and puts a fatherly hand on Raz's shoulder. 'Come on now. You know what happened last time, Raz. No more trouble . . .'

'Don't worry, I'm going. I reckon I've won that bet, anyway.' He grabs up his cue case and jerks one finger violently in my direction. '*She* can pay for the table. Only thing women are good for. Paying for my pleasure.'

'Dream on, Raz.'

Bob seizes hold of his arm. 'Leave her. She's not worth it.'

Raz shrugs off Bob's restraining hand. The situation, if that's what you can call it, appears to be under control. But as he passes, Raz leans into my face and smiles. It's not a pleasant smile. I can smell lager on his breath. 'You're going to regret this, Zoë. No one calls me a cheat.'

When I get back home, I'm shaking so much that it takes three cups of hot tea to calm me down. I don't know why I'm so upset by his threat. I should be laughing. I should be chalking it up to experience, or whatever it is you do after stupid things like this happen. But I'm not. I'm scared. I start thinking wild thoughts, like giving up snooker for ever and staying away from the club. I need never face Raz again. But then I start thinking about women snooker players in general. I think about those Victorian ladies who played billiards with their fathers and husbands while no one thought anything about it, and how everything subtly changed somewhere in the early decades of the twentieth century. Maybe the two great wars changed attitudes towards women. Not just for the better, you understand. Maybe men tried to curb that sense of freedom women had experienced whilst the country was at war, and in some areas of life it worked, but in others it didn't. Women fought back about careers and child-care and most sports. I don't know what happened with snooker and billiards, but somewhere along the line women snooker players got forgotten about, or pushed out, or simply forbidden to play.

Now, men like Bob and Raz come along, see that what their forefathers have done is good, and agree to perpetuate the myth that women can't play snooker, or that it's somehow insane or unnatural for a woman to want to play snooker. In some cases, as happened this afternoon, they are even prepared to threaten women with physical violence to ensure they stay out of the clubs. I start feeling angry that this should still be the case, and all I want to do then is get back to the club, and give the men as much hell as they give me.

Even with all this shit flying around, I'm more in love with snooker than ever before. I'm in Saffron Walden for my next world-ranking tournament. The kids are with my long-suffering mother. It's a beautiful morning. The tables are so green they look like paradise. My cue is humming in its case. I'm walking with a bounce in my step. Out of the way, everyone. Zoë's on form.

Originally, Tricksy offered to book the accommodation for this tournament, but it turns out that Saffron Walden is not exactly overflowing with places to stay, and in the absence of any obvious choice, I have turned up today to find that we have nowhere booked because Tricksy thought she'd wait until I was there to make the decision for her. The Tournament Controller tells us there are rooms in the main hotel, but the club's quite a way from the town centre, and besides, a hotel would be way beyond our means. As far as I can see, there's absolutely sweet F.A. available within our price bracket. I've got some extra cash from the Parker's Pump & Shoe Company, to help with tournament expenses, but the car exhaust is hanging off and I was hoping to use that money to get it repaired.

'There's a double room. And I mean double . . . not a twin. But it costs forty-five quid a night for two people. That's over twenty-two quid each. I don't think I can even stretch to fifteen. The train fare was steep enough.'

'No car?' I ask Tricksy, frowning.

'It's fucked.'

Fair enough. That's not a situation I'm exactly unfamiliar with. But her money problems still leave us stranded as far as accommodation is concerned. 'What do you suggest? That we roll up in our coats under the stars tonight, or shall we just persuade the club to stay open twenty-four hours so we don't have to go to sleep?'

'Ho bloody ho. I've got an idea, actually.' Tricksy's ideas are notoriously bad. But our options are limited, so I might as well hear her out. 'Katie Number One's brought her younger brother, Chris, to the tournament. He wants to watch her play or something. He was going back home tonight, but he says . . .'

'No. Whatever it is, no.'

Tricksy looks disgruntled. 'You haven't heard my suggestion yet.'

'I can imagine.'

'No, it's all perfectly innocent. We get the double bed at the guesthouse. I sneak Chris up there when the landlady's not looking, and then he'll pay for the room. He's got a job. In a hardware store. He can afford the whole whack . . . forty-five quid, the lot.' She smiles. 'He was really sympathetic when I told him I was skint.'

'Let me get this straight. Katie's brother is offering to pay for our room if we share a double bed with him?'

'That's right.'

'Piss off.'

'It's true, I swear.'

'I'm sure it is. The question is, what's he going to want in return?'

Tricksy opens her eyes very wide. 'Zoë, he's only twenty-one. Are you calling me a cradle-snatcher?'

'Given half the chance, yes.'

'All right, he's good-looking. I admit it. But I'm only thinking of the money.'

'You slut.'

She nudges me in the ribs. 'Go on. You can sleep in the middle.'

I'm going to regret this. 'Okay. Set it up. But don't let him get any ideas, for God's sake. The last thing I want to find in my bed tonight is an over-sexed male octopus.'

'Speak for yourself,' she grins. 'I'm game.'

Tricksy dances off to phone the guesthouse before the first-round draw is called. I've never met Chris, but I pity him already. The poor little bastard doesn't have a clue what he's letting himself in for.

It's a classic tournament. You know how sometimes you get the feeling that a situation is about as perfect as it will ever be, and that if you died there on the spot, at least you would die with a stupid grin on your face? Well, that's exactly how everything feels today.

Saffron Walden is my favourite tournament of the year, mainly because it's also my favourite club. It's a tiny little place, only about ten tables and an open bar area you could just about swing a cat in, with a knee-high wall separating the bar from the tables. Because you know how exposed the tables are, you keep your conversations at a low pitch. There's none of that usual jostling at the bar, or a rabble hanging round the public phone, and no yelling across the room at players you haven't seen for months. The chatter is subdued, almost a murmur. The atmosphere is civilised. It's how I always imagined snooker tournaments would be before I started playing the world circuit and learnt about life's realities.

The only hitch about Saffron Walden, due to the club size, is that matches are played over fewer frames than usual. But it's a great one-day event, even if the tournament rarely finishes before eleven o'clock at night.

I start off on table three, flush against the wall and near enough to the bar to catch the occasional conversational highlight. There's an intimacy about that sort of situation that lowers your guard, makes you friendlier, more open to the vagaries of human nature.

I'm playing Bo, the pregnant girl, and when she stretches over the table for a long shot I'm almost alarmed for her. She must be nearly full-term now. The bulge is straining at her green maternity dress like a mole about to pop out of the ground. Feeling particularly good-humoured today, I help her replace the rest several times, and even suggest she takes her shoes off to play. 'Your feet must be killing you.'

Bo grins. 'They're not too bad. It's this I'm worried about.'

I stare at her swollen abdomen. 'You're kidding, right?'

'No. I was due last week.'

My jaw drops. 'You should be resting, not playing snooker.'

'The midwife said I should keep active. So here I am.'

I try to stay calm. It's her choice, after all. None of my business. I lean over and re-spot the blue for her. 'Well, I hope it's not planning on making an impromptu appearance during this match.'

She fluffs the next shot, probably because we're talking. I keep quiet, embarrassed that I may have put her off her game. Still, I'm not sure she's done the right thing by playing today. It could really disrupt the tournament if she goes into labour.

You don't get this sort of situation in men's snooker. There's never any danger of an opponent waddling off to call an ambulance because his contractions have started. But it gives our game a close-knit atmosphere that the men's circuit lacks. It's not easily explained, and it's not entirely a sense of sisterhood that binds the circuit together, we're all too bitchy for that, but it is something akin to mutual understanding. So when Bo staggers past with the extended spider, I have to admire the determination that makes a woman carry on playing at full-term. 'Want a hand with that?'

'I can manage, thanks.'

Bo's got courage, I'll give her that. Her coloured hair-beads click quietly against each other as she bends to replace the extended spider on its hooks, having successfully navigated a path for the white through the cluttered reds and back to baulk. But when she straightens, she exhales sharply, putting a hand to her stomach. Her face goes very pale.

I hope it's a false alarm. 'You okay?'

She nods, puffing slightly. 'I get a lot of these twinges. Nothing ever seems to happen. I'm beginning to think it's staying in there for good.'

I sincerely doubt that, my dear, and I speak from experience. But I say nothing, even managing a wry smile as I wander round to see what Bo's left me. Not much by the look of it. I tap the edge of the table softly. 'Good shot.'

A good safety shot is as hard to play as a good pot. It deserves applause, consideration, respect. What it requires is foresight, a sound knowledge of the angles, the ability to judge pace correctly, and most of all, patience. The impatient player will never execute a safety shot well, if they play one at all. You need to know you can't win a frame by force alone, that potting is simply the means to an end, not an end in itself. Another means to the same end, which is required in the majority of frames, is the safety shot. Of course, you can't clip and run forever. At some point, you have to put your cue where your mouth is, if you see what I mean, i.e. not literally, but in terms of break-building. But to get to that point where a potential break becomes reality, you need to force your opponent into making a mistake. And that's where the 'attacking' safety shot comes in.

Bo has played this one to perfection. I'm tucked up sweet as a nut on the back rail. One loose red is clippable, but only just. I'm partially obscured by the green, still on its spot, but the obvious route back to baulk is blocked by a maverick red. The black is sitting over the pocket. The pack is still relatively intact, but there are enough deserters for Bo to make a tidy break, assuming I fail to bring the white back up. I raise my eyebrows. There's only one word for this situation, and it isn't repeatable with a referee hovering within earshot. Swearing at the table is strictly *verboten*.

But I'm calm. And that's the key. You have to look at it like a mathematical problem or a logistical puzzle. It's pointless bringing terror to the table. It only clouds your decision-making. Okay, I'm one of the worst offenders when it comes to letting emotion get the better of my game. But not today. The club is so silent. This is the first match of the day on this table. The baize is still gleaming where the iron caught it. Everyone seems incredibly calm and focused, even Bo, who has frozen like a statue beside the wall, knowing that any sudden movement may distract my concentration. I like her for that. There's nothing worse than a player without etiquette.

I make my decision and play the cocked-hat escape, just missing the red on the cushion which might have caused a problem. Unfortunately, I fall slightly short of the back rail. The ball loses momentum as it slides gently off the side cushion, but there's no major damage done. I've left her on the wrong side of the table for any of the loose reds now. It's not a return snooker, but it's a reasonable first-frame effort.

Bo starts heading off in that direction, then stops abruptly, clutching the side of the table. 'Shit,' she hisses, getting a sharp glance from the referee. She puts her head down slightly and I can hear her panting under her breath. 'Do you mind if I nip to the loo?'

'Nip away. Will you be all right on your own?'

'Uhuh.' She disappears rapidly down towards the toilets.

The 'floating' referee sidles up to me, adjusting his white gloves. A 'floating' referee is one that handles several tables at once. The kitty won't always stretch to one referee per table, but this system seems to work okay as long as no one starts making a nuisance of themselves, i.e. wanting the white cleaned every other shot, or continually questioning an opponent's free-ball decisions. He keeps his eyes steadily on the next table while he whispers: 'She shouldn't leave the table mid-frame like that. Want me to have a word when she gets back?'

'Have a heart. Bo's pregnant. You can't just cross your legs in that state. When you gotta go, you gotta go.'

He shrugs. 'Okay. Your decision. But you may feel differently if you lose.'

'I won't.'

'What, feel differently?'

'Lose,' I whisper back.

He glances at me then, and grins. 'Fair enough.'

But Bo doesn't come back. Ten minutes pass and Bo still does not emerge from the ladies' toilets. In the end, catching the referee's eye, I lay my cue down on the table and slip quietly past the other players and through the bar area. When I push open the door to the toilets, I hear her immediately, panting heavily. She's slumped on the floor in one of the cubicles, with the door slightly ajar. The floor is slightly wet, and so is her dress.

'Bo? Are you okay?'

It's a stupid question. I realise this as soon as I've said it, but Bo just looks up at me, grimaces, and then starts panting again, hunching her shoulders. 'I . . . want . . . to . . . push.'

Christ. She's in labour. 'Hang on. I'll get the owner to ring for an ambulance.'

She grabs at my arm. 'My boyfriend . . . John . . . his number's in my bag.'

'Ambulance first, Bo. I take it your waters have broken? Right. I'll be back in a minute. Just . . . don't push, okay?'

She nods. Her face is an awful grey colour, and there's sweat on her forehead. As I dash out of the door, I can hear her whimpering softly under her breath. I feel a twinge of pain on her behalf. God, I remember how it felt, giving birth. But at least she seems fairly advanced in labour. I was in that bloody first-stage labour ward for eighteen hours before my waters broke. She probably doesn't realise how lucky she is, skipping the interminable agony of waiting.

As the ambulance pulls out of the club, the Tournament Controller declares the game conceded. I go through to the next round, and lose. Just as some players get stuck on people (players they can never seem to beat, however many times they draw them), so I seem to be getting stuck at the last-sixteen stage. I may know one end of a cue from the other but when it comes to the crunch, I always seem to bottle it. I run away from winning. Maybe I haven't got what it takes. Okay, maybe I'm even a fairly crap player. But it's not simply a question of ability. It's as much to do with visualisation again, the inability to 'see' myself in a quarter-final, or even to consider myself as being quarter-final material.

Sylvie, of course, has no trouble seeing herself in the final. What happened at the World will be an eternal mystery to everyone, but she's back on sparkling form for Saffron Walden and takes the first three frames without any trouble. Tracey, still struggling with the heavy mantle of World Champion, is having trouble concentrating her energies. She beat Rebecca the Wondergirl again to reach this final, but Sylvie is proving very hard to get rid of.

Tricksy comes bounding up out of the semi-darkness, dragging a reluctant Chris by the arm. 'We're going out for a pub meal. Want to come?'

I politely decline, glancing swiftly back at Sylvie's match as the small gathering of onlookers groans. (Sylvie has just played a spectacularly bad in-off.) Tricksy has that look in her eyes that says 'I'm offering, but don't you dare accept'.

She clearly wants to be on her own with Katie's impressionable younger brother. He's not bad-looking, nearly six foot, with that muscular outdoor air of the weekend footballer. Tricksy has never admitted her age, but I suspect it could be anywhere between thirty and thirty-five. She's incorrigible, seducing a boy of twenty-one. I take the spare key to the guesthouse, slip the scribbled instructions on how to get there into my handbag, and wish them both a pleasant evening. Especially Tricksy. She has that rarest of smiles on her face tonight, a grin of the 'hoping to get laid' variety.

After Sylvie has won, shaking hands with a tearful Tracey, she looks over at me and crooks a little finger in my direction. This is clearly a signal to approach.

'Some of the girls are going for a meal. There's a restaurant in the town centre that's staying open late for us if we can get at least eight people. Want to come?'

Frankly, I'm surprised. She hasn't spoken to me since what happened at the World Championships, and an invitation to join her and her cronies for a late supper is the last thing I expected. 'Do you really want me there, or is this a "making up the numbers" thing?'

'I don't know what you mean.'

'Who else is going?'

'I told you, some of the girls.'

Ah, subterfuge. She knows I don't like her friends, but she's not going to rise to the bait. Two can play at that game. 'Heard anything of Matt recently?'

Something flashes in her eyes, and is hastily veiled. 'No,' she says coldly. She puts her cue away, obviously fighting against the temptation to enquire further. After a few seconds of silence, she gives up the struggle. 'Why?'

'Oh, I just wondered. So. Where's this restaurant?'

Let me explain this exchange. I don't like Sylvie's friends or her politics, but I like her, and it irritates me that she lives the way she does. I suppose I'm one of those interfering people who can't bear to stand by and watch other people mess up their lives. I want Sylvie to see that I'm not prepared to brown-nose like her other 'friends' do, so I'm winding her up, reminding her of what I know and how I know it. Actually, I want to walk away from her and stop playing silly buggers, but I can't help liking her. You know the type of person I mean. They irritate the hell out of you sometimes, and their other friends make you puke, but you like them enough to want to persevere.

Women. They say men are hard to know. But friendships between women are far more complex and demanding, like those 5000-piece jigsaw puzzles which you know from experience are going to drive you crazy and take up your entire coffee table for three years, but you still can't help wondering which bit goes where.

The meal is a total disaster. Dani and Lou and Sara turn out to be in the middle of some long-running feud. Somewhere in between dessert and coffee, for some reason which will never become clear, Sara pulls Dani's hair. Dani screams. Lou gets up and decks Sara. A chair goes flying. Wine is spilt. The restaurant owner insists we pay immediately and leave. Sara stumbles off with a black eye, and Dani and Lou disappear into the night arguing vehemently.

Sylvie, Tracey, Julia and I are left standing outside the restaurant, waiting for a taxi. Sixteen-year-old Ruth has already gone back to her hotel, under severe threat of grounding by her coach, who turned up half-way through the main course and dragged her off by her ear.

I light a cigarette and stand there for a few moments in silence, wrestling with my desire to comment on the situation and the awareness that I may get my own shiner if I push it too far. Eventually, I can't help myself. I turn to Sylvie. 'Is this fairly representative of your nights out?'

Sylvie shoots me a poisonous look. 'Piss off. This isn't my fault.'

'Oh, shut up! Shut up, both of you!' Tracey exclaims, bursting into tears. We all stare at her, appalled. Her voice is barely coherent as she dives into her pocket for a tissue and blows her nose. 'Isn't anyone worried about poor Sara?'

No one says anything. I feel awkward about this, and make the mistake of trying to smooth things over. 'She'll be fine, Tracey. It's only a black eye. I'm sure she's had worse.'

From Sylvie's heavenward roll of the eyes at this comment, I've obviously hit the proverbial nail on the head.

Julia retouches her lipstick using the restaurant window as a mirror. She is a tall blonde in her early twenties, well built, with shoulders as broad as a rugby player's. She looks like the sort of woman you wouldn't want to get into a fight with, so I've been studiously avoiding her gaze all evening. She took an instant dislike to me when we first met, several tournaments ago, and all remarks thrown in my direction tonight have been deliberately provoking. As she puts her lipstick back in her bag, Julia turns her head and stares at me. She has the precise, clipped diction of someone who knows they're drunk, but is determined not to sound it. 'Who asked your fucking opinion? You remind me of someone else I used to know. She talked too much. I put a bottle in her face.'

Sylvie laughs nervously. 'Here comes the taxi. Come

on, girls, no more bickering. Let's be friends.' As we pile into the taxi, she squashes up beside me in the back and whispers in my ear. 'Don't say another word to Julia, for God's sake. Do you want to die?'

When the taxi drops me off in front of my guesthouse and I stumble up to Room 13 (had to be, didn't it?), the light's on under the door. I can hear the creaking of bed-springs and the alternate 'ooh' and 'argh' of Tricksy and Chris going at it full-tilt.

I turn the key and go in, too tired to give a monkey's. It's my double bed too. Tricksy looks over Chris's shoulder and giggles, red-faced. 'Hi! Nice time?' Then she digs her nails into his back, obviously a hint for him to carry on. By the time I'm in my nightshirt, teeth brushed, and ready for bed, they've finished and are both asleep, one on either side of the large double bed.

I climb over Chris and curl up between them, exhausted. Unfortunately, both my bed-partners have omitted to mention that they snore. Within minutes, he's making a noise like a creaking door, and Tricksy's doing a fairly good impersonation of a whinnying horse. I stare up into the darkness. So this is life on the circuit.

I would like to be able to say that we woke before dawn, and enjoyed an erotic threesome, but it wouldn't be true. Well, not entirely. Chris did roll over at one point and put his tongue in my ear . . . completely by mistake, as he later explained. He had felt a female body beside him and thought, befuddled by sleep, that it was Tricksy. If he hadn't subsequently reached out to discover a pot-belly instead of something resembling an ironing-board, I might have rounded off my tournament in style. Pity, that.

9

'You're moving where?'

'Spain,' my mother says, more than a little nervous. She gestures down the table. 'Pass the butter, Jemmy darling.'

Jemima passes the butter dish, her eyes shiny. She looks as if she's going to burst into tears. 'But that's thousands of miles away, Gran.'

'It's only an hour or so on the plane. No time at all.'

I stare at my mother. 'So this is why you invited us round. What's Dad said about it?'

'It's none of his business now. I've kicked him out for good.' My mother taps a minuscule amount of butter on to her jacket potato. She doesn't meet my eyes. 'I have to be so careful what I eat. Do you know how many units of fat there are in that little bit of butter? Hundreds. Literally hundreds.'

'You've kicked Dad out? Where is he now?'

'With Sharon, I expect. She's got a flat. He's not on the streets, if that's what you're worried about.'

'Dad can take care of himself. I just wondered . . . this

is very sudden, Mum. Are you sure? I mean, why *Spain*, for God's sake?'

My mother bends her head, examining her salad minutely. 'Goodness, I think that's greenfly. What, dear? Why Spain? Er . . . an old friend of mine's lived there before. We're getting a nice little villa together.'

'What's his name?'

She catches my sharp tone and looks up. 'Now listen here, miss. I can do what I want, when I want, and with whomever I want. I'm a free agent now. You and the others are all grown-up. You don't need me around.' She helps herself to a larger knob of butter, spreading it on her potato defensively. 'Gordon's a very nice man. He'll take good care of me.'

'When are you leaving?'

'In a few months. After Easter, I think.'

'And what about the kids?' I hiss, looking at Jemmy and Tom, who are both listening to this conversation, pale and uncertain.

'They can come and visit. Would you like that? A holiday in Spain every few months?' She smiles as they nod shakily. 'There's a pool with a water-slide, and a garden, and the beach is only a few miles away. You'll love it, I promise.' She looks at me defensively. 'It's all settled, anyway. You can't stop me.'

'Good God, what makes you think I'd try?'

She shrugs. Her lip trembles slightly. 'It is a big step. I'll be leaving all my friends behind. But Gordon . . .' She pauses, looking at me guiltily. 'Gordon already knows lots of people out there. People our age. After what happened with your father, I just want to . . . start again.'

I get up and give her a tight hug. 'Don't be silly, Mum. I'm pleased for you, honestly. It was just a shock at first.' I look at her. She's still got that uncertain expression on her face. That's what my mother's like. Bites your head off and then ruins the effect by apologising afterwards. I try to lighten the atmosphere with a weak joke. 'I mean, Spain's a bit drastic, isn't it? Most people your age move to Bognor Regis.'

She manages a smile then. 'I hate Bognor.'

'I know you do. Remember that time Dad took us?'

We both laugh, and talk about my childhood holidays for a while. But although I know it's probably the right thing for her to do, and I actually envy her a little, throwing off convention at her age and moving to Spain with her new man, I'm also secretly rather worried. With families, you get into habits very easily. Sunday lunch, Christmas Day, having the relatives over at Easter, even knowing you can pick up the phone at any time and find a babysitter in an emergency. All that's going to change. If I need someone to look after the kids, I'm going to be thrown back on Adrian again. I can't ask Dad to have the kids. He wouldn't have the first clue how to handle them, and I don't fancy Sharon getting her maulers on them. I can hardly keep asking the other mothers to mind them while I'm away at a tournament. And although I could probably stretch to a few days of cheap childminding, I hate the idea of a stranger looking after Jemmy and Tom. It goes against the grain. And you hear such horror stories about unregistered childminders.

'Zoë? What's wrong?'

I smile at her, shaking my head. 'Nothing, Mum. It sounds marvellous. All that sun, sea and sand. I'm jealous, that's all.'

But what I'm really thinking is, how the hell am I going to manage once she's gone? It's strange, isn't it? You get to your late twenties and you think you're a grown-up. In fact, you advertise the fact by doing all those things you've always imagined grown-ups do . . . getting pissed and stoned, getting a job, settling down, having kids, looking round for a post-children career – and some young mothers like myself even manage to find one – then you find yourself suddenly deprived of your mother, and you realise that it's all been a sham, that you're not grown-up at all, you're not even close to being grown-up. You still rely on her, not for pocket-money or washing your clothes like you did when you were younger and still living at home, but just to be there for you. To be alive. To exist somewhere, so that at any time you can phone her up or turn up on the doorstep, and be reassured that you don't ever have to be really grown-up, so long as she's there to be older and more grown-up than you. It's a comforting thought.

But once Mum's gone, I won't have that buffer zone between myself and full grown-up status any more. Then I'll have to be the responsible one. The one who's always there for Jemmy and Tom. To be their buffer zone.

And snooker will have to disappear from my life for ever.

I get a phone call from Kevin on Friday. I'm just scooping clothes out of the washing-machine when the phone rings. I answer it awkwardly, juggling an armful of damp knickers. Kevin has a knack for choosing the worst possible moments to ring, and never pays any attention to a 'Can I call you back?' plea.

Today, he doesn't waste any time getting down to business. 'When's your next tournament, Zoë?'

'In a fortnight. If my mother will still have the kids, that is. She's busy making arrangements to move out to Spain.'

'Spain?' Long pause while Kevin digests this information. 'Well . . . I think I'll come with you, if that's okay?'

I don't know what to say. Kevin's never offered to come with me to a tournament before. It feels strange, almost unsettling. I rearrange the armful of underwear now creating a damp stain on the left side of my T-shirt, so that the right side gets wet as well. 'Why?'

'Because I'm your coach, and it's about time I acted the part.' He hesitates, then coughs awkwardly. 'Separate rooms, of course.'

'Of course.'

I don't know if it's my hormones, or the gentle note in his voice, or even because I've just soaked my clean

T-shirt, but after I've put the phone down, I start crying. I sit there on the kitchen floor, surrounded by a pile of damp socks and knickers, and cry as though my heart is breaking. Which it probably is, at this moment. Kevin doesn't realise it, but his sudden gesture of solidarity is the last straw.

I've been steeling myself for days now, ever since my mother told me she was going to Spain for good, preparing myself for the fact that I will have to give up playing snooker. I'd just managed to convince myself that I enjoy being a single parent, that washing underwear and tidying up toys are the everyday joys I live for. But as soon as I heard Kevin's voice on the phone just now, I knew it was a lie. Snooker is what makes me come alive, what makes my world bearable, and without snooker, a light will go out in my life which, once extinguished, could never be rekindled by anything else.

'This is Kevin. My coach.'

The girls nod. Someone passes the raffle book and money-box. 'Got a quid for a raffle ticket, Kevin? There's a Cheddar Classic leather cue case up for grabs. It's really smart.'

Kevin digs dutifully into his pocket for some change.

Tricksy nudges me in the ribs. 'Coach?' When I nod, trying to look cool, she raises her eyebrows. 'Don't forget us when you're rich and famous, will you?'

'No one gets rich and famous in the women's game.'

'Nit-picker.'

'Prat.'

'Sticks and stones . . .'

Katie Number One interrupts this slagging match. 'Hey, look! A new player. I've never seen her before.'

We all glance across the bar. Fresh blood. It's always worth sizing up a new player as soon as she walks into the club. If you don't check her out, it's odds on you'll draw her in the first round, and waste half the match doing the checking-out you should have done when she arrived.

'Bloody hell. It's Joe 90.'

We all giggle. The unfortunate girl is wearing huge up-turned glasses, reminiscent of the ones Dennis Taylor wears, but on her they look ridiculous. She even walks in that robotic way, glancing jerkily from side to side as she heads into the bar area where we're all sitting, waiting for the draw.

'Very sensible glasses.' I can tell from Kevin's tone that he disapproves of our little bitching session. He may know more than I do about snooker, but he's got a lot to learn about women. 'Much better than normal frames. You can't see the ball properly otherwise.'

In the ensuing embarrassed silence, I light a cigarette. I've noticed I smoke more at snooker tournaments than at home. At the average tournament, I go through almost thirty cigarettes, although it's true that other players always seem to be delving into my packet too. At home, I rarely smoke more than ten a day, although I never used to smoke at all before I started playing. I've decided it's because the atmosphere here is so tense that

I need something to keep my hands from tearing my hair out. 'Anyone heard from Bo?'

Tricksy shakes her head. 'Probably still recovering. God, who'd want to give birth? Ugh.'

'It's not that bad,' I say mildly. 'Besides, you soon forget about the pain.'

'I wouldn't. It must be like Japanese water torture.'

'Talking of water torture.' Katie Number Two leans forward in her chair. 'There's a karaoke tonight. After the quarter-finals have finished. I think they're trying to encourage people to stay who don't get through to tomorrow's matches.'

'Sounds fun!'

I laugh at Tricksy's sudden enthusiasm. 'Can you sing?'

'Sure . . .' She demonstrates, tipping her head back as she dismally wails a few lines from 'Stand By Your Man'. 'I love the old Country and Western stuff.'

Kevin winces. This conversation is obviously going from bad to worse for him. He perches on the side of my chair, looking around the bar. I've never seen him so nervous. He's even wearing a clean shirt today, one that I've never seen before. He probably bought it specially. New or not, he looks decidedly uncomfortable in it. Maybe he already regrets coming to this tournament. After all, as a man, he's outnumbered by quite a sizeable margin. Okay, there are referees here, but even some of them are women now. I know I'm grinning, but I can't help it. No profession is safe.

'Can I get you a coffee or something?'

He nods at me gratefully. 'Strong. Black, no sugar.'

Sylvie's at the bar, ordering herself a suitably bland-looking cup of tea. Even in flat shoes – black leather pumps, standard tournament wear – she towers over me. I'd sort of forgotten how tall she is. You know, you think 'God, that person's tall' when you meet them the first couple of times, and then as you get used to seeing them, you just think 'oh, there's so-and-so' and you forget, or more correctly, adjust to the fact that they're incredibly tall. But today I notice again. Maybe it's because I'm feeling fairly depressed about my future in snooker, and being depressed always makes me feel shorter than I am. Or maybe I really am that short, but I only realise this when I'm feeling down. Whatever the explanation, today I feel short and Sylvie looks tall. This observation depresses me even more.

'Hi,' Sylvie says cautiously, stirring her tea. She doesn't look at me properly, which is puzzling, since I thought we'd parted on reasonable terms at the last tournament. Then I remember Dani and Lou and Sara, and wonder whether she's embarrassed because of that scene in the restaurant. After all, Sylvie probably doesn't make a habit of inviting someone for a meal, and then have her other friends start a fight so that everyone gets thrown out on the street. Although, as I recall, I accused her of something along those lines at the time.

'Hi.'

She hesitates, obviously trying to think of something suitably light to say. Something that won't remind either of us of the past. 'How are your kids?'

I didn't even know she knew I had kids. 'Fine, thanks. They're with my mum this weekend.'

'Doesn't she mind having them?'

'I think it takes her mind off my dad, actually. They've just split up.'

She looks shocked. 'I'm sorry.'

'Don't be. It's been on the cards for years . . . ever since they married, in fact.' I feel surprised after I've said this, suddenly realising that it's true. I'd never thought of it like that before, but my mum and dad aren't suited to each other. Why they got married in the first place is beyond me. Probably for the same reason that Adrian and I started a family when we were so young; sheer blind stupidity, though some people call that love. 'To be honest, I think my mum's glad to be free of him at last.'

'Well . . . that's a good thing, I suppose.' Sylvie looks almost embarrassed, as if she didn't expect me to be so blunt about my parents' relationship in front of her. She picks up her tea. 'Well, I'd better . . .' She gives me a little smile, leaves her excuse hanging in the air, and disappears down the other end of the bar.

Her friends have left a space at their table for her, and I can see Dani getting up to move her cue so that Sylvie can squeeze through. Somebody must have just said something very funny, because they all start laughing within seconds of Sylvie's arrival. She glances back over her shoulder at me, still looking vaguely embarrassed. Let's face it. Sylvie has her corner and I have mine, and never the twain shall meet, because when they do, people get punched, wine gets spilt, and brief acquaintances threaten you with a bottle in the face. That's to be expected though, when you hang round with people who scratch a living from the snooker circuit.

The game responds to mood as the tide responds to the moon. With astonishing accuracy. I often wonder whether this is the prime difference between male and female snooker players. Men are notoriously such insensitive bastards. Women are far more subject to mood swings: you argue with your best friend, your goldfish dies, you're having your period, the room's too hot, too cold, too noisy, someone laughs at your new outfit etc. It is those women players most capable of controlling their reactions to external stimuli who rise to the top of the game.

It should come as no surprise then that some of those players become insensitised over time, almost masculine in their reactions. This is the sports equivalent of the woman politician, taking voice classes to deepen and broaden her range, to avoid projecting the higher pitch of the female, with its connotations of hysteria and, by association, unreliability.

I struggle against my own personality in the same way. But I'm on to a loser here. I was born to burst into tears at the end of a weepy movie. It's a knee-jerk reaction. Totally uncontrollable. Pretending otherwise is gradually eroding my true sense of self. Other women, intended by nature to be ball-breakers, succeed far more easily in this. And good luck to them. Women deserve some breaks in snooker (pun intended). We've got the game. We've got the ambition. All we require now is the emotional constitution of a steel vault.

I'm reminded of this fact when I get to my familiar glass ceiling, the last-sixteen stage, and again it refuses to break. I'm playing Dani, whose petite figure and charming heart-shaped face hide the intense focus and determination of a snooker-playing Joan of Arc. The last time I saw her, she was smack bang in the middle of a shrieking cat-fight, with Sara yanking at her hair, and Lou leaping to her defence. Today, at the table, she is cool and courteous. There is a flicker of something unidentifiable in her eyes as she shakes my hand before breaking off. But once the game is underway, I could be playing a complete stranger.

I admire this ability to shut off the outside world. There's also something hilarious about it, some mischievous impulse in my nature that wants to remind Dani of our last meeting, but I have too much respect for her handling of the situation. She is totally in character here, entirely the professional snooker player. Who am I to break the concentration of an artist at work?

I am out-classed. Dani, vampire in girl's clothing, sucks the reds from the table as though her cue were a vacuum cleaner. I sit back in my chair, lean my cue gently against my inner thigh, and admire her style. Her cue action is not perfect. But it works. You can see the hand of a good coach in her approach to the table: step into the shot, square to the ball on, one, two, three feathers at the white, long pull-back (almost heart-stoppingly too long), then a swift but controlled punch straight through and beyond the white. Lovely finishing position. Still motionless, down on the shot, waiting until the ball drops.

Afterwards, shaking my hand, Dani meets my eyes for the first time. 'Good game, Zoë.'

As I walk back into the bar area, I'm still reeling from this breach of unspoken top-player/crap-player rules. Dani took my hand and called me Zoë. Okay, it's standard practice to shake the loser's hand and say 'good game', but there is absolutely no necessity for the loser's name to be tagged on to the end. That almost constitutes an act of friendship. Or, at the very least, an act of recognition.

I'm not sure whether to be shocked or elated. What does this indicate? That I 'belong'? No, that would be impossible. I could never in a million years 'belong'. I'm just not made of the same stuff as them. I'm not talking about talent here. I'm not even talking about performance on the table, or how many ranking points a player has. 'Belonging' is something only permitted to an élite group of players, all of whom are similar people, with similar goals, ambitions, ideas about the game. To that world, I will always be an outsider.

Back in the beginning, when snooker was still virgin territory to me and anything was possible, I saw that élite group in action, and I burnt inwardly to be one of them. But now, older, wiser, and slightly shell-shocked from what the game has thrown at me, I can see that I no longer want to be a part of their world. There's something infinitely false about those players. Possibly (my God, am I about to commit an act of heresy?), there is even something false about competitive snooker itself. To play for any reason other than a deep and abiding love for the game is false. Once you get to that level, once you are admitted to that magic circle, everything revolves around ranking points, revenge, who played whom and in what position you will finish the season. That isn't what drew me to the game. I started to play because I was in love, and I still play because I am in love. When I fall out of love, that will be the time to hang up my cue and disappear back into the shadows.

Talking of love, I have no idea why karaoke is so bloody popular. You get up, sing badly and off-key to a song which you realise half-way through you actually hate and can't imagine why you've chosen it anyway, people laugh at you, the microphone emphasises your inability to breathe properly by amplifying every gulp of air snatched between lines until you sound like a fly-past by the Red Arrows, and you usually have to share this battered mike with someone even less talented than yourself, who bears such a striking resemblance to Mrs Worthington's daughter in the eponymous Noël Coward song 'Don't put your daughter on the stage, Mrs Worthington', that you almost recommend it to them. It's at times like these that you appreciate exactly why you will never fulfil that childhood dream of being a pop star.

'That was great!' Tricksy runs her finger down the list of songs. She has to shout to make herself heard over the noise in the bar. Most of the players have turned up for the karaoke: the ones who lost today are getting steadily pissed, knowing there's only the Plate competition to play tomorrow, and the ones still in the main tournament are conspicuous by their ability to walk straight. 'Let's do "Summer Loving". You can do the high bits.'

'Give it a rest, will you?'

She looks at me, surprised. 'What's wrong?'

'Dunno. Just feeling pissed off.'

'You due on?'

If only it were that simple. Periods. Perennial excuse of the depressed, the angry, the overweight, the underweight, and the generally fucked-up woman. I wish Kevin was here, to take my mind off things, but he's gone back to the hotel for an early night. I shake my head, getting up. 'I hate this. My head's splitting. Let's go outside for a minute . . . get away from all this noise.'

Outside the club, it's cool and relatively quiet. The car park is full, but there's no one about. Tricksy walks down past a few rows of parked cars, looks around furtively, then pulls something out of her coat pocket. 'Fancy some of this?'

It's a joint. I've seen a few in my time, even smoked one or two when I was younger. This one is decidedly sorry for itself, wrinkled, slightly bent in the middle, the roach almost hanging out. I raise my eyebrows. 'Where the hell did you get that?'

'My brother. It was a Christmas present.'

'Tricksy, it's nearly March.'

She shrugs defensively. 'So? I saved it. Thought it might come in handy.'

Oh, what the hell. Anything's better than sitting in the club, listening to hits of the sixties, seventies and eighties that deserve no better fate than to be relegated to a second-rate karaoke list. Smoking cannabis may just take the edge off what I'm feeling, this bewildering awareness of my ambivalence towards the game, and the appalling sense of loss that such awareness entails. 'Here, borrow my lighter.'

It's only later, leaning on the dirty bonnet of a Citroën, that I stop laughing and sober up rather abruptly. 'Tricksy . . . We're both playing in the Plate competition tomorrow, aren't we?'

'Of course we are.'

I look down at the smouldering dog-end on the ground. 'Random drug testing. Does that ring a bell?'

'Random *what*?'

'You know, they pick a name out of the hat, hand you a specimen bottle, you trot off to the loo . . . sound familiar?'

'Oh shit.'

'Exactly.'

We both stare down at the roach, now fully extinguished.

'We'd have to be very unlucky if . . .'

'Tricksy, are you a lucky person? Am I?'

She fingers her 'lucky' blouse thoughtfully, then

peers at me through slightly unfocused eyes. Her nervous giggle confirms my suspicions. 'Maybe not.'

'How long does this stuff stay in the bloodstream?'

'Dunno.'

Great. Perfect. This is just what I need right now. Being banned from the world circuit for taking drugs. I wouldn't mind if it was for game-orientated purposes, by which I mean smoking it so that I could be more relaxed at the table, play better, rise up through the rankings by circumventing the terrors of the game, but no. I'm just smoking it because I'm an arsehole. Pure and simple.

I look up at the sky. It's dark. I can see tiny flickering points of light which I assume to be stars, never a safe assumption in these days of multiple orbiting satellites, but the moon is up there too, reassuringly large and unmistakable, half-veiled now by a thin wreath of cloud. I close my eyes fiercely. Please, God, if you exist, don't make it *my* name that's drawn out of the hat tomorrow. I couldn't stand the humiliation of summary expulsion from the circuit. Not for this.

When I open my eyes again, the moon is no longer obscured. It glows above me, a huge luminous disc of light, like a giant white ball on the snooker table of the heavens. Keeping my fingers crossed, I strike it dead centre with my heart, hoping for a clean contact. It rolls across the sky and sinks a black hole into the top left-hand pocket. Seven points. That must be why they call it pot.

We never were called upon to provide urine. The odds were against it from the start, I suppose, but guilt plays on the nerves until the uncovering of your crime seems not only possible, but downright inevitable. This is what happened to King Claudius in *Hamlet*, which may be stretching an analogy rather further than it will go, but at the time I certainly felt as though I had murdered my brother and married his wife, at least in terms of sickening guilt. Okay, maybe not guilt, but fear of discovery and punishment. It was lucky for me that Kevin never found out about our little misdemeanour in the car park. He might have refused to coach me any more. But I learnt a valuable lesson about the pros and cons of smoking prohibited substances that night. In future, I shall stick religiously to tobacco or, failing that, dried banana leaves.

At the moment, though, avoiding the temptation of illegal drugs is the least of my problems. Absorbed in my snooker career, focusing on the table and nothing else, I have forgotten that life still goes on around me, and that, however much I try to hold it back, the outside world is about to come crashing in on me.

My mother has fixed a date for moving to Spain. She's going over at the end of April now. That only leaves one more tournament before I'm left without my chief babysitter. Mrs Bottomley seemed less than impressed with Jemmy last time she had the kids, saying something about her 'wetting the bed', which I suppose is a fair enough complaint. Jemmy rarely wets the bed at home, but I suspect it had some connection with her dislike for Mrs Bottomley's eldest son. He used to sneak into the bedroom while she was undressing and take Polaroid pictures. I was all ready to go round there, up in arms about this behaviour, when I discovered that Mrs Bottomley had already confiscated the camera on scene, and sent eleven-year-old Paul scampering back to his own room with severely boxed ears. Meanwhile, Adrian's moved his new girlfriend into his flat, and the last thing he wants is the kids hanging round while he's trying to impress her with his lifestyle, or whatever it is men do when new girlfriends move in.

Let's face it. This next tournament could be my last. Things have been going steadily downhill since the World Championships. I look ahead, and all I can see is a long dark tunnel with nothing at the end but a dreary slipping back into housewife mode. It looks like my heydays on the world circuit will soon be over. It's my own fault. If I hadn't had kids, maybe even if Adrian and I hadn't split up . . . a thousand reasons why I could have done this better, planned out my life more competently. But I didn't. Now here I am, stuck with a single-parent lifestyle I never wanted, aching to be something I never shall be. It's ironic, really. I've been mentally slagging the game off for months, but now that I face losing it, I'm filled with confusion. Only when something's about to be taken away from you, do you really start to appreciate how important it is in your life.

As far as an exit bow is concerned, this last tournament is not exactly the high point of my snooker career. It's the old old story again. I hit the last sixteen, and *bam*, I'm out.

I hang around the bar for a bit, not wanting to face Tricksy yet. I know she will enjoy hearing that I lost. She isn't comfortable with the fact that I'm now ranked twenty-five places above her, and relishes every opportunity to take the piss. 'I'm surprised you want to be seen talking to me,' she murmurs at every new improvement in my world ranking. 'You're practically a seed now.'

In between matches, Sylvie seems to live at the bar. I bump into her, literally, just as she's turning round with a full cup of tea in her hand. 'Shit, I'm sorry,' I hastily apologise. Fuck it, I'm so clumsy. I grab a cloth from behind the bar and wipe up the spilt tea on the floor. 'I didn't see you there.'

'Evidently. Not playing?'

'I'm out.'

Sylvie raises her eyebrows. 'I thought you were

playing quite well before. I caught some of your match on my way through to the toilets.'

'Appearances can be deceptive. I scraped the first frame, lost the second on the black, and she took me to the cleaners in the third. After that, I couldn't seem to pot a ball.'

'It happens.' She orders another tea. Her voice is husky. 'You know, there's still some unfinished business between us, Zoë.'

I suspect I know what's coming. Three guesses and two don't count. This has got to be about Matt.

She confirms my suspicions. 'I was very angry about Matt. But I've been doing a lot of thinking since Geneva. I know it wasn't your fault, Zoë. I think Matt only did it to wind me up.'

I'm stung by the suggestion that I could have looked like the rear-end of a horse and Matt still would have slept with me, but at least she's not foaming at the mouth and swinging a length of lead-piping. Not that behaviour like that would be entirely in character if she did, but sometimes men can have a funny effect on women. I hoist myself up on to the leather-topped bar stool and order myself a coffee. 'It certainly looked that way at the time.'

'Did he tell you that's why he did it?'

She sounds surprised. 'As good as,' I say, manipulating the truth a touch. If Sylvie wants to think he only fucked me because of her, then where's the harm in that? Personally, I'd like to think mutual attraction came into it somewhere, even if only on a very basic 'I've got to fuck *somebody*' level. Sylvie looks at me, her eyebrows raised as if my slight hesitation has been suspicious. I fumble for a diversion, feeling my cheeks turn red. I've always been incapable of direct face-to-face lying without giving the game away with some sort of tell-tale sign. 'We were both very drunk. I'm sorry, Sylvie.'

There. I've apologised for shagging her husband.

'It's not important.' Sylvie leans back on to a bar stool, able to put both feet on the ground, unlike me. The only way I can touch the ground is by sliding forward slightly and stretching my toes out in a ridiculously uncomfortable posture, so I haven't bothered and am perched on top of the stool like a gnome without its fishing rod. 'I don't know why I reacted like that, anyway. It was totally illogical. We split up months beforehand. He doesn't belong to me.'

'Well . . . theoretically.'

She shakes her head firmly. 'No. I've got to make my mind up about Matt. It's no use pretending I don't still . . . love him.' She makes a face. The husky Finnish accent intensifies. For a moment, her voice reminds me of the mad Muppet chef, juggling his chickens in the air, but I suspect that this is not a good time to make a joke about it. Besides, I seem to remember that the Muppet chef was Swedish, so maybe it's not an entirely appropriate analogy. 'See? I can hardly bring myself to admit it. I know Matt. He can be very persuasive with women. I don't blame you at all.'

'You looked pretty angry at the time.'

Ooops. Perhaps I shouldn't have reminded her of that. Her eyes flash. 'Of course I was angry about it. What do you expect? I thought you were my friend.'

Friend? This is news to me. Actually, I thought Sylvie was trying her bloody hardest to avoid becoming a friend. I'm suddenly irritated. I'm a reasonable person, or so I like to think, but putting me in the same category as her cronies is just not on. 'I'm not your friend, Sylvie. Tracey's your friend. Dani's your friend. That blonde girl, Lou, she's your friend. You don't "hang out" with me on the circuit. That's what friends do. We're not friends.'

'Tracey and Dani and Lou are just people I know. They aren't friends, not really. If we . . . what was it you said? . . . "hang out" together during tournaments, well, it's because we've known each other for ages and we're all at about the same level.'

'That's an exact description of "friends".'

'No, you don't understand.' Sylvie sighs. 'Friends you make on the circuit are like friends other people make in the office. You see them when you're working. You don't necessarily want to invite them round to your house, or on holiday, or to see a film. That's what you do with your other friends. The ones who don't play snooker.'

It's a fair point. I struggle to disagree though, aware that I'm being obstinate and bone-headed about this, but arguing for the sake of arguing, an irritating trait of mine that anyone who has ever known me has commented on at least once. 'Okay, but the point is, you said you thought I was your friend. And I said that Tracey, Dani and Lou were you "friends". And I suppose that I didn't want to be put in the same category as them because . . .' I pause, but not long enough to stop myself saying it. 'Because they're arse-lickers.'

There. She asked for that. She pushed me to say it. Her friends lick arse, there's absolutely no question about it. Sylvie's a great player. They all know she could be World Champion one day. They're not interested in Sylvie, only in what she stands for. Watching them jostle for position, to be the first one she turns to after a match, it's enough to make me puke. In fact, they're so far up her arse, they could brown-nose for Britain.

Sylvie knows that expression. Her cup of tea pauses on its way to her mouth. After a few minutes of stunned silence, she recovers enough composure to put it down. 'What gives you the right to say something like that about my friends?'

'But you said they weren't your friends,' I point out, logically. 'You said . . .'

'I know what I said.'

'Well, then.'

She shakes her head. 'You're unbelievable.'

'Why? Because I'm honest?'

'Because you're so bloody rude.'

'Fair enough, but it doesn't make it any the less true.'

Sylvie exhales sharply. 'You remind me of Matt.'

I'm confused. And possibly insulted. 'Why?'

'He never liked any of my friends either.'

Maybe I was wrong about Matt being a stupid, misogynistic bastard. He may actually turn out to be an *observant*, misogynistic bastard, but I'm not prepared to allow my argument here to be simplified down to a man's point of view. 'Men never like their wives' friends. It's a question of hierarchy. They don't see why a woman should need any emotional sustenance other than that already on offer from them.'

'You really don't like men, do you?'

'Of course I do. I've just never met one worth knowing.' That's not true, actually. I like Kevin, and I like my father. I like the guy in the High Street record shop, although that's mainly because he never laughs at the albums I buy. I even like Adrian, in a sneaking still-remember-the-good-times sort of way. But that's not the point. The point is that I don't want my brilliant analysis of Sylvie's current relationship with her friends on the snooker circuit to be squeezed down to something which will fit into her recollection of Matt's emotionally insecure, knee-jerk reactions. 'Look, I'm not being funny. Your friends are brown-nosers *extraordinaire*.'

'But why? Because they talk to me? Hang round with me? That's rather insulting, really. Isn't it possible that they could genuinely like me?'

I may be mistaken, but I think I've offended her. She thinks I'm saying that no one in their right minds would hang around with her, unless there was an ulterior motive. Social climbing, in this case. Why do people always get the wrong end of the stick when I'm trying to explain something? Similarly disastrous conversations of the past loom large in my memory. Hastily, I attempt to retrieve the situation. 'Of course it's possible. That wasn't what I meant . . .'

'I know what you meant. And I think you're jealous of my friends. I think you're jealous because they're better players than you, and always will be. And if my friends *are* arse-lickers . . . well, it takes one to know one.'

I wasn't mistaken. Sylvie is definitely offended.

'Lost again?' Tricksy asks idly, playing cards with Katie Number One and a new girl she's taken under her wing, Faith. It's a good name for a snooker player. Unfortunately, I'm running out of it myself. Fast.

'Yep. I think I'm going to head home soon.'

Tricksy stops playing and looks up at me, surprised. 'Already? But it's only eight o'clock. Aren't you going to stay for the karaoke? They're running a competition this time. Best impersonation of a pop star, living or dead.'

This I can do without. 'That decides it. I'm off.'

'Spoilsport.'

'Piss off. Karaoke's strictly for sad people.'

She shrugs defensively. 'So I'm sad. Who cares? It's still good fun.' She puts her cards face-down on the table, carefully avoiding a pool of spilt lager, and gives me her version of an old-fashioned look. 'You're just pissed off because you lost. Why don't you admit it,

Zoë? You're no better than any of the rest of us. If you can't come to terms with that, you're going to drive yourself crazy.'

Great. Amateur psychologist Tricksy strikes again. Earlier she was telling me that she hits the white badly because it reminds her of her grandfather's bald head, so she doesn't have the nerve to give it a good smack. I'm still stinging from Sylvie's analysis of my snooker ability. 'Save it for the new players, will you?' I gesture towards Faith, who's listening to this exchange with every evidence of fascination. 'She may believe your psycho-babble nonsense, Tricksy, but I don't.'

She makes a face. 'Oh, go home then. I'll see you at the next tournament.'

'I doubt it.'

'Why? What's wrong? Not money problems again, is it?' At last I have her genuine, undivided attention.

'Not this time. It's the kids.'

Faith stares. 'You've got kids?' she breathes, rapt.

Oh, for the innocence of the young. 'Yes, two of them. And no one to look after them for the foreseeable future.' I shrug at Tricksy's expression. 'My mum's kicked my dad out and she's off to Spain soon. With her new boyfriend. And Adrian's got someone new . . . he's not going to be exactly over the moon if I dump two kids on his doorstep several times a month.'

'They're his kids too.'

'Well . . . *technically*, yes,' I mutter, looking away. She doesn't understand the situation. I like Adrian. He's still a pain, but I like him. He's been dragging himself round like a dog with a sore leg for months, but now he actually smiles when he comes over to see the kids. Jemmy's stopped referring to him as 'Dreary Dad', and Tom sprints down the garden path to meet him, instead of lagging behind his sister like he used to. Since he met Ms Right, Adrian's almost a new man, if you'll pardon the expression. And I don't want anything to interfere with that transformation.

'So you won't be coming to the next tournament?'

'It looks unlikely.'

Faith shakes her head. 'That's awful. And you're such a good player, too.'

I look at her, unable to resist that warm glow of received praise spreading through me. Okay, she's just a kid, but hell, she could be right. I wish Sylvie could hear this. A promising career is being blighted by maternal responsibilities. It's a bloody tragedy. Not quite of *Romeo and Juliet* proportions, admittedly, but a tragedy none the less. In an instant, I see myself hanging by the neck from an exposed beam. Flicking the lid on a bottle of Valium and swallowing the lot. Driving into a brick wall at speed. Hold on . . . what would be the point of suicide? If you're giving up snooker for the sake of your kids' mental and emotional welfare, killing yourself wouldn't exactly fulfil that brief, would it?

Tricksy is nodding. 'Maybe I could look after the kids one time while you go to a tournament?'

Wonderful logic. 'And then you wouldn't be able to play either.'

'Good point. Okay. Well . . .' She looks uncertain. 'Give me a ring sometime.'

And that's it. No tearful farewells. No waving hankies from the club doorway. No promises to write. Just 'give me a ring sometime', which, roughly translated, means 'I'm sorry you can't play any more, but frankly, I've got problems of my own to worry about'. Friends, eh? Suddenly, and with great bitterness, I remember what Sylvie said to me about the difference between friends in snooker and friends in 'real life'. This life, playing tournaments every month, watching your ranking points grow and fluctuate with each match, it's more of a snooker circus than a snooker circuit. You're only accepted by the others while you're a performer. Once you've fallen off that dizzying high-wire, you might as well not exist any more, because snooker is life, life is snooker, and anyone outside that definition is simply one of the audience.

I get to the M1, and the car starts coughing. I nurse it gently down towards the M25, but by the outskirts of St Albans, it's smoking more than I do at tournaments. I pull off the motorway and start looking for a garage, but I know I can't really afford to have the car mended or towed or whatever it's going to take to get me home tonight. It's nearly eleven o'clock at night and I'm getting rather nervous about the prospect of being stranded at this time of night, when the engine conks out.

I try to restart it, but nothing happens.

I get out, walk round the car, and give it a few kicks

for good measure. The metalwork groans slightly, but there's no sign of life from under the bonnet.

I want to sit down, there in the damp grass by the roadside, and have a good cry. But I know I can't. The road isn't particularly well-lit, and several lorry drivers have already slowed down, leaning over to the passenger side to shout 'Need a hand, love?' through the window. I wave them on, smiling, but I know it may only be a matter of time before someone stops who won't take my polite 'no thank you' for an answer.

I scrabble about in my handbag, looking for change for the telephone. Perhaps I can get a garage to pick me and the car up, even though I don't have any cash or credit cards on me. They might take a cheque without a guarantee card, you never know. I could always do my helpless female act. That usually fools them.

I know I saw a pub a mile or so back down the road. The lights were still on when I passed it. I can probably get there in about fifteen minutes, even in these soft-soled pumps. It's been raining and the verge is soaked, but at least it's only a fine drizzle now. My hair is already wet from standing over the open bonnet, but that's the least of my worries at the moment. I lock my cue in the boot before setting off. There's no way I'm going to risk losing that. And I haven't even got a proper coat with me, only my tournament jacket which is flimsy and unlined, so I know I'm going to freeze. But it's better than waiting for Jack the Ripper to pull up and offer me a ride.

I get stared at in the pub, which isn't surprising really.

I'm wearing black dress trousers, a maître-d'-style white shirt (I've sensibly *removed* the pink bow-tie and cummerbund), and I probably look like an escapee from a nearby restaurant. When I walk into the lounge bar, half of them look round in anticipation as if they expect me to come over and offer them a choice of hors d'oeuvre.

I stand in the corner by the bar, trying to look inconspicuous, and rifle through the Yellow Pages for a local garage. Not for the first time, I realise what a prat I've been for letting my AA membership lapse. I could have been home by now. Well, practically.

'Sorry, love. Not without a credit card.'

'But I've broken down. I'm on my own.'

'And where are you going to? Oh no . . . that's out of our area.'

The second garage number I try is endlessly engaged, and the third is no longer recognised. I put the phone down in despair. Then it occurs to me that I could ring someone I know in this area, and offer to give them money later if they'll come out now and tow me home, or at least to a railway station before the trains stop running. But I'm about thirty miles from home. I don't know anyone in this area. Except . . .

From the bottom of my handbag, I produce a card with a phone number on it. Creased, slightly bent, but still legible. I check the address with a feeling of acute embarrassment. No, it's not more than five miles from here. I don't see what other choice I have.

He answers after only three rings.

'Matt? It's Zoë. I'm in a spot of trouble.'

'Better?'

I nod, looking up at Matt from under the fluffy blue towel. My hair's nearly dry now. The shower was hot and invigorating, and although I'm still rather embarrassed about my bare-faced cheek in asking him to rescue me, Matt's being far more understanding about the situation than I expected. Perhaps I've been overly harsh on him. After all, he was very upset over Sylvie when we parted in Geneva. Losing your wife would be enough to make most men inclined to lash out verbally at the nearest person. 'It's a very powerful shower.'

'That's the way I like them. Wakes you up.'

I smile. I'd forgotten how good-looking Matt is.

It's somewhere round this point that I realise I want to have sex with him again, even at the risk of a) appearing pathetically stupid for wanting to sleep with someone so obviously of the common *totus bastardus* species, b) teetering on the verge of promiscuity and c) revealing myself as a complete bitch for sleeping with Sylvie's ex for the second time (I'm not sure of the sexual 'ethics' here – if they're separated, but not divorced, or even undergoing divorce proceedings as far as I'm aware, is Matt fair game or am I still poaching?). Whatever. Something inside me is saying 'Don't do it,' but I've got my fingers in my ears and I'm yelling 'I can't hear you! I can't hear you!' to that little voice – metaphorically speaking, of course. If I did that literally, Matt would probably think I was going mad, and lock himself in the airing-cupboard, assuming he has one in this luxurious but undeniably *small* flat.

He hands me a steaming cup of coffee. 'It's home-ground.'

I'm in one of those coffee adverts, aren't I? It had to happen one day, I suppose. Real life emulating art, instead of art emulating real life. If television advertisements can be said to come under the heading of art, that is. It's a moot point. 'Thanks,' I say, then hesitate, sensing it's my line but not seeing the auto-cue anywhere. I improvise. 'Mmmm. That's lovely.'

Okay. The obligatory coffee has been served. Now what? Matt hasn't yet suggested a cab company that does long-distance trips, and the fact that he's slipped his shoes off probably indicates that he's not planning on driving me home tonight. My car is tucked up tight outside, still attached to his Saab by a length of old rope. So, does this mean I'm staying the night?

'I'd better phone my mum. Let her know what's happened.'

He leaves the room discreetly while I make the call. My mum's worried, of course, and irritated that she'll have the kids overnight, but I tell her I'm at a friend's house and will get the car towed back first thing in the morning, which mollifies her a little. Mothers never quite believe that their kids can look after themselves, do they? Even when you're grown-up with kids of your own, you still get the feeling they'd like to check behind your ears or investigate the contents of your fridge, just in case you're not washing or eating properly. Fathers are much more *laissez-faire* about the whole 'cutting the apron strings' process. My mother's not exactly Attila the Hen in these situations, but she goes through the motions anyway, as if she feels her maternal instincts may be called into question otherwise.

Matt comes back into the room just as I'm putting the phone down. 'Everything okay?'

'Yeah, but she wants me back as soon as possible.' This is me testing the waters. If he says 'I'll run you back now', I'll know where I stand. But if he says nothing, well, I still may not know where I stand, but at least I've given him the option of turfing me out.

He nods. 'There's a garage number on the fridge door. They're good . . . I use them myself. They can probably arrange to tow you back home.' He sits down next to me on the sofa – well, I'm calling it a sofa, but it's one of these low Japanese futon-style jobs – and puts his arm along the back in a meaningful fashion. 'In the morning, of course.'

'Of course.'

'I have to leave for work at around seven. But you're welcome to sleep in . . . have some breakfast before you leave. There's some stuff in the fridge, I think.'

'That's great. Thanks.'

I'm playing it cool, because that's how it's done. I'm not about to be out-done in the sophistication stakes. It's a tall order though. Matt's highly sophisticated. In his bathroom, I noticed he had a state of the art open-and-close liquid soap container fixed to the shower wall. No soap on a rope for him. And although I scoured the bathroom for evidence of tampons, Mum underarm deodorants, disposable razors and all the other paraphernalia that women bring into a man's bathroom, I couldn't find anything to make me suspect he was seeing anyone. I even looked in the cupboard under the sink, running the tap loudly in case he heard me rummaging about. *Rien. Nada.* Zip. As far as other women are concerned, Matt looks as clean as his bathroom shelves.

'There's no more coffee in the percolator, I'm afraid,' he murmurs, glancing at my empty cup on the glass-topped coffee table. Don't you hate people with glass-topped coffee tables? It's a sure indication of a childless inhabitant. Tom would put his model train through that in five minutes. 'But maybe you'd prefer something more substantial?'

I'm just about to say 'No thank you, I'm not hungry', when he leans over and I realise belatedly what he meant. Smooth bastard. We kiss for about ten minutes – an improvement on the previous occasion, when foreplay ran a very poor second to time spent on actual intercourse – then he takes my hand and leads me through into the bedroom.

Matt sits on the edge of the bed and starts undoing the buttons on his shirt. He undoes them one by one, slowly and deliberately, keeping his eyes on my face the whole time. I'd forgotten how muscular his chest is. The little dark wiry hairs curl down the centre of his chest. I want to tug my fingers round them and pull. He drags his shirt free of the waistband of his black jeans, and starts sliding it down over his shoulders. I'm not sure what comes over me, maybe I'm too horny or too impatient for his 'I'm a cool stud' persona, but I lean forward, drag the shirt off backwards and kiss him passionately. It's all lips and tongue and teeth for a few breathless seconds, then Matt pulls back. 'Hey, slow down!'

'I thought you wanted this?'

He blinks. 'Of course I do. But at my own pace.'

'Well, I can't wait any longer for Mr Tortoise to poke that sexy little head out of his shell.' I unzip his jeans in one smooth movement. My mouth is watering. 'Come on, Matt. We both know this is why you asked me to stay the night.'

I pin him down to the bed with my knees. Throwing off the flannel bathrobe he lent me, noticing with relief that I haven't ruined the gesture by getting tangled in the belt, I lean forward and brush my breasts along his rough chest. He stares up at me, speechless. But I can feel his penis getting hard under my bottom. I wriggle slightly. 'Ever been tied to the bed?'

Matt's eyes widen. He shakes his head.

I raise my eyebrows, glancing sideways at the long white belt of the flannel robe, now lying across the bed like the world's longest strand of cooked spaghetti. My voice drops to a husky whisper. I hope Matt thinks it's sexy and not that I'm starting a cold. 'Well, there's a first time for everything.'

Matt pushes me away suddenly and struggles off the bed, landing on the floor with a painful thud. He jerks to his feet, his hair sticking up comically where I was running my hands through it. Seeing my hungry stare,

Matt glances down at his wide-open jeans, then grabs the white duvet and wraps himself in it protectively like an Eskimo. 'You're sick.' He looks me up and down, his face dark red. 'Look at yourself! Didn't your mother ever tell you the *man* is meant to be in charge in bed? You didn't act like this last time, you . . . you pervert!'

'Matt, where's your sense of fun?'

He stares at me, wide-eyed, from inside the white cowl of the duvet. Suddenly, he reminds me of E.T., and I can't help laughing. His face hardens. 'I'm sleeping on the sofa. And don't get any ideas about coming through in the middle of the night.' Matt stalks off to the living room. 'I don't go in for pushy women.'

When I wake up, Matt's gone. There's a note for me on the coffee table. 'Garage number on fridge. Tea in left-hand cupboard. Let yourself out.' Wryly, I wrap myself in his flannel robe again and stumble through to the kitchen. I put the kettle on, ring the garage and arrange for someone to come out and tow my car home, relieved to hear that this garage *will* accept cheques without a guarantee card so long as they have an address to pin you down to, then start rummaging through the cupboards for some breakfast cereal. I don't usually eat before midday, but today I feel like having a binge. I eat one large bowl of Kelloggs' Frosties, and am just helping myself to a second one, when I hear someone unlocking the door to the flat.

I freeze, cereal box in hand. Someone is coming quietly down the hallway to the kitchen.

The door is pushed open, and a glamorous young woman stands in the doorway, staring at me. The suitcase in her hand drops to the floor with a dull thud. 'Who the fuck are you?'

Absolutely bloody marvellous. Thanks, Matt. I think you forgot to mention you had a girlfriend. Still, these things happen. The poor sod was probably so busy anticipating shagging my brains out that it slipped his mind. I'm slightly surprised though that her name didn't come up in the 'tieing-to-the-bed' department, as an example of nice girls who *don't* take the initiative in bed. Surreptitiously, I put the half-empty packet of Frosties back on the table, hoping she hasn't noticed them. Why did it have to be Frosties? Couldn't it have been Alpen, for God's sake, or All-Bran, or even something sort of nineties-trendy like Cornflakes? Being caught with a bowl of Frosties destroys all hope of cool in these situations. 'I'm a friend of Matt's.'

No, she's not biting. This is not going to wash. I'm going to end up with a meat-cleaver in my head. The most unfair thing here is that I won't even have deserved one. The closest I got to Matt after last night's fiasco was when I stumbled past him at about four in the morning, heading for the loo.

She's one of these strawberry-blondes who deliberately choose lipstick to clash with their hair. Under the unbuttoned hip-length black jacket, she's wearing a short tight skirt and a ribbed green tank-top which emphasises her large chest, helped by the fact that she's clearly not wearing a bra underneath it. Okay, I'm being mean. She's curvy in a pert sort of way . . . not plump, or sagging slightly in the middle, which is more my department, but all the same definitely not slim . . . just sort of, well, *curvy*. I reckon she's somewhere in her very early twenties, so still firm-looking skin, but another ten years and gravity will be taking its toll. This knowledge softens my bitchiness into humour. I gesture at the Frosties. 'Want some?'

Her mouth is trembling. 'He said . . . he said, it was the last time.'

'The last time?'

She's holding on to it, just. Her huge green eyes, which I would personally kill to possess, fill up with tears but she's not going to cry. Her chin is jutting out, shaking but determined. 'Other women. He promised.'

Oh shit. I'm in the middle of a domestic. It's worse than I thought. I'm not the first Matt's brought home, and judging by the suitcase, she thought he'd changed for the better. The pattern comes clear on the loom. And she's only a kid. 'What a bastard.' I pull out another chair. 'Come on. Sit down. You look like you could do with a coffee, er . . . sorry . . . what's your name?'

One tear rolls silently down her cheek. But she still doesn't move, looking at me stiffly. There's something disturbingly familiar about that proud gaze. 'I'm Kristin.'

11

There's always someone worse off than you. I'm at home, cleaning my cue for what will probably be the last time, when I remember Kristin's face as she realised I knew Sylvie. There was hope in her face for a second, bright blinding hope, quickly eclipsed by despair and the memory of what she's done, which must lie between those two sisters like a drawn sword, waiting for one to use it against the other. But I wasn't wrong about what I saw. Kristin wanted to patch things up with Sylvie.

'It's obvious Matt's a bastard, isn't it?' she said bitterly over a cup of his specially home-ground coffee. I didn't like to tell her whose hands had done the grinding. She might have choked. 'It's only me who hasn't seen that from the beginning. Sylvie must hate me.'

I ought to have reassured her on that point, even if I had no evidence to support me, but something along the lines of hell having no fury like a woman scorned tugged at my memory. I didn't particularly want to be responsible for Kristin turning up on Sylvie's doorstep, expecting to be forgiven, and being admitted to the Casualty department with a kitchen knife stuck in her back.

I have to hand it to Matt. He knows how to cause trouble, big-time. Marry one sister, bang the other, then simply move on to new pastures, leaving them to sort out the mess. And all this time, Sylvie's been playing world-class snooker as though her private life's running as smoothly as Richard Branson's Virgin empire. No wonder she flunked the World Championships when Matt showed up . . . in my hotel bedroom, of all places.

Still, I think Matt genuinely cares, or cared then, about Sylvie, in his own inimitable way. He certainly wasn't happy to let her go. She was probably the best thing that had ever happened to him. Maybe that's why he slept with Kristin. Because he felt angry and inadequate next to Sylvie, talented rising star of the snooker world. Okay, it may not mean much to people outside snooker, but he only had to turn up at a few tournaments to see how she's idolised by her band of followers, and to be on the receiving end of some of her arrogant behaviour, to suspect that he was a nobody in comparison. To someone like Matt, that must have hurt. And he certainly got his revenge in the end. Shagging her sister in their own bed was a brilliant parting shot.

Poor Kristin. She may have betrayed her sister's trust, but I'm not sure she deserves the punishment of being trapped in an emotional no-man's-land. Because she's caught in the middle here. Sylvie doesn't want to know her. Matt clearly doesn't want to keep her. Kristin told me he'd been sleeping around for months, right under her nose, and whenever they rowed about it, he would start packing for her and only stop when she started crying. Matt must have been wondering what he had to do to get rid of her. Even when Kristin eventually left, she came creeping back within a week, only to find *me* sitting at the kitchen table. If I hadn't been there, she would probably have stayed. That would have been true poetic justice for Matt. Getting stuck with the wrong sister for ever.

'Would you ask Sylvie if she'll see me?' Kristin asked at last. 'I'm too scared to approach her myself.'

Déjà vu. I recalled someone else saying that, and the disastrous events that followed. 'I don't know when I'll be playing snooker again. Never, probably.'

'You couldn't ring her?'

Stupidly, I agreed, and she scribbled Sylvie's number on a piece of Matt's note-paper for me. But I haven't even looked at the number yet, let alone lifted the phone. I don't know where I stand with Sylvie at the moment, or what her reaction will be if I start acting as go-between for her and Kristin.

I lay my cue carefully in its case, *lovingly* even, and put the lid back on the bottle of linseed oil. Just that one tiny drop should be enough to keep the wood from drying out over at least the next six months, prevent it from cracking at any extremes of temperature it might be exposed to.

The fact that my cue is highly unlikely to be exposed to any extremes of temperature whilst stuck in an aluminium case at the back of my built-in wardrobe is not something I consider relevant to this situation. It *might* get cold in there. The boiler might break, and the pipes freeze over in winter, and icicles might form in my wardrobe. It's a very remote possibility, but a possibility is still a possibility, you will concede. Alternatively, we may get an Indian summer this year. The ozone layer is disintegrating. The temperature in this wardrobe could easily reach the nineties. You hear of that happening all the time . . . ninety in the shade, they predict cheerfully on the weather forecast. Well, a wardrobe is undoubtedly 'in the shade', so why not? It's conceivable. Just.

At this point, I'm sort of going through the motions, staying calm about my enforced retirement from snooker. After all, it's not really enforced. I could carry on playing after my mother goes to Spain. I could ignore the letters from the bank. I could turn to prostitution to cover the bills. I could allow my children to be taken into care because no one's looking after them. These are all feasible options. Actually, I'm just whining about not being able to play snooker because I'm a lazy cow with no interest in finding a way round this, who doesn't really give a stuff about the game and who just wants to paint her toenails on the sofa in front of *Home and Away*.

Okay. You get the picture. If I want to keep my life within the bounds of common decency, then snooker is no longer a possibility for me. Maybe decency is the wrong word. It's more akin to a sense of responsibility towards my kids than anything else. Whatever. To be honest, I'm disgusted with myself. What crap timing. I hate myself for suddenly discovering a maternal streak that I need about as much as I need a hole in the head. All I know, or care about at the moment, is that I've just packed my cue away and I don't know if I will ever get to use it again.

'Chin up, Jemmy. Be brave. You'll see Gran again soon.'

She clings on to my mother, not making a sound, but her shoulders are shaking uncontrollably. It's been hardest on Jemima, because she understands rather better than Tom does what 'moving to Spain' entails and what it means in the long-term. No more flying visits from Gran with toys or chocolates or new videos. No more Sunday lunches where they get to drink as much pop as they like and play in Gran's garden afterwards. Possibly no more big family Christmases where even Grandpa shows a reluctant face, and intriguingly wrapped presents are distributed like water. Worst of all, no more Gran.

'I'm not dying,' my mother points out, disentangling herself with difficulty from Jemmy's weed-like arms. She laughs nervously, pinching Jemima gently under her chin. 'I'm just moving house. It's not the end of the world.'

'Yes, it is . . .' Jemmy says tearfully, adds something

too incoherent to follow, then sinks back on to the airport seat, burying her face in her hands.

My mother ruffles the top of Tom's head. 'You'd better learn to swim properly, little man. Otherwise you won't be able to use the pool when you visit.'

'I can swim,' he protests.

'Of course you can. With armbands.' She looks at me over his head. 'Make sure he can swim alone before bringing him over. I don't want any tragedies.'

Gordon has come back from the Tie Shop. He puts his arm round my mother. He's younger than her, in his late forties, but he's tanned from his frequent visits to Spain, and very muscular for his age. My mother knows a good thing when she sees it. 'Ready, love?'

'Please don't call me "love",' she hisses at him, then smiles at us, holding out her hands for a last group hug. 'Right. No more time left. Kiss me goodbye.'

It's only at this point that I realise what's happening. I mean realise properly and with full understanding. Before today, it was just 'Oh, Mum's going to Spain with her new boyfriend'. It was never something I took seriously, apart from the obvious ramifications for my snooker career, and now here she is, leaving. And there's no more time. What if she has a heart attack on the plane? What if she slips on the pool edge and drowns? Other possibilities, each more horrific than the last, flash swiftly through my mind, and each one leaves behind the indelible message: *I might never see her again.*

'Zoë! You're nearly breaking my ribs.'

'Sorry, Mum.' I'm in tears. She's staring at me. 'Sorry.'

Gordon reaches out and squeezes my shoulder. His smile is obviously meant to be reassuring. 'Don't worry. I'll take good care of your mum.' He looks down at her and a little smile passes between them. It's one of those excluding smiles that I've seen on the faces of other couples, but which I never expected to see my own mother using in front of me. It says, 'We're together and they'll never understand what that means to us.' I feel an illogical stab of jealousy. Gordon's a nice enough man, but he's taking my mother away from me and my children, taking her as far away as Spain. I've never even been to Spain. What does he have to gain by taking her away from her family? Does she have a Swiss bank account that I don't know of? Maybe a huge life insurance policy that he could benefit from? His smile suddenly seems sinister. 'She'll be safe with me.'

She had better be, buster. I give Gordon a fierce look, to which he responds, quite reasonably, with mild surprise. I'm then forced to give myself a swift reality check. This isn't a rerun of *Eldorado*. Gordon's simply in love with my mother, and is kindly taking her to a place where she can swim, sunbathe and drink Pina Coladas well into her twilight years. I'm being ridiculous. 'Of course. And we'll come and visit as soon as I can afford it.'

'I'm sure we can work something out about that.'

My mother puts her hand on his chest. It's a possessive gesture. In fact, I could almost suspect it's aimed more at the wallet in his breast pocket than anywhere else. 'We'd better go, darling. We'll miss the plane.'

In the airport café, Jemmy sits by the window for the next hour and waves every British Airways plane off, convinced each time that it's one bound for Spain. 'I can see Granny! I'm sure I can.' Her hand drops slowly. 'I think it was her, anyway.'

'Come away, sweetheart. They're long gone now.'

She turns away from the window. Her face is haggard, her blue eyes red-rimmed and swollen. 'She isn't coming back, is she?'

I shake my head. 'No, sweetheart.' God damn it. Now I'm crying too. People are staring at us. I pull a surprised Tom towards me and squeeze him tight, just wanting to feel them both. I hold out my hand to Jemima and she takes it, leaning against me silently. 'Granny isn't coming back.'

Eventually, Jemmy lifts her head and dries her wet face on her sleeve. For God's sake. A new dress, too. How many times have I told her not to do that? But before I can remind her of the handkerchief in her pocket, Jemmy straightens and looks up at me. 'We're all going to have to be brave now, aren't we?'

No money for practice, no babysitter, not even a coach at the moment, since Kevin's so pissed off with my decision to quit the game. I can see his point of view. He's put a lot of time and effort into me, not to mention the money I've borrowed on loan perpetual, and now I must seem like the worst sort of time-waster. Someone with talent but no commitment.

That couldn't be further from the truth if it was on Mars. I love the game. I worship the game. Nothing else has the power to stop me in my tracks the way snooker does, literally as well as figuratively.

Passing an electrical showroom yesterday, I found myself fixed to a window display as Stephen Hendry compiled a devastating break in one of the televised tournaments. Passers-by must have thought I was mad, standing in the middle of the pavement, clutching my plastic carrier bags with whitened knuckles, completely unaware of how I must look until some exasperated woman tapped me on the shoulder and asked if I would let her get past with her double buggy. I shook myself as though waking from a dream. For Kevin to think I couldn't care less about the game is a gross misjudgment of my character and motives.

So when Kevin rings me again, he hardly lets me get a word in edgeways. 'You're too good to stop playing now. It's ridiculous. I know you think you're doing it for your kids, and that's commendable, but you're not doing them any favours. Without snooker, you'll be bloody miserable to live with.'

'Kevin, I've told you . . .'

'You can still practise while the kids are at school. I could come to tournaments with you, help look after them . . .'

'Listen to me for a minute. Once I'm out of the loop, I stay out of the loop. You can't give up your spare time to look after the kids. And I'm not fiddling about with an hour here, an hour there, playing the odd tournament whenever I can afford the child-care. You know as well as anyone, once you stop playing full-time, your game goes downhill. Even if I played part-time, I'd never get my form back. I'd certainly never achieve anything near a top-ranking position.'

'So you're just giving up?'

'It's over.'

'Sod you then,' Kevin says after a brief silence, and puts the phone down. He doesn't slam it down. He doesn't snarl or raise his voice. And that's the worst thing. There's quiet despair in his voice, and disillusionment, but not anger.

I don't blame him. It must look to Kevin as though I don't give a toss, hiding my cue away, refusing to even try. But he doesn't understand. Snooker isn't a pastime for me. It's all or nothing. It's patently clear that I can't have it all, so nothing is the only other option I can choose with honour. It's like suicide among the Japanese. There are some circumstances where it seems the only dignified way out. Well, that's what I'm doing. I'm choosing snooker suicide. The ceremonial putting away of my cue was an essential part of that. And once you're dead, you stay dead. You don't come back for one more episode, or to save the day, as those retired spies in John Le Carré novels do. There's no such thing as a miraculous resurrection in this game.

It's sort of bizarre not having my mother around. Not

that she was ever really 'around', but you know what I mean by 'around'. I mean being on the other end of a phone. Being in the same postal district. Being there, not as in the strange Peter Sellers film of the same name, but as in being available when I need to query the exact birthday of a distant relative or if I want to know how long I should defrost a chicken or what the recipe is for lemon soufflé. Okay, I never actually cook exotic stuff like lemon soufflé and the number of distant relatives I'm still in touch with could be counted on the fingers of one hand, but I do occasionally defrost chicken. It's also fair to point out here that she *is* still on the other end of a phone . . . they have phones in Spain too, believe it or not . . . but it's just not the same. 'Hi Mum, when's Great-Uncle Edwin's birthday again? Yes, I know it's costing me an arm and a leg, but while you're there, any tips on exciting new ways with paella?' Doesn't sound right, does it?

When I do ring her, the conversation does not go exactly as planned. 'I've given up snooker. It's just too difficult, trying to cope . . .'

'Well, thank goodness you've come to your senses.' My mother has her sensible hat on today. 'You'll be much happier this way. Believe me. You were getting quite grumpy, always losing. If you'd been any good, you would have won more matches. I don't know why you didn't give up months ago.'

'Because I love the game.'

'Oh, rubbish. You're just bored. Do you know what you need, Zoë?' She pauses, but I can't bring myself to make even sarcastic noises. I know what she's going to say. Mothers are the most predictable breed alive. 'You need evening classes.'

'Flower-arranging?'

She hesitates, deadly serious. 'Well, actually, I think your talents might lie more in the wok area of things. Chinese cookery. I've seen you do wonderful things with a stir-fry. And the best way to a man's heart is through his stomach. Are you still seeing that Kevin person?'

'I was never "seeing" him, Mum. Kevin is . . . was . . . my snooker coach.' I frown. 'I thought you didn't want me to get involved with anyone else for a while?'

'It's different now. I'm not around to listen to your complaints when it all goes wrong.'

Thanks, Mum. Cheer me up, why don't you? 'Well, don't worry, I'm not seeing anyone.'

'You should. That snooker thing was making you . . . a bit strange, to be honest. What you need is a man.'

'I thought I needed a wok.'

'Please don't be facetious, Zoë. Cookery is a serious subject.'

It's only now that I realise what pathetically limited conversations I've always had with my mother. I mean, we never discussed my break-up with Adrian, or my vague and fairly pointless yearning to be World Champion, or even what she must have been going through when she split with Dad, although we skirted the issue. However, we did manage to cover frozen chickens. I never saw her in the light of a confidante. My mother represented babysitting more than friendship, and it's only now that she's gone that I feel any sense of shame about that, thinking of all the opportunities we missed to develop our relationship beyond the freezer level.

Okay, there's always the phone. I can try to reforge my relationship with her, gradually, by long-distance phone calls. But it feels too late. She's got Gordon and I've got my kids. We must each live in the holes we dig for ourselves. If mine's deeper than hers, that's down to my over-enthusiasm with the shovel, not due to her inability to show me how to use one.

I ring Sylvie as I promised Kristin I would. Her reception to the idea of seeing Kristin again is not exactly warm. 'Why on earth would I want to speak to that bitch? She slept with my husband.'

'Kristin's really sorry. She realises now what a bastard Matt is.'

Sylvie seems unconvinced. Then the question I've been dreading raises its ugly head. She sounds suspicious. 'But I don't understand where you met Kristin . . . or how you can possibly know each other.'

'We . . . er . . . that is, I . . .'

'Have you been seeing Matt again?'

'Sort of.'

'Well, either you have or you haven't.'

'Okay, I have, but only by accident.'

'And where does Kristin come into all this?' Sylvie

hesitates. Her voice is harsh. 'Is that bitch living with him?'

'Yes. No. Well, not any more.'

Long silence. 'Christ, I've been a complete fool, haven't I?'

'No, not at all. Matt's taken both of you for a ride. He's very convincing, you said it yourself.'

I can't persuade her to see Kristin again, but she does take her new phone number. I'm not entirely certain why I'm doing this for Kristin, but I suppose there was something in her eyes that morning that made me feel sorry for the poor cow. She's only a kid, after all. 'Well, you've got her number now. Just in case you change your mind.'

'I won't.'

'She's your sister, Sylvie.'

'Not as far as I'm concerned.'

Afterwards, it occurs to me that Sylvie and I aren't really that different. I can't have a full-time snooker career, so I shut the game out of my life for good. Sylvie can't see her sister in the same light as before, so she shuts her out of her life. Maybe we're both being ridiculous. Possibly even pig-headed. But there's something grimly satisfying about being an extremist, and at the moment, it's all I've got.

All you need is someone to accidentally pick at the surface of your life, and the whole thing peels off, leaving no protective buffer zone in between you and those furry brown hats bag-ladies wear. Talking to Sylvie, current hot-shot of the ladies' circuit, reminds me that I'm going nowhere fast.

Of course, when I was playing snooker, none of this shit really mattered. I had a goal, an ambition, even a potential destiny. Now what do I have to look forward to? How can you work seriously towards an ambition like 'I will now only take three minutes to mop the kitchen floor' or 'By next year, I will have mastered the art of getting a duvet into a duvet cover without actually having to climb inside the bloody thing'? The limitations of these ambitions are undeniable, and other women in the same position would probably take courses towards a post-children career, and they'd be right to do so, but the only talent I've ever had, all right, sod it, the only thing I've ever *wanted* to do is play snooker.

I'm panicking. I can feel it. I see the rest of my life flash before my eyes and it's not a full-length feature film, it's a sound-bite commercial for boredom. What happens to people when you take their dreams away? Okay, in this case, I have allowed it to happen, or, more accurately, executed the final *coup de grâce* myself. But there is a bitterness involved, as if someone had forced my hand, which, I suppose, they have. To a certain extent. People survive though, don't they? People can survive anything. The man in the iron mask clung on for years in his prison, locked in surely the most terrible struggle of all: the battle to remember, and affirm, if only to himself, his own identity.

So when I wake up this morning and ask: who am I?

it's not entirely a rhetorical question. I feel as though I have been walking on stilts for the past few years, elevated above reality, in an atmosphere so thin I needed to change my lungs in order to breathe it. Re-design them, so they could cope at that higher altitude. And now, stilts suddenly knocked from under me, I'm struggling to breathe this thicker air, choking like an inner-city cyclist on the exhaust fumes of reality. Adjustments have to be made, a peculiarly unpleasant re-tuning process that leaves me with the knowledge that I will never again . . . Christ, that's a hard word, *never* . . . feel the way I did at the table. Never live fully again. Because that's what snooker was, in the final analysis. Not just an extension of myself, easily removed and packed away, as I've done with my cue, but something that *grew* me, like a plant or a tree being given oxygen, light, water. I feel smothered without it. Cut off from life. Disorientated. I became someone else when I was playing. Someone new. Different. Possibly even unique. And now, I can no longer be that person, and yet, I *am* still her.

In the beginning, the snooker world felt alien to me. I wasn't prepared for how it works on people, how it changes them. But I wanted to belong, I *needed* to belong, so I let those changes happen. Even welcomed them, not knowing that one day I would have to discard that persona and gradually reclaim my former identity, however unwilling I might be to do so. Even the way I speak has to change now. Snooker is a hierarchical society, like any other, and it has its own language, designed to distinguish outsiders from insiders. I learnt that language. I know its mysteries, its unspoken rules. I am an adept now. You don't 'beat' someone. You *get through*. You don't 'play well'. You are *on form*. You don't 'clip' a ball. You *kiss* it. Most bizarrely of all, there is one language for the bar and one for the table. This dichotomy derives, on the one hand, from the particular social class in which club snooker has its roots, and, on the other, from the urgent, media-driven need for the game to drag itself away from that image. In bar-time anecdotes, you never simply won a game. You *cleared the fucking table*. You don't just drink. You get *absolutely rat-arsed*. And you don't make love any more. You *shag*. But at the table, you keep your mouth and your game clean.

Now, back in the grim light of day, I have to unlearn everything. I tell my neighbour I got *absolutely rat-arsed* last night, and she stares primly, then shuts the door in my face. I knock a pile of tins over in the supermarket, swear roundly, and the woman next to me drags her young child out of earshot, later shooting me a filthy look three aisles down. I tell myself this is unacceptable language in these situations, in this society, and I do understand *why*, I appreciate the differences, but there's a sickness inside me at the same time, an inability to decide which is the better approach to language: honest club-level crudity or this starchy, tight-lipped world outside, where white may well be black, or even red, but we would never say so, except, of course, within the safety zone of our own four walls, where words are containable, can't whisper their vile way under the door and out into the street, for others to hear and judge us by.

You'd think it would be easy, going back to something once so familiar, but it's not. You can't do the things I've done, live that different life, and then expect to slide back into a lifestyle you no longer desire or even recognise. No one could do it. I was unprepared for change in the first place, and now, second-time round, I'm still clinging on to the remnants of a world I'd only just started to feel comfortable in.

So here I am. Scouring the newspapers for any reports of women's snooker. Watching televised matches, it doesn't matter who's playing, just the sight of the baize is enough to satisfy my longing for an hour or two. Armchair snooker, they call it. Is this how low I've sunk? I despise myself. It's eating me up from the inside out. Passing the club every other day and looking at the number-plates of cars parked outside, working out who's in, and wondering what they're doing, how well they're playing, whether life goes on without me, as cold logic tells me it does. No one is indispensable. Least of all me.

This sickness. This desire to play. It's like having a great black shadow at my back, a creature hunched over my shoulders, which I can never shake loose. And when I look round, desperate to release myself, I can see it has my face. That creature is me.

12

I've never been so busy. How the hell this place didn't fall apart while I was playing snooker is beyond me. Everywhere I turn, something needs mending or cleaning or replacing. It's a madhouse. But I'm going to sort it all out. I've got a list drawn up of minor repairs that need doing, and I've set aside a week each for the bigger jobs. I bought a new mop yesterday, because the old one was fit for nothing but the bin, and the difference is incredible. The kitchen floor is immaculate. I'm serious, you could eat your dinner off it. Even Adrian commented when he came round to see the kids. 'I can see my face in that lino.' It was a fantastic moment. Well, you had to be there.

I'm at home, I'm wearing heavy-duty pink rubber gloves, it's about twelve-thirty, and outside the sun is shining. It's coming through the kitchen window in one huge block of light. On the outside, the cooker is gleaming. But inside, well, you don't want to know what it's like inside. I can hardly bring myself to admit it. I'm ashamed. There's twenty-four months or more of grease, grime, and bits of blackened food like little lumps of charcoal littering the bottom, clogging up the electric element. When I turn it on, the smell is awful and it smokes. Frankly, I'm surprised the neighbours haven't complained.

It needs a complete overhaul. I've bought and assembled Brillo-pads, a tin of that special cleaning foam for cookers, scrubbing pads, cloths, a plastic spatula for particularly stubborn bits, and a bucketful of warm soapy water for the base of the grill and the sides of the cooker, which I haven't dealt with yet either. This isn't the sort of thing you can just throw yourself into. That's how mistakes get made, essentials get missed. So I'm gearing myself up for it, walking up and down past the cooker, up and down, pacing myself, staring at the open door and the blackened mess inside.

The doorbell rings. I hesitate. It can't be anyone important. It might be the electricity meter man. I don't have any friends who 'pop over', so it isn't likely to be anyone who's going to be upset if I don't answer the door. The cooker is more important. Time's ticking on. The water in the bucket will be turning cold. My day's already half-gone. Before I know it, the kids will need picking up from school.

It rings again, twice. It's an insistent kind of ring, the sort that tells you whoever it is knows you're in there, and they're not giving up until you've opened the door.

It's Kevin. He stares at my rubber gloves. 'Have I come at a bad time?'

'Yes.'

'Can I come in?'

'No.'

'Thanks.' He shoulders past me.

I eye his raincoat. It's still stained. 'Is that machine washable?'

'I haven't the faintest idea.'

'Come here.' I check his label. 'Take it off. I'll give it a quick spin, since you're here and you're obviously not going to leave until you've said whatever it is you've come to say . . .' As he opens his mouth, I shake my head, stripping off the rubber gloves with what I hope passes for venom. 'And I know what that is, and the answer's still no.'

'You're a stubborn woman.'

'I'm a realist.'

'That's what I mean.' He watches me poke the raincoat into the washing-machine and slam the door on it. 'There's nothing wrong with dreaming, Zoë. Dreams are important.'

'So are cookers.'

He glances down at the pile of assorted cleaning implements at his feet. 'You're serious about this house-wife and mother thing, aren't you?'

'I'm not married. Never was.'

'Same difference.'

'Not entirely. What's your point?'

'Have you ever seen that film, *Dead Poets Society*?'

This is too much. 'Oh, please!'

'Have you?' Kevin persists. When I nod wearily, he

makes a sudden sharp gesture of despair. '*Carpe diem*? And you still don't get it? That there's more to life than . . .' He looks at the cooker as I kick the door shut, embarrassed by the blackened interior. 'Do you think I care whether you've cleaned your cooker? Do you think anyone cares? Do you really believe that's important?'

'Keeping a cooker in good running order isn't important, is that what you're telling me?'

'Of course it is, but Zoë, just listen to yourself. This isn't the Zoë I remember, the woman who said "Fuck the lot of them" when they tried to stop you playing, when the babysitters and the money ran out, even back when you were losing every bloody first-round match you played. What's happened to you?'

'I got real.'

'You got stupid.'

'Is it stupid to give up when there's no hope left? I'd call that intelligent, actually. Logical.'

'What's logical about this?' He kicks the cooker.

'Hey! That's my cooker. Do you mind?'

'Yes. Yes. I mind very much. I've put too much time and energy . . . yes, and money . . . into you to stand back and watch you . . .'

'Go on, say it.'

He looks at me. 'Flush your life down the toilet.'

'Oh, I see. Is that what I'm doing?'

'That's what it looks like to me.'

'And did it never occur to you that I might be

happy doing this? That I might actually enjoy being a "normal" person again?'

'No, frankly.'

I stare at him. The conversation, all right, *argument*, has been cheerfully rocketing along so far, but I've just hit an unexpected brick wall. I open my mouth and nothing comes out. No sharp retort. No self-justifying comment to set Kevin straight. No explanation that will prove to him, beyond a shadow of a doubt, that I *am* happy, thank you very much, that snooker was a mistake, a blip, a wrong turning I took years ago and have only just managed to correct. Because he's right. The bastard's right.

'Well?' Kevin's expecting a comeback from me, and I don't have one. He's watching my face for a reaction. 'Am I close?'

'Go away. I'll post the raincoat.'

'Don't be ridiculous.'

'Why not? I feel like being ridiculous. Go away.'

'No. I refuse.'

I pick up my packet of cigarettes and light one, although I know I'm meant to be giving up. I can feel his eyes on my face. 'Okay. If you won't leave, I will.'

'You can't leave, this is your house.'

'There aren't any rules here, Kevin. I can leave if I want.'

He shrugs. 'Okay. Go on then.'

'I didn't say *when* I was going, did I? Give me a minute, I'm smoking this cigarette.'

Kevin reaches over, takes the cigarette away from

me and stubs it out in the ashtray. He shakes his head. 'Don't do this, Zoë.'

'I'm giving up.'

He almost laughs. 'I meant the game, not smoking.'

'I know what you meant.'

He leans back against the washing-machine, watching me. I start to feel nervous, which is stupid, because this is only Kevin, and I have no reason to feel nervous about Kevin, well, not nervous in the way some women might get nervous about having a man alone in their house with them, not like that, because, after all, this is *Kevin*, but I can't get the nervousness out of my head, and it's getting worse, which may have something to do with the fact that I can't explain why I'm nervous in the first place.

Then, just when I'm starting to feel panicky about my inability to guess why I'm nervous, Kevin opens his mouth, and I suddenly realise I'm nervous because he's asking all the questions I want to ask *myself*, but daren't. 'What's all this in aid of, Zoë? Have you got some crazy idea in your head about not being a fit mother if you don't do ... *this* ... to yourself?' He looks down at the bucket of soapy water with acute dislike. 'So your mum's gone to Spain. So what? Does that give you *carte blanche* to sink back into your kitchen and play out this sad charade for the outside world, because you're ... what, guilty? Terrified?'

I stare at him, speechless.

'I know the game's scary. It scares the shit out of me, Zoë, but that's not a good enough excuse to just give up and walk away. Christ, you love this game!'

'Define love.'

He points to his stomach jerkily. 'It's in here. In your guts.'

'There's nothing in my guts but last night's supper.'

He shakes his head. 'I'm wasting my time, aren't I?'

'And mine. Do you know how long it takes to clean an oven?'

'Get your cue. Let's go for a game.'

'Kevin, I'm not interested in playing snooker.'

'Bollocks.'

I'm shocked. Kevin never swears. Well, not anything worse than 'bloody', although admittedly he managed a 'sod you' last time we spoke, which was bordering on the epic. In this relationship, I've always been the one who swears. I stare at him. Hearing Kevin swear is like seeing your goldfish stand up and whistle an aria. 'I think you'd better go.'

'Fine. Okay. Get back to your oven. I hope you'll both be very happy together.'

When he's gone, I launch myself into the bowels of the cooker with a Brillo-pad, and scrub the blackened walls until my nails are hanging off and my skin's sore. Then I remember the rubber gloves, still lying limply on the kitchen surface. Fuck-a-doodle-do. It's all Kevin's fault. Even from beyond the grave, snooker is still reaching out to strangle my attempts at domesticity.

★ ★ ★

I cruise by the club on Tuesday afternoon. I don't mean to, but somehow I just find myself there, slowing to a crawl outside the car park, engine coughing as I ease the gearbox down into second. Kevin's car is not there. Hardly surprising. He rarely went to the club unless I was there. By the look of it, there aren't many people in at all.

As though in a trance, I find myself pulling into the snooker club car park. I'm getting out of the car. I suddenly remember putting my cue into the boot of the car this morning, telling myself I should take it to a sports shop, try and flog it to someone second-hand. But of course it's all nonsense. I have no intention of selling my cue, and never did have. I put my cue in the car so that I could play this afternoon. I deliberately drove the long way round to the supermarket, so that I could pass the club and think hey, why not stop in for a quick knock?

I'm so transparent.

Half an hour, I promise myself. Half an hour. No more, no less. Just a quick sweep of the table, a few magic passes of the cue, and I'm out of here.

But as soon as I walk in through those blue double doors, the atmosphere hits me like a freight train. My knees weaken. My eyes blur. I have selective hearing, tunnel vision. The table is all I see. The click of the balls is all I hear. The lights dazzle me. The acrid smell of the chalk is once again under my fingertips and in my mouth. I can almost taste the game on my tongue. Up close, the lure of the baize is intolerable. It shimmers under the hanging lamps like a green lagoon. I am powerless to resist.

Bet's cleaning the optics behind the bar. I ask her to flick the light on over table three. I can see Bob sitting in the bar behind a raised newspaper, apparently oblivious to my presence. There are a few lads playing the fruit machines, but I don't know them. It's strange. Only a couple of months ago, I thought I knew everyone in this club. But once you move out of circulation, things change. People drift away and newcomers take their place. It's a fluid world, the club scene. You can't afford to be gone too long or you quickly lose your place in that society.

Then I start hitting balls. For the sheer hell of it. A sense of peace descends. Gradually, my mind clears like a wiped-down slate. While I am here, caught in the grip of the game like a carved piece in the hands of a great chess-master, nothing else matters. There is nothing else. There is only this. Removing all questions, dissolving all boundaries, bringing no purpose beyond this present, is the greatest gift snooker can bestow on its players. This isn't a match, where player must struggle against player to win the game's favour. Solo practice is an act of sheer worship. Ball contacts ball. White contacts cushion. Fingers press gently into baize and, underneath that, into cold slate. The eyes focus. The mind narrows to a single thought. Nothing intrudes, because there is nothing beyond the table but darkness and empty space.

Later, I play the line-up. It's like a mantra.

The methodical click-click-clunk of white ball hitting object ball hitting pocket removes the need for deliberation, slides the mind up on to a higher plane.

Somewhere between potting the final ball and putting my cue away, I realise why I came here today. Why my unconscious mind engineered this impromptu trip to the club. Because this is where I belong. To be a woman snooker player is to adopt the role of Persephone, living in the dark halls of Hades during the winter season, only emerging to sunshine in the spring. This baize is the River Styx, bringing forgetfulness. And each bright snooker ball under the lights represents another pomegranate seed placed in my mouth. I tore myself away during the dead season, before I was meant to leave, and nothing in the outside world can ever replace the darkness of the snooker hall.

I go to the bar to pay for my table. Bet is hunched on a bar stool, watching MTV, a long menthol cigarette dangling from the corner of her mouth. She gets up reluctantly. 'Finished, have we?' When she wishes to sound patronising, Bet always uses the royal plural. I notice she's now plucked her eyebrows entirely, and drawn them back in a mocha shade, with a rather unsteady hand by the look of it. She pats her bleached hair, coiled on top of her head like one of those *brioches* the French eat instead of cake, and glances idly at the computer screen. 'That's five pounds exactly.'

I hand over a tenner, then see Bob lean forward as she goes to the till, whispering something. Bet looks back at me over her shoulder, takes a fiver out of the till, then shuffles back in her toe-thong pink sandals. She doesn't quite meet my eyes. 'Bob's just reminded me, love. There was a committee meeting the other week. The men decided you weren't to be allowed back in here.' She clearly takes my astonished silence for compliance. 'I knew you wouldn't mind. You barely play any more. I would have said when you first came in, only I forgot.'

'I'm being banned?'

'It's for your own good, love.' She raises her brown pencilled eyebrows at my expression. 'It got back to the committee that you'd had trouble with Raz. You were cheating, or something? Well, I'm not fussed what you get up to as long as you pay for the table, but the committee don't hold with cheating.'

'I didn't cheat. It was Raz who cheated.'

'Hey, you watch what you're saying. He's my nephew, he works behind this bar, and I won't hear ill of him.' Bet slams my fiver down on the bar. 'Bob told us the whole story, anyway. Now take that and get out. You're banned.'

I look over, but Bob has slunk back behind his newspaper. Bet is waiting for me to leave. The lads at the fruit machine have fallen silent and are watching me with sly grins on their faces. Young and scrawny in their leather jackets, they look like hyenas. What am I meant to do? I can feel the heat in my cheeks. I lift my chin up as far as I can manage and walk out, but by the time I fumble my car door open, the world has dimmed to a shiny haze. What was it Kevin once told me? *Don't let the bastards grind you down.* But what choice do I have in this situation? When people like Bob and Raz can twist the truth back in on itself, and ruin someone's reputation for their own ends, there's nothing to do but walk away.

Good news travels fast in the snooker world. Two days later, I get a phone call from Kevin. 'Is it true?'

I can barely contain myself. 'You bastard. You don't seriously believe I'm a cheat?'

'Don't be soft,' Kevin says sharply. 'I mean is it true you're playing again? You actually went to practise at the club?'

'Of course it's true. How else do you think I found out about being banned?' Slightly mollified, I don't see why I shouldn't admit the truth. 'I couldn't help myself. I was just passing and . . . you know how it is.'

'Uhuh.' Pause. 'Look, don't worry about this ban. I can find you somewhere else to play. Ther's a golf club outside town, with a couple of tables out the back. Nothing special, but I'm a member there. I could probably get you some free practice time.'

'As long as the owner's not friendly with Bob.'

'It's unlikely.' He sighs. 'Look, don't drag this around with you, Zoë. Let it go. They're a bunch of mindless prats at that club. They proved that by taking Raz's word over yours.'

'You do believe me, don't you?' I don't think I could stand it if Kevin thought I was dishonest. 'I'm not a cheat, Kevin.'

'Of course you're not. Problem is,' he pauses, 'not everyone knows you as well as I do. Mr Parker was on the phone this morning. He's already heard about the ban.'

'From Bob?'

'Probably. But the damage is done. Parker's withdrawn his sponsorship.'

I close my eyes. 'That's the end, then. I can't go on without funds.'

There's a long silence. When Kevin eventually speaks, he sounds almost angry. 'So you're letting them win?'

'I don't have much choice.'

'Rubbish. I've offered you that golf-club table for practice. I've agreed to look after the kids at tournaments . . .'

'I can't take my kids to a tournament. It's not exactly a suitable place for kids, is it?' Kevin doesn't understand. Why should he? He's not a father. Over the past few years, I've struggled to keep my kids out of snooker clubs, away from the circuit, to give them as normal an upbringing as possible. I can't expose them to life on the circuit now just because it's convenient to do so. 'Okay. Look. I'll try this golf-club table for a while. But don't get any ideas. I'm not practising towards a tournament. This is just for fun.'

'Just to keep your eye in, you mean.'

'No,' I say wearily. 'I mean just for fun.'

'Well, if you do change your mind, I want you to

know I'm here for you. You were meant to play snooker, Zoë. Don't fight against it.'

'You're not listening to me, Kevin.' I close my eyes and try to sound resolved. But who am I trying to convince here? Me or him? I feel as though I'm chasing my tail with all these 'ifs' and 'buts', never getting any nearer the truth. I'm hanging on to my sanity by a thread. That abyss of nothingness I've been facing for weeks is still only one step behind me. But I can't go back on my decision, however painful this separation process becomes. 'From now on, snooker is strictly reserved for fun.'

Like a headache pill, this half-hearted resolution only alleviates the symptoms for a while, then the problem comes back again, stronger than ever. I wake up a few days later, with the nagging question in my head: *why not?* My mother need never know. Why shouldn't I take the kids along to a tournament? Kevin says he'll look after them. It's not such a big deal. These aren't dirty back-street clubs. As long as I can get them back to a B&B or a hotel by early evening, I could keep them away from the worst of the drinking or the socialising that goes on. Tournaments are fairly sedate until night falls. Kevin could keep them occupied with books or colouring pads while I was at the table. The only problem would be the expense. I could share with Jemmy and Tom, but Kevin would need his own room, and I couldn't expect him to pay for it. Not with him looking after the kids all weekend.

I turn over in bed and bury my head under the pillow. What am I thinking about? This is ridiculous. Without Parker's sponsorship, I've got no chance of playing full-time and, in my book, that's the only way to play the game. My money could just about stretch to a couple of nearby tournaments, but why should I waste it on snooker when there are bills to pay, the mortgage to keep up, and food to put into the kids' mouths? I must be mad. I get reasonable maintenance from Adrian, but I can't justify using that money to finance my snooker playing.

Maybe if I play one more tournament, just to see how it goes. One more. That's not so awful, is it? I look out from under the pillow at my alarm clock. It's seven-forty. A thin sunlight is already struggling through the curtains. I can hear someone further down the street starting their car. The engine is sluggish, coughing repeatedly until finally it flares into life. The world turns without snooker. People come and go without snooker. You could ban all snooker playing tomorrow and few people would notice. Only the players. It's pathetic, really, being this obsessed by a wooden stick and twenty-three balls on a green cloth. But I can't help it. At some point in the past, snooker crept under my skin, and now it will always be with me. Like a scar I can never entirely hide.

Listening to the kids trashing their bedroom next door, I come to a decision. I shall play one more tournament. If I fail to do myself justice, I shall quit for ever. And this time, I *mean* for ever, not just until my next comeback. I'm not a pop star. I'm not going to trot myself out every so often for one more farewell appearance. I can't live like that. But it's obvious I can't throw it all away without being bloody certain I'm doing the right thing. If anything happens to the kids because I can't stay away from snooker, I'll never forgive myself. Thinking of it like that, my mother wouldn't forgive me either.

Okay, my mother's thousands of miles away in a foreign country. Theoretically, she need never know. But maybe I ought to tell her. You never know, she might be pleased. She's happy. She's got Gordon. Why should she be so upset about this now that we have such separate lives? Okay, her reactions have never been exactly easy to predict. It would probably be wiser not to mention the tournament. But there's a sneaking part of me, a 'good girl' hidden away beneath this 'screw the lot of you' exterior, who's wagging her finger at this situation and threatening to tell. Frankly, I want to punch her lights out, but no, she's too cunning for that. The little bitch always stands just out of reach.

A few days later, I come back from the club and there's a message on the answerphone. 'Zoë? This is your mother speaking. I hate these machines. Gordon gave me your message and I think it's disgraceful. You can't take my grandchildren to a . . . *snooker* tournament. I'll never forgive you. Call me back.'

When I've picked the kids up from school and settled in for the evening with an extremely large glass of

Rioja, I sit on the stairs and contemplate the message on the answerphone.

I haven't deleted the message. I should have done. I should have wiped it off the tape and out of my memory as soon as I listened to it. I should never have made that call to Spain in the first place. It was madness. I thought, correction, I *hoped* she would be pleased for me. Gordon said he'd tell her when she came back from the health club. I can imagine the scene. At this very moment, my mother will be pacing the villa, waiting for my return call. She may already have booked her seat on the first available flight home. Even if I've got the rest wrong she'll definitely be practising those de-stressing yoga exercises in front of a silent telephone. Because I'm not going to call her back.

Sod you, Mother darling. I make a face at the answerphone and sink my nose deep into the Rioja. This is as close to Spain as I'll ever get now.

But mothers aren't that easy to get rid of, are they? They linger around in your head for years, like the smell of bad drains. I want to be brave. I want to stand on my own two feet and say 'no' to her demands, her screw-turning, her long-distance emotional blackmail. But when I open my mouth, all this other stuff comes out: horrible whining excuses, scared bleatings, some Oprah Winfrey-style crap about mothers and daughters, and how important it is to stay friends. *Friends*. Being 'friends' with my mother is like having a close personal relationship with a torture chamber. And she always seems to know which instrument will inflict the greatest pain.

I pour myself another glass of wine. Wine has this amazing ability to blur the edges, red wine in particular. I never discovered that until Adrian left. Okay, it's not ideal, because a) it gives you a hangover, b) it can be fattening in large quantities, and c) that fucking 'good girl' in the back of my mind is always reminding me that I shouldn't drink whilst in charge of my kids. This last is a fair point, but it doesn't mean I have to thank the little cow for nudging my conscience every time I lift a glass to my lips. If it was up to her, I'd be sipping carrot juice at this very moment and discussing shades of wallpaper with my mother. But I'm not, because I still have the upper hand here. Instead, I'm perched on the third stair up, partially slumped against the wall, and I have no intention of either picking up the phone or redecorating, thank you.

I bang my head wearily against the wall a few times. Why on earth did I dream I could take up snooker again? Especially after getting banned from my own club. Why did I have to give myself these false hopes? I must have known that once my mother found out, it would all be over. She's been adamant all along that Jemmy and Tom should never go to a tournament with me. I'm not entirely sure why. Maybe she thinks they'll catch some fatal disease from the other players, or end up like me: a lost cause. But being stupid, or overly optimistic, or whatever the right description is for someone who could tell their mother something that they know *for certain* is going to upset her, I had to race off to the phone and give her the glad tidings.

Maybe I was testing myself. Working my way round

the obstacle of not having a home club to play at any more. Pushing myself back up to standard with no one but Kevin to practise against. Seeing exactly how far I'm willing to go to play one more world-ranking tournament. But I've certainly been answered. At the moment, it doesn't look as if I'm going any further than the end of the street.

After a while, it strikes me that I'm crying. I've done a fair bit of crying recently. It's becoming a nervous tic. But this time, it's different. I'm not sobbing. In fact, I'm hardly making any noise at all. One tear has just rolled down my cheek and into the corner of my mouth. I lick at it, speculatively. It tastes salty. Definitely tears, then. Another soon follows it, and then another. How the fuck can I go to this tournament and play my best, when I know my mother despises me for what I'm doing?

The stairs behind me creak. It's Jemmy. She's dressed in her pyjamas, clutching a teddy bear. She watches me in silence for a few minutes. 'You're crying.'

'Go to bed, sweetheart. Mummy's just tired.'

'When Grandma went away, you told me not to cry. You told me to be brave.'

'This is different.'

'Why?'

'Because . . .' I look at her, suddenly uncertain. Why is it different? Is this situation any more insurmountable than my mother going away? So she disapproves of my behaviour. But when has she ever approved? Maybe I'm just using this as an excuse to back out, before things move too far and I'm staring another pressure match in the face. Maybe snooker always terrified me. But how much of that would Jemmy understand and should I burden an eight-year-old with my pathetic fears anyway? I take a deeper swallow of my wine, closing my eyes. There's not really anyone else to confide in. 'Because this is grown-up stuff. And I'm scared.'

Jemmy creeps down to where I'm sitting. She hands me her teddy, not looking at me now as if she's embarrassed to see me crying close-up. 'Here, Mummy. Mr Bear's scared of the dark. If you look after him, maybe he'll look after you.'

Mr Bear has one ear missing and a comical expression. I look away too, poking the loose stuffing back into his head. I'm not sure which of us is more embarrassed: me, Jemmy or Mr Bear. 'Thanks.'

On her way back up the stairs, Jemmy hesitates. 'I'd *like* to go to that snooker thing, Mummy. Don't worry about Gran. She just thinks snooker's for boys. But we know it's for girls too, don't we?'

'Yes, we certainly do.' I hide my face in Mr Bear's rough coat. I'm shaking. Jemmy's only eight now, but she's already a hell of a lot braver than I am, over three times her age. Here I am, sobbing on the stairs into a glass of wine because someone *disapproves* of me. I'm totally spineless. What sort of mother am I anyway, if I can't even get it together when I've got someone like Jemmy on my side? I've got to make a decision and I've got to make it now. 'Go to bed, sweetheart. I'll be coming up soon to tuck you in. First, I've got a phone call to make.'

13

It's a historic moment. Here I am, walking through the smoked-glass doors into the Scottish club, shoulder to shoulder with Tricksy. I clutch Mr Bear to my chest, ignoring Tricksy's look of disbelief at the tatty old bear. If Jemmy thinks he'll bring me luck, I'm prepared to give it a shot. Besides, Mr Bear's already helped me through the early rounds. I've reached the quarter-finals of the Ladies Scottish Classic, and I'm playing Sylvie. What more is there to life than this?

There's an unearthly hush in the club. Tricksy dashes to the loo before the draw's called for her Plate competition, and I wander over to the table where my name is written up on the board beside Sylvie's. Carefully, I perch my teddy bear on the cushion rail. The table has just been brushed and ironed. It looks like a bowling-green at the start of the season. I hardly dare put my heavy aluminium case down along the table. It seems sacrilegious to disturb the fine green nap, though I suppose that in another half-hour, it'll be scored to hell by fingers and chalk and screw-shot lines.

I balance the case along the cushion rail and I'm just undoing the catches when Jemmy comes running over from the bar, closely followed by Tom. Her face is filthy. 'Mummy! Kevin bought us ice cream for breakfast!'

'Ssssh . . . remember this is a snooker club.'

'Is Mr Bear going to bring you luck?'

'Fingers crossed. I hope you're on your best behaviour for Kevin.'

'Course we are.' Jemmy hugs the teddy bear. 'Can I look after Mr Bear while you play?'

'If you want. I'm sure he can bring me luck just as well from the bar.' I open my cue case, watching them dance around the table. 'Tom, leave the white ball alone. You'll get it sticky.'

He looks up at me slyly. 'Kevin let us roll them on the table.'

'I'll have to have words with Kevin about that.' As he approaches, I start screwing my cue together, smiling in what I hope passes for a cheerful manner, but my stomach is turning cartwheels. Is it possible to go through the menopause before the age of thirty? I'm having hot and cold flushes at the thought of playing Sylvie in the quarters. What am I doing here? How the hell did I get back into this? I'd forgotten how bad nerves can be before a match, unless it's just because of the occasion, who I'm playing, and at what level. 'What's all this about letting the kids mess around on the tables?'

'Only before they were ironed. Come back here,

Tom. And you, missy. Your mum's going to need all her concentration for the next few hours. You two are going back in the bar with me.'

'Thanks for doing this, Kevin.'

He shrugs and turns away, clearly embarrassed. 'Just play your best, Zoë. That's all anyone can ask.'

Play my best? My hands are shaking so much, I'll be lucky to hit the ball in the first place, let alone pot it. But at least I'm back with a vengeance. I was so scared that I'd come back to the circuit only to flunk pathetically in the first round.

But something seems to have happened since I left. Something marvellous. All the pressure I felt has gone, all those long-winded inner dialogues have been silenced, the dissection of each shot that stopped me seeing the game as a whole. The only reason my hands are shaking is because it's Sylvie I'm playing. And Sylvie is . . . well, things are complicated there, aren't they? She's not just another faceless seed. She's not one of those top players I loathe and despise and would give my eye teeth to beat. She's someone who almost, very nearly, became a friend. And there are so few real friends in this game. Okay, I slept with her husband, and tried to get her back together with her hated sister, but my life was out of control in those days. I was living in the eye of the storm, and everything outside was a blur. Now, shit, I don't know, do things get better or do we just kid ourselves that they're better, looking back and unable to believe the things we did? What was it? Six months ago?

Less? It seems more like a century. And I feel like a different person.

Quite suddenly, I'm not scared any more, I'm terrified. This is a defining moment in my life. In the golfing film *Tin Cup*, Kevin Costner's character, archetypal talented loser Roy McAvoy, says that 'when a defining moment comes along, you define the moment or the moment defines you'. I have about twenty minutes before break-off. But which way will I swing? Will I define the moment, or will it capture me in loser's mode, seizing the moment of my defeat like a snapshot, for ever unalterable?

Okay, you may arguably say, but Sylvie's a great player. You may end up being unable to beat her, however well you play. Right? Wrong. Theoretically, there's no such thing as an unbeatable player. Like chess, this game is all in the mind. It's about choices. Giving yourself permission to win. Refusing to admit the slightest doubt. Doubt is like a cancer. It eats away at a player until the cue arm gives and the whole game collapses like a line of dominoes. An opponent can only win while they're at the table. You have to keep them in their seat. That means potting balls. Alternatively, it means an attacking safety shot that forces an error, an error which leaves you down among the reds, facing a winning break. And if the frames start slipping away, you have to keep your head above water, playing each frame as if it were the first, undaunted by the scoreline.

Easier said than done. But fortune's meant to favour

the brave, isn't it? And while talent may still elude me, I'm not short on courage under fire. I have to remind myself of that constantly. Anyone who can ring their power-crazed mother and calmly tell her to stop meddling in their private life must be brave. Brave or very stupid. I can't decide which, and neither could my mother, judging by her silence on the other end of the phone. But no one can say I'm not making an effort. I've walked through hell to get here. I've practised constantly since I decided to make a comeback. I've gone over earlier matches, point by point, with Kevin, until I'm sick of explaining how or why I lost them. We've discussed the nature of defeat. The possibility of victory. The mysteries of snooker. The very essence of the game itself. And now, all I have left to do is play my heart out.

There's some commotion at the doors. Sylvie walks in, cutting it fine as always. A skinny little man with a microphone, who I assume is a reporter, is snapping at her heels like a whippet. Sylvie pays no attention to him, striding past to the bar on those unfeasibly long legs. She's been growing her hair again. If you've got long hair, you're not meant to play with it loose, which is probably why she's tied it back chignon-style. Somehow it makes her look taller than ever.

Tricksy appears at my elbow. Her 'lucky' blouse is looking rather the worse for its umpteenth outing. If she wears it to many more tournaments, it'll be nothing but a faded orange rag. 'Scared?'

'Should I be?'

She shrugs. 'I would be. Sylvie's a scary player.'

'I'm not you.'

'Fair enough.' Tricksy peers at my face. 'You're very pale.'

'I've been dieting.'

This seems to satisfy her. 'Did I tell you? I've got a new man.'

'*Another* one?'

'Hey, none of the rest were serious. This is the real thing.'

I fiddle with my cue. This isn't the time or the place to be discussing Tricksy's love life, but she's about as sensitive to atmosphere as a wart-hog. Unless that's being unfair to wart-hogs. 'I'm very pleased for you.'

'In fact, we're getting married.'

Now she has my attention. I stare. 'When?'

'Next summer. He's American. A rancher. His dad's got a cattle ranch in Texas . . . we're going to move out there after Christmas.' She smiles. 'We met a few months ago on a train, when I went over to see my aunt. It was so romantic, Zoë. There was only one space left in the luggage rack, and Rex let me have it. He had to sit with his rucksack on his lap all the way from Paddington to Bristol Temple Meads.'

'Rex?'

Tricksy shrugs. 'His dad likes dogs.'

'And what about snooker?'

'What about it? It's just a game, Zoë.'

'But you'll miss it terribly.'

'Miss losing? I don't think so.'

I don't know what to say. I had Tricksy pegged as the sort of woman who would *never* stop playing. There are plenty of them on the circuit. They lose in every first-round match they play, but keep coming back for more, plugging away at the game with the tenacity of a bulldog. Their limited vision and obstinacy prevent them from seeing that they will never rise any higher in the rankings, that the great break-through they secretly long for will never come. But the game needs these suckers. Like any other sport, snooker's shaped like a pyramid. The cannon-fodder at the bottom supports both the rising stars and the top players, up there with their heads in the clouds. 'You won't even miss your friends?'

'I'll miss you.' Tricksy frowns. 'I mean . . . well, you know.'

'Yeah. Ditto.'

'Bad timing, huh? Just when you're coming back on the circuit . . .'

'One door opens, another closes.'

'Something like that.' She runs a finger along the cushion rail. 'I *will* miss you, Zoë. You're the only one round here with any . . . I don't know. You're just different.'

I look away, not wanting to catch her eye. That's probably as close to a compliment as Tricksy will ever get. She's never been a particularly articulate person. I wonder vaguely what Rex is like, and whether he realises what he's letting himself in for. Still, he *is* an American cattle rancher. Without wishing to stereotype American ranchers, Rex isn't likely to be highly skilled in the conversational department himself. It's all that cowshit, I expect. Tricksy should feel right at home with it after the snooker circuit. 'Thanks.'

'You're welcome. And good luck. Don't let Sylvie give you the runaround.' Tricksy hesitates, looking at Sylvie across the club. Then she leans closer, whispering, 'She's not been playing well recently. Tracey's flavour of the year since winning the World. Even Sylvie's fans are starting to swop sides. I'm sure you can beat her, Zoë.'

If this is meant to be a comforting piece of information, it has the opposite effect. So Sylvie's game has gone downhill since we went to Geneva. The chances of that phenomenon having nothing to do with me and Matt are fairly slim. Which makes me feel as guilty as hell. I look across at her at the bar. She's in animated conversation with the Tournament Controller. The reporter is still hanging around, adjusting his microphone as if in anticipation of an interview. He hasn't bothered speaking to me, of course. I'm a nobody. I'm a no-hoper. Because I've been out of the game for so many months, I've slipped to the mid-thirties in the rankings. Tricksy may consider I've got the game to beat Sylvie, and I may possibly dream that I have, but no one else will think so. Not with any seriousness. And the way I've fucked Sylvie's head up, I don't think I deserve to beat her.

What am I saying? That winning isn't everything? Or that there are different ways of winning, and that some are less *worthy* than others? Yes, I suppose I am saying that. So what happened to that 'take no prisoners' attitude I started out with? Somewhere along the line, the end result has become less important than the means of getting there. Which means I've either lost my competitive edge or gained something people used to call a soul, better known in snooker as weak-wristedness. Whichever it is, I'm screwed.

Tricksy's watching me closely. 'You all right?'

'Bit nervous, that's all.'

She looks relieved. 'Never thought I'd hear you admit it.'

The Tournament Controller is calling for quiet. I can feel my insides clench repeatedly like a fist. 'You'd better go. Your Plate match must be due to start.'

Tricksy fumbles a pat on my back before leaving. Through the glass partition, I can see Jemmy and Tom sitting in the bar. Jemmy is hugging Mr Bear to her chest. Tom is grinning, and giving me the thumbs-up as Kevin taught him, only he can't quite manage to do it and is making a face of excruciating concentration as he squints up at his hand. Kevin is talking to one of the referees, oblivious to my dilemma out here at the table.

If I beat Sylvie today, will it be a hollow victory, knowing that what's gone on between us has thrown her game? If she beats me because I can't bring myself to win, will I have acted unprofessionally, allowing my personal feelings to get in the way of my game? And if I try my hardest, and Sylvie still beats me, will I be able to live with my own staggering inability to play snooker at this level?

Sylvie appears at the table, cup of tea in hand, followed by the referee. 'Good luck,' she says in a perfunctory manner, not meeting my eyes. I can't tell what she's thinking. The coin is tossed, we shake hands, wipe down our cues and wait for the referee to finish writing out the scoresheet. Sylvie won the toss, so she breaks off and leaves me tight up on the cushion behind the green.

I walk to the head of the table and stare down at the far end. The pack has hardly split at all, so I could get away with a loose safety, unless I leave her a chance to tie me up somewhere more unpleasant than this. Only top-spin is possible, with the ball right against the cushion, but a smooth shot off the bottom cushion, clipping the pack, then swinging past the blue and back up to baulk should do the trick. It's not a particularly hard shot, but I feel nauseous. The lights are dazzling. I can sense her eyes boring into my head.

What's the matter with me? This is what I wanted, isn't it? To face Sylvie across the snooker table. To decide, once and for all, whether I'm up to her standard. Not even simply that, but whether I can beat her. I've played out of my skin to get to the quarters again. But now I'm here, my head feels as though it's stuffed with cotton wool. I stare down the length of the table, and all I can see is a curved glitter of light from the colours, the untouched cloth gleaming under the hanging fringe, and beyond that, the darkness of failure.

I've been here before. It's a familiar feeling, freezing up at the table. But not today. Please, not today. My cue arm feels like a stiff wooden board. My back is hunched as I get down on the shot. My wrist has tightened like the washer on a tap. I can't get it to relax. When I feather the shot, I feel like a marionette, jerky and uncoordinated. Somebody else is pulling the strings.

I fluff the shot, clatter into the pack, spin off and leave the white wide in the centre of the table. Several new reds lie open for the picking. The pink has been cleared for the middle pockets.

I glance at Sylvie. That shot must have told her everything she needs to know about my state of mind. But there's not even a flicker of expression on her face as she moves to the table. She has it all under control. She is the ice-maiden. She chalks her cue with the utter contempt of a born winner playing a born loser. When she gets down on the shot, her eyes focus on the red like a snake, waiting to strike.

I've only seen this act from a distance. I've never been on the receiving end before. The cold burns my skin. It's like being forced to put my hand in a freezer compartment for several hours. But I can't complain. I wanted this. I worked for this. All I can do now is get my shit together and try to beat her at her own game. Okay, as Yoda points out in *The Empire Strikes Back*, 'try' is the wrong word: 'Try not. Do or do not. There is no try.' Yoda may have looked as if he were made of Play-Doh, but he would have made a good coach. If it's cold Sylvie wants, I must give her cold. If it's pain she wants to inflict, I must hand it straight back to her on the table. I can't even afford to think about it. At this stage, thinking will only destroy my game.

I've got to start thinking. Sylvie's two frames up. This is the best of seven. She only needs two more and I'm out. I'm fighting for my life here. All consideration of right and wrong has gone out of the window. At the moment, all that matters is beating her off, point by painful point, forcing her back into her seat, leaving her nothing. But Sylvie keeps pulling pots out of the hat. I think there's nothing left on, then her eyes sharpen, she's seen something, and *smack*, there's another red down and another destructive break under her belt. I feel like King Canute, trying to hold back the waves. All I need to complete the picture is a crown and soggy feet.

I clip off a red and back to baulk for the hundredth time. This isn't snooker. This is sheer desperation. She never leaves me a pot when she misses, but I seem to be all thumbs when it comes to safety. I tie her up somewhere impossible. Sylvie steps in and magics a break from that position. I can't believe my eyes. I'm playing the queen of darkness.

I can't even shake her tempo by speeding up or slowing down. Sylvie has no particular tempo to shake. She just plays. In the past, I could have sworn she was an automaton at the table, almost robotic. Now, close up, in the full glare of her talent, I realise there's nothing robotic about her game at all. It's more like watching a prima ballerina in action. Minus the tutu, of course. She knows all the moves. She never misses a cue, never falters a step. It's as though the match is playing to music in her head and she's following it smoothly, irrevocably, to its conclusion.

What have I got compared to this? A handful of raw talent, a few years' worth of technique, the odd outrageous pot to surprise the onlookers. My game is all about playing to the gallery. Hers is all about winning. Until I played Sylvie, I thought I respected the game more than anyone else ever could. Now I realise that there are different levels to that respect. Mine is the respect of the devoted club player. Hers is the respect of someone whose bread-and-butter is also the love of their life. Mary Lauretta, a dedicated nun, once said: 'In order to be successful, you must first fall in love with your work.' Sylvie is a living example of that dictum. I may be in love, but it's more of a helpless desire than a lifelong partnership. When it comes to the crunch, the game will always elude me.

As I'm getting down to break off for the fourth frame, a movement in the crowd catches my eye. It's Kristin, watching me across the table.

I stand up again, chalking my cue furiously to recapture my concentration, but it's too late. What the hell is Kristin doing here? Sylvie made it plain she didn't want to see her again. I glance over at Sylvie. She's seen her. Her face is tight and she's staring at her sister with every evidence of hatred. This is all my fault. Last time Kristin rang, I told her I was coming to this tournament. She must have decided to brave Sylvie on her own territory. I've got to hand it to Kristin. She knows how to make an entrance.

I play the break-off okay, but my hands are shaking. I can imagine the storm waiting to break over my head. Sylvie's too cool to make a scene about this in public, but I'm probably inextricably bound up with Kristin and Matt in her mind. When she looks at me, she sees them. There's no other explanation for her coldness towards me since the World Championships in Geneva. So she's probably going to blame me for Kristin's impromptu appearance at this tournament. Maybe Sylvie will think I've planned all this, even Kristin's dramatic mid-match entrance, to help swing the game my way. Looking at it like that, I have to admit that it does seem likely to increase my chances of pulling a frame or two back. But now, I feel almost too guilty to take advantage of it.

We play a little cat-and-mouse game with the white for five minutes, then I foolishly take my eye off the ball and leave her in. If I thought Kristin's presence was going to affect her performance, I was wrong. If anything, Sylvie is even more determined to win now. I can hear her anger in every shot. Each ball hits the back of the pocket like a clap of thunder. Sylvie's not playing safe now. She's not playing wildly either, but there's a certain recklessness in the shots she's taking on, as if she's simply been toying with me up until now, letting me feel I can play. Now she's going at the game full throttle. And it hurts.

Now she's three frames up. One more and I can kiss this tournament goodbye. I don't know what I can do to stop her. I'm playing flat out. My cue arm has relaxed now and the pots are flying in like birds. I'm putting stuff away that I could barely even manage in practice. Kevin is staring at me from the bar, astonished. Jemmy and Tom are pressed up against the glass partition, grinning. I can hardly believe it myself. It's as if simply competing against such a great player has raised my game. But it's not enough. Not nearly enough.

I have to face facts. I just don't have the game to beat her. To be honest, I don't think I'll ever have the game to beat her. Sylvie has completely outclassed me. The strange thing is, I don't seem to care any more. I'm actually enjoying myself. I'm playing a fantastic game on a fantastic table against a fantastic player, and life, surely, will never get any better than this.

Seven points in it. I've actually brought her to the margin of one black only. And it's the last black. She's three frames up. This black is to save the match. I know, deep down, I've got no chance. But somehow *this black* symbolises the game for me, the match, even my entire snooker career to date. If I can pot this black, pull just one frame back at least, I'll know I have it in me to be a great player. So, as you can imagine, this is a bit of a pressure shot.

Sylvie's left the black in the middle of the table. The white's, ooh, let's say two inches away from the yellow spot. It's an almost dead-straight shot, down into the left-hand bottom pocket. I must have played this shot a thousand times in practice. And missed it about seven hundred times. So, ignoring the added pressure, this is a thirty per cent possibility. Now, snooker is a game of percentages. Only lunatics ignore these all-important statistics. Anything under about sixty-five per cent is a no-go. Taking on a thirty per cent shot is like being sick over the side of a ferry when the wind's blowing in your direction. The chances of not getting your lunch back immediately are fairly remote.

So what do I do? Do I ignore the low statistic shot and go for the sensible cocked-hat safety shot? Do I fuck. My cue arm's working like a piston now. I'm hitting the cue ball sweet as the proverbial nut. This shot's almost straight. If everything's correctly aligned, that black should go soaring into the bottom left-hand pocket as though it had wings. No sweat.

I get down on the shot. My spine dips elegantly into a curve. My feet are well spread for balance. My shoulder's loose. My wrist's firm. My three light feathers almost touch the cue ball, they're so deadly accurate. Everything's on for the pot. Down the full length of the cue, past the white, past the black, over the vast green expanse of the baize, I can see the pocket gaping like a huge mouth in the corner of the table, waiting, waiting. I pull back slightly, I hesitate for a heart-stopping second, then drive the cue through the white, through the black, and on into the heart of the pocket.

But the little sod rattles, doesn't it?

Sylvie steps in, leans over and gently, ever so gently, sinks the jawed black into the pocket.

I'm reaching out, automatically. It's over. Briefly, my hand is in hers. 'Well played.' I don't know if Sylvie said that or I did. Maybe we both did. It's all a blur. Someone pats me on the shoulder. The other games are still going, so we have to be quiet. Someone is whispering something. I'm unscrewing my cue, staring round for my case. Out of the corner of my eye, I can see Kevin on his feet in the bar, holding back Jemmy and Tom who are obviously dying to rush out to me. The club's so dimly lit. I think I've got tears in my eyes.

'You were unlucky. That black should have gone.'

'No, Sylvie. You out-played me.'

Sylvie says nothing for a moment, not meeting my eyes. 'Why is Kristin here? Did you tell her to come?'

'No. She knew this tournament was on though.'

She looks back at me sharply. 'You've kept in touch with her?'

'It was the other way round.'

'But why?' Her voice is so low I can hardly hear it. Sylvie looks completely changed. It's bizarre to see such a transformation. This isn't the woman who so coldly dispatched me a few minutes ago. Now she has the eyes of a little girl, scared, apprehensive. It's almost as if the whole thing had been an act, a show put on for her sister, and anyone else who wanted to attack her.

'I think she just wants to patch things up.'

'You don't know Kristin.'

'Maybe you're too close to understand her properly.' I slide my case up on to the table and open it. I may as well put my cue away. I'm not going to need it again today. Maybe not ever again. I haven't decided yet. That game was so terrifying, so embarrassing, so incredibly tiring, yet so exhilarating at the end. I can't make my mind up. I look down at the cue in my hands. 'Maybe I'm too close to the game to win.'

'Rubbish,' Sylvie says dismissively. 'You just don't want it enough.'

I stare at her. 'Of course I do.'

'No. You think you want it, but you don't want it enough. There's a difference.' She closes her eyes briefly. 'I've got to play the semis now. And I've got to win. Then I've got to play the final. How the hell am I going to do that with Kristin watching me?'

'Talk to her. Cut her some slack.' I put my cue slowly in my case and snap the lid shut. I can see Kristin hovering near the bar door. She looks pale and strained, her hair swept up into a ponytail. She must have immense courage to have turned up here like this, after the trauma the two of them have been through. Matt certainly has a lot to answer for. 'You said yourself Matt could charm the birds out of the trees. Your sister fell for his smooth talking just as much as you did, Sylvie.'

'And you.'

I wince. 'Yes. I fell for him too. I'm not denying that. But you forgave me. Let me put it like this. How would you feel if Kristin died tomorrow?'

Sylvie hesitates, then sighs. 'Awful, I suppose.'

'There's your answer then. Go and make it up with her, Sylvie. She's come all this way just to apologise. Give her credit for effort, at least.'

Sylvie nods wryly at the table. 'You didn't get credit for effort.'

'Piss off.'

She smiles. 'You're too hard on yourself, Zoë. You may not want it enough to make a great player, but you love the game, and that's something far rarer than ambition. Don't let it go.'

I run a hand slowly across the lid of my case. 'No. Maybe I won't.' I smile up at her. She's so bloody tall. 'Go on, Sylvie, go talk to your sister. You're giving me a crick in the neck.'

She turns to go, then hesitates, looking back. 'By the way,' she says lightly, 'I owe you an apology.'

'About what?'

'Those so-called friends of mine. You were right. As soon as Tracey started to overtake me in the rankings, they all disappeared.'

'I'm sorry.'

Sylvie manages a half-smile. 'Don't be. It's taught me not to be so trusting in future. Besides, I got a lot of free drinks out of them.'

Jemmy and Tom are tiptoeing down past the other players to reach me. Tom headbutts me with a grin, and I put a finger to my mouth. 'Ssshhh . . . there are still other people playing.' As Jemmy hugs me, I throw my arms around her and lift her off the ground. She smells of shampoo and fabric conditioner. It seems so strange to have the kids here, in a snooker club. It feels dangerous, almost like having my cake and eating it too. 'I lost.'

'Mr Bear forgot to say good luck, that's why.'

I glance at Mr Bear, squeezed between her hands. His smile looks lopsided. 'He'd better remember next time.' I put Jemmy down and kneel beside her. 'Would you like to come to another tournament or were you bored?'

'Can I play next time?'

'You?' I laugh, then stop, realising she's serious. 'Would you like to?'

Kevin is behind them now. 'You've got a budding snooker player there, Zoë. She was playing every shot with you from the bar.'

I look up at him. He's smiling, but in a serious way. I know that look. Kevin's already coaching Jemmy in his mind, watching her climb the rankings, become the youngest women's World Champion. Maybe even taking the men on at their own game and beating them. I stand up, dusting my dress trousers down. All around me I can hear the quiet click of balls, subdued whispers from the bar, the swiftly murmured score from a nearby referee. Along the hall, table after table is lit up under those gold-fringed shades. Sylvie is right. Snooker's in my blood now: the ambition, the long hard days of practice, the fear, the disappointment, the despair. I can't shake it off even if I wanted to. But is this the world I want my daughter to join?

Through the glass partition into the bar, I can see Sylvie and Kristin talking. Their heads are both lowered, but Sylvie smiles as she glances out into the snooker hall briefly, then looks back at her sister. Kristin puts a hand on her arm, and Sylvie doesn't shrug it off. They seem to be deep in conversation. That's one battle Matt will never win again. I wonder why he did it in the first place. Men. Their minds are a total mystery to me.

Jemmy looks up at me. 'Can I have a cue for my birthday, Mummy?' There's a brightness in her eyes I've never seen before. In fact, I feel as though I've never really looked at her before today. I've always thought of her as a child, her personality not fully formed, but I was wrong. She knows what's going on. She knows what she wants, just as I finally know what it is I want. I feel as though I've spent my whole life asking the same question, when the answer has been here, all around me. I don't want Jemmy to go through life as blind as I've been. 'A really good cue, like yours? I want to beat Sylvie for you.'

A ball thuds forcibly into a pocket somewhere. There's an excited round of applause. I can't wait for another tournament. Another chance for revenge. In my mind's eye, I'm already potting that next blue and kissing the pink. I ruffle her hair. 'If that's what you really want, Jemmy. But it's not easy.'

Kevin grins. 'Nothing this good ever is.'

I'm not sure what it is about snooker, though it could

be the biblical-style resemblance between a billiard ball and an apple, but one taste and we're hooked. Somewhere along the line, however, men got wise and tried to keep that delicious find to themselves. Looking back, this is probably how it started. God turned up in his referee's outfit, Adam guiltily dropped the apple, Eve gave it a smart shove with her hoe, and it rolled across the green lawns of Paradise into a rabbit-hole. The game of snooker was born. The reason male snooker players get paid more than women is because Adam cheated and claimed *he'd* potted the apple, not Eve. Women have been trying to even that score ever since.

A selection of other books from Sceptre

Magpie	Jill Dawson	0 340 65385 X	£6.99 ☐
Singling Out the Couples	Stella Duffy	0 340 71561 8	£6.99 ☐
Tourist	Matt Thorne	0 340 70865 4	£6.99 ☐
A Sort of Homecoming	Robert Cremins	0 340 71723 8	£6.99 ☐
Your House is Mine	Hugh Brune	0 340 71867 6	£6.99 ☐

All Sceptre books are available from your local bookshop or newsagent, or can be ordered direct from the publisher. Just tick the titles you want and fill in the form below. Prices and availability subject to change without notice.

Hodder & Stoughton Books, Cash Sales Department, Bookpoint, 39 Milton Park, Abingdon, OXON, OX14 4TD, UK. E-mail address: order@bookpoint.co.uk. If you have a credit card you may order by telephone – (01235) 400414.

Please enclose a cheque or postal order made payable to Bookpoint Ltd to the value of the cover price and allow the following for postage and packing:
UK & BFPO – £1.00 for the first book, 50p for the second book, and 30p for each additional book ordered up to a maximum charge of £3.00.
OVERSEAS & EIRE – £2.00 for the first book, £1.00 for the second book, and 50p for each additional book

Name _____
Address _____
_____
_____

If you would prefer to pay by credit card, please complete:
Please debit my Visa/Access/Diner's Card/American Express (delete as applicable) card no:

Signature _____
Expiry Date _____

If you would NOT like to receive further information on our products please tick the box. ☐